Ex Libris

Tory's foot slipped and she fell back

For one frightening moment she swayed, held only from falling into the deep, dark waters below by Julian's viselike grip.

"Hold on, Tory," he said, stretching his other hand toward her. She managed to clutch it and slowly, achingly, he pulled her to safety. His arms closed tightly around her. Tory leaned against him, struggling to get her breath.

"That was a near thing. I'm sorry," he said. "I didn't expect you to react quite so violently."

She said shakily, "I... it was my fault, too. I'm sorry."

"Shall we seal a pact of mutual forgiveness?" he asked, and slowly bent his head and put his mouth against hers.

There was thunder in her ears, her lips opened beneath his, and she was transported. Her arms went around his neck and everything and everyone was forgotten....

Harlequin Premiere Editions

Harlequin Premiere Editions

THE CHANGING STARS

Nan Asquith

Harlequin Books

TORONTO • NEW YORK • LOS ANGELES • LONDON
AMSTERDAM • PARIS • SYDNEY • HAMBURG
STOCKHOLM • ATHENS • TOKYO • MILAN

Original hardcover edition published in 1975
by Mills & Boon Limited

ISBN 0-373-82114-X

This Harlequin Premiere Editions volume
published September 1982

CHAPTER ONE

TORY was thinking about Ralph as she locked the school house door and put the key through Miss Ewing's letter box. Miss Ewing had earlier in the day departed to the dentist's at Kirk Newton for emergency treatment of a painful wisdom tooth and Tory had been left to take school on her own that afternoon. Now the children were gone, their voices sounding high and starling-shrill as they scampered along the road to the Scarsfell village.

She wondered how Ralph's uncle was. It was not expected that he would live much longer and she knew the last months had been an anxious time for Ralph. She tried not to think of what he had said the last time they met, but the memory persisted. He had kissed her and said, 'When my uncle dies everything will be different for us, Tory, you'll see.'

She had protested, moving away from the circle of his arm, not wanting to think that their future depended on an old man's dying. She remembered Ralph saying sharply, 'Face facts, Tory. You know the salary Uncle Harold pays me for managing the estate is quite inadequate for these days, but he's so old-fashioned *he* thinks it's princely. God knows I don't want anything to happen to the old boy, but when it does, I shall be his heir. And that will alter the entire situation.'

Tory turned down the path as if turning from her own thoughts, and as she did so, she saw the man.

He came riding out of the sunset, a tall figure on a tall horse, silhouetted black against the winter sky. He was hatless, his dark hair falling untidily across his forehead and curling on to the back of a black polo sweater. He wore a tweed jacket and dark cavalry twills, and he was so unexpected a sight that for a moment Tory could only stare at him.

He reined in at the sight of her standing on the roadside and said, in a deep almost drawling voice that held a trace of some accent, 'Good evening. I'm afraid I'm on the wrong road. Could you please tell me the way to Ravensholme.'

'*Ravensholme*?' She was so startled she could hardly speak. She said again, 'Ravensholme?' and then, hurriedly, 'It's that way—down the hill. When you come to the bridge at the bottom you have to turn left and go along the road by the river. You'll come to some big iron gates—that's the house.' She stared up at him, aware of a sombre frowning face, eyes so dark they looked black under level black brows, a straight nose and a deep-cut mouth above a firm chin.

'Thank you. Is it far?'

'Quite a way. About six miles to the bridge and a farther three to the gates.' She hesitated. 'There is a short cut a few miles down the hill—a stone stile leads to a track through the woods, but if you don't know the way it might be difficult for you to find. It will soon be dark.'

He nodded gravely.

'Yes. Thank you, I'll go by the road.' As he spoke Tory saw, past his shoulder, something flash low in the western sky. It was moving and very bright, a strange curving apparition, blue-silver in colour, with a long V-shaped tail.

She couldn't help crying out.

'Look! Oh, look over there. It's the comet. It's Grandfather's comet—he's been watching out each night for it. How fantastic!'

The man swung the horse's head round and gazed at the sky, at the brilliant spectacle before him. Tory stared too, fascinated. As she watched, the comet seemed to become stationary and hang suspended for a few moments and then, slowly, it faded and was gone.

She let out a long breathless sigh.

'I can't believe it—that we've seen Kahoutek. It *must* be Kahoutek, for the whole world has been watching for it. I only hope my grandfather has seen it too.'

The man was still staring at the sky, at the place where the comet had shone so brightly. He said slowly, as if to himself.

'When beggars die there are no comets seen

The heavens themselves blaze forth the death of princes.'

His voice was sombre yet musical. Tory found herself staring at him again, thinking that his unexpected appearance was almost as strange and dramatic as the comet's, sitting there, tall and broad-shouldered on the tall black horse he looked like someone out of a book or a film. There was a formidable quality about him. She could imagine him a man from another century—a duellist with guard and rapier, or a highwayman in mask and caped greatcoat. As if answering his words she heard herself saying,

'A comet never seen in heaven without implying disaster.'

He looked round at her.
'Claudius. You're well read.'
'I'm a schoolteacher.'
'Back there?' He gestured towards the stone school house.
'Yes.'
He shrugged.
'I shouldn't think you have many pupils. It seems very sparse of people up here.' He lifted the reins and the horse moved forward. 'Thank you for directing me. Good evening.'
'Goodbye.'

Tory watched him ride away down the road and then she turned to where she had parked the Mini. She wondered who the stranger was and why he was going to Ravensholme. It was at Ravensholme old Mr. Brierley lay ill. Perhaps the man was a doctor? But hardly. Doctors didn't ride around on horseback any more, they drove fast reliable cars. Perhaps he was a friend of Ralph's, for Ralph was staying at Ravensholme. He and his widowed mother and his sister Carole had gone there just before Christmas when Mr. Brierley became so seriously ill.

As she drove up the winding road toward the moors she thought about Ralph again. If his uncle died he would inherit Ravensholme, the big stone house in the valley and the three thousand acres that went with it, land and farms and cottages, including the village of Scarsfell. Even the school, for it belonged to Scarsfell church and was run by a Board of Governors.

Tory had known Ralph most of her life. They had always

been friends, but it was only since she had returned from London to the North Riding that their relationship had deepened into love. She had been at school with his sister Carole until Carole had gone away to Switzerland to finish, and Tory had left to take up a teacher's training course.

The road levelled out, the moors rolling away in shadowy dusk on either side of her. It was too dark now to see the fells and the bulk of Great Scar rising above them, but ahead of her she could see a twinkle of lights and she knew that she was home.

Wether Bell Farm had been home to Tory since she was a child. Her parents had died in a train crash when Tory was five. She could remember her grandparents coming to take her back to Yorkshire with them on a supposed visit, and it was a long time before she realised that she would not see her father and mother again. She couldn't remember the words in which she had been told this, but she remembered one dark winter day when she had felt sad and cried and her grandfather saying to her, 'Take hold on this, Tory,' and folding her fingers over something small and smooth, and when she opened them to look it was to find the prettiest little white egg she had ever seen. As she stared in wonderment at it her grandfather said, 'Run into the house and tell your grandma to cook it for your tea,' and her childish grief was forgotten as she scampered away, the bantam's egg clutched close to her dress.

She had been named Victoria Mary after her grandmother. Her grandfather always insisted that Tory was exactly like her, but Tory could never see it, for her grandmother had been a tall beautiful woman with red hair and blue eyes and a rose-leaf skin. Tory was tall too and she had the red hair, but when she looked in the mirror she saw irregular features and grey-green eyes and a scattering of freckles across a skin that was clear and smooth but far from rose-leaf.

Four years ago her grandmother had died, but her grandfather insisted that Tory was to continue her training and go away to work.

'I can manage well enough on my own,' he had affirmed. 'Young folk don't want to be tied down by old 'uns. You've your life to live, Tory. Sam Dyer and Bessie will see after me,' and so, until six months ago when he had fallen from a hayrick and fractured his hipbone, he had been stoutly independent. After his accident Tory refused to listen to him but gave up her post in London and came home to the farm. Then, luckily, she discovered that the school in Scarsfell required an assistant to the headmistress and because there was no rush of applicants to work in a remote fell village in a school so small there was talk of it being closed, she got the job without difficulty.

The wind blew round her as she left the Mini in the barn and crossed the yard to the house. There was no moon, only a prickling of stars. That brought back the remembrance of the comet, and she could hardly wait to tell her grandfather about it.

He was so excited by the news that he got to his feet, leaning on his stick to say, 'I can't believe it. That you and this chap just saw it as clear and bright as could be? And here's me been watching night after night through yon telescope and binoculars and never had a glimpse of it.' He sat down again with a thud. 'It beats all.' He shook his head and leaned back in the big leather armchair. 'Tell me again what it looked like. You say the head pointed downwards?'

'Yes. It sort of—oh, I don't know, hovered. Like a hawk does. The tail wasn't big, but it seemed to be V-shaped. It was—it was sort of mysterious—almost awesome. Do you think it was Kahoutek, Grandfather?'

'Ay, that 'ud be Kahoutek all right. Some say it was like to be the comet of the century—' He shook his head again. 'But it's a chancy thing—hasn't come up to expectations so far. And to think you *saw* it, Tory lass.'

She said doubtfully, 'Perhaps it's not a good omen. Aren't comets supposed to be portents of disaster? The ancients said they presaged flood and fire, earthquakes, windstorms, war and the death of kings.'

'That's a long list. I doubt a comet would bring all that in its train. Some people reckon they have good effects—the comet of 1811 coincided with such good harvests and rich vintage seasons in Europe that some of the best wines of that year were called "Comet wines".'

'You know so much about astronomy, Gramps. It's a real hobby with you. Do you remember how you taught me to know the stars and constellations?'

He shook his head.

'It's but a smattering I have. Though I admit that the more I read and get to know of such things the more absorbing I find it.'

Tory was already laying the table for the meal that was half high tea and half supper. Bessie Dyer, the spinster sister of Sam Dyer who had been Mr. Webster's shepherd for many years, came in three mornings a week to tidy round and she did some of the cooking, leaving a midday meal for Tory's grandfather on the days she worked at the farm.

The farm was centuries old and built of stone with walls several feet thick and low latticed windows now cosily curtained against the moorland gales. In the great inglenook a log fire burned day and night, never going out all winter through. Before it, on the old-fashioned rag rug made for them by Bessie as a Christmas present one year, lay Troy, Mr. Webster's old black labrador, and close beside him Topaz, the marmalade-coloured cat. The ceiling was beamed, a fine oak dresser stood against one wall, the fire-light glinting on copper jugs and patterned china plates. The rest of the furniture was a mixture of practical comfort and old pieces that had been there so long no one took any account of their almost priceless value, for Websters had farmed at Wether Bell for over two hundred years.

The meal over and cleared away, Tory was washing up in the kitchen which, although stone-flagged and old-fashioned, boasted the comfort of a gleaming Aga range, when she heard a knock on the back door. She opened it against a gust of cold wind to find Ralph standing there.

'Ralph!' She stared in surprise. 'What are you doing here so late? Come in—please.' She pushed the door to behind him. 'How is your uncle?'

Ralph stared down at her for a moment without speaking, his handsome face pale and frowning. Then he said slowly, 'He died yesterday morning.'

'Oh! Oh, Ralph, I'm sorry—so very sorry.' She put a hand out to him and he caught her fingers in his but made no attempt to kiss her. As he came into the light she saw now how tired he looked with lines of strain about his mouth.

'It's the devil—oh, not just his dying, but everything else that's happened. It's unbelievable. I can't begin to tell you—'

He let go of her hand and pulled off the heavy sheepskin jacket he was wearing. 'I must talk to you, Tory. I must talk to someone.'

'But what—what is it? What's happened? You told me it—your uncle's death was to be expected.'

'Yes. We knew from what Dr. Spicer had said that there wasn't much hope. That's why we moved up from Bramwick to be with him. What we didn't know was—' He broke off, pushing a hand through his thick fair hair in distraught fashion. 'The most damnable thing. Something we'd never dreamt—had no idea of. Uncle Harold has a son.' He paused as if waiting for Tory to assimilate the fact.

It took her a few moments.

'A *son*? But where?—Where is he? Why didn't anyone know about him?'

'He's here—he's at Ravensholme. They sent for him. I mean, Mr. Earnshaw, Uncle Harold's solicitor, sent for him, at my uncle's request. A sort of deathbed thing. All these years he's kept it a secret and never had anything to do with this—this Julian. Oh, we knew he *had* a son, but it was supposed that he'd died as a child, because he never came to England. No one ever saw him.'

Tory was still trying to take the news in. Now frowningly she said, 'Where was he living then—wasn't he in England?'

'As it turns out, he was. He's been over here some time from Canada, where he was born. You *must* have heard the gossip, Tory—that my uncle married a French girl after the war when he went out to Canada for a couple of years. She—her people had left Paris and immigrated to Montreal—Quebec, rather, and lived with relatives or friends. People said she died in childbirth, but I think it must have been later on. Anyway, she's dead and so are her parents, but my cousin, can you believe it? my *cousin* Julian, is very much alive.'

'But—what does it matter that your uncle had a son and he's here? Why are you so upset?'

His mouth tightened, the blue eyes hardened.

'Because, my dear simple unthinking Tory, Uncle Harold has left practically everything he possessed to this son.'

Tory bit her lip, realising now the full extent of Ralph's chagrin and dismay. After all his hopes and expectations this news must be a bitter blow to him, dimming even the grief at his uncle's death.

She said slowly, 'How can you know this? I thought—I thought wills weren't known or read until after the—the funeral.'

'They aren't, but Earnshaw gave me a pretty clear hint as to how things were going to be. I asked him outright if my uncle had made a will—I knew he had been called in for this purpose and he told me that prior to the discovery of my cousin's whereabouts no will had been made but that my uncle was anxious to settle his affairs and had done so in favour of—the words were—"his issue". I said, "Does that mean the bulk of his money?" and old Earnshaw answered, "I am not in a position to tell you that until the will is read, but I had better warn you, Ralph, not to expect too much." '

'I'm sorry. You must be—be disappointed, but it isn't the end of the world. After all, it's only natural that your uncle should put his own son first, and it seemed he had left you something—a legacy—'

'A *legacy*!' Ralph broke in, his face so contorted with anger that he looked like another person. 'A legacy, when I'd expected to inherit Ravensholme and the estate. It's damnable—an outrage. What's my future to be now?'

She was startled by his outburst, the bitterness in his voice. She wanted to say something to comfort him, but she could only think of trite phrases. His angry voice must have penetrated to her grandfather, for the door of the kitchen suddenly opened and Mr. Webster looked in to say, 'Oh, it's you, Ralph. I wondered who'd come.' He gave a quick glance at Ralph's unsmiling face and said, 'Is anything wrong? It's not your uncle, is it?'

'Yes, he—my uncle died yesterday, Mr. Webster.'

'Eh, I'm sorry. Very grieved indeed to hear that. Come in to the fire and take something to drink. Tory, fetch the glasses, Ralph here looks as if he could do with a stiff whisky.' He put a hand on Ralph's arm and pushed him gently toward the door. In a few moments Ralph was sitting in the big chair opposite to Mr. Webster and sipping at a glass of whisky while Mr. Webster drew on his pipe and said, with a shake of his head, 'Your uncle'll be missed,

Ralph. Although he was never a sociable man and not one to mix with the county folk he did a lot for Scarsfell. He fought like a tiger against that new road they wanted to build through the dale, wouldn't sell a foot of land, and in the end the County Council had to give up. They were going to build two bridges across the Scar—not one, mind you, but two. That would have brought a pile of traffic and spoilt the dale for ever. Mr. Brierley wouldn't have it—he loved Scarsdale and said he wanted to keep it just as it was.'

Ralph stared down into his glass.

'I doubt if I shall have any say in the matter, Mr. Webster. My uncle had a son—did you know?' He glanced up, his blue eyes narrowed angrily. 'It's expected that he will inherit the Ravensholme estate.'

For a moment Mr. Webster stared blankly at him, then slowly he nodded, taking the pipe out of his mouth. 'That's right. He had a son, but it was thought he died as a baby. Mrs. Brierley died young—I remember that. She never came to Ravensholme and folks thought it a sad thing for your uncle to be in that big house alone, with neither wife nor child to cheer him. He was always a bit of a recluse, never an easy man to know, and he was in his thirties before he married. This son—he'll be your cousin, Ralph? Has he come to Ravensholme, then?'

Ralph explained a little of what had happened, ending with the words, 'He arrived yesterday, but too late. My uncle had died a few hours earlier.'

Mr. Webster shook his head.

'A tragedy. Reckon he was counting on seeing the lad.' He frowned consideringly. 'Well, man he'll be by now. Your age, or older, Ralph?'

'He's a few years older than me.' Ralph put his glass down on the table at his side, and stood up. 'I think I'd better be getting back, Mr. Webster. Mother will be wondering where I've got to—I couldn't telephone Tory, so I came to tell her what had happened.'

'Of course. You'll have plenty on—best get back.' Mr. Webster put out his hand. 'Goodnight, Ralph. I'm sorry you had to bring us such sad news.'

Tory went to the door with Ralph. As he pulled on the sheepskin coat she said slowly, 'I met someone tonight—

near the school. He was on horseback—a tall dark man. Would it—could it have been your cousin?'

Ralph buttoning up his coat, turned to look at her.

'On horseback? Yes, that would be Julian. He went out riding late this afternoon, of all things. Said he needed some fresh air or something. He took Uncle Harold's old hunter. Did you speak to him?'

'Yes. He asked the way back to Ravensholme. I was just getting the car out to come back here.' She nearly said, 'We saw the comet—saw Kahoutek,' but something in Ralph's frowning preoccupied gaze stayed her. This was no time for such topics.

'He's an odd devil. Takes after my uncle, I expect.' Ralph turned away. 'I must go, Tory.'

They went out into the yard where the wind blew fresh and cool off the moors, and the silence around them was infinite. Ralph drew Tory close to him and said, 'I'm sorry to be in such a mood tonight, darling, but I'm just about knocked out by all this.'

Tory laid her fingers against his thin cheek.

'I know. But try not to worry. Things may turn out better than you expect. And—and money isn't everything.' She wanted to say, 'We have each other. That's all that matters,' but it sounded like another banal phrase.

'It's a hell of a lot. I've got Mother round my neck, and Carole. Oh, I know she's got a job, but she's still living at Bramwick and I'm responsible for the upkeep of everything. Without a decent inheritance from Uncle Harold I can't see ahead to make any plans.' He looked down at her. 'For myself, or for us, Tory.'

For us. The two words rang like a little bell through her head. Although Ralph had never asked her in so many words to marry him she knew that only his responsibilities held him back from doing so. Only indirectly did he ever reveal to her his feelings. *'For us,'* he said, and Tory was comforted by such words. When he bent his head and kissed her, she put her arms round his neck and kissed him back with all the warmth and love she felt for him, and all the sympathy and consolation she wanted to give him in his troubles.

He released her to say, 'I wish you were on the phone

up here, darling, but I'll be in touch. I'll let you know what happens.'

'You can ring me at Miss Ewing's—she won't mind in the circumstances. I mean, if it's something important or you want to arrange a meeting. She'll take a message.'

'I'll do that, if necessary. Goodbye, angel.'

She watched him drive away, the red taillight of the car fading out of sight on the lonely windswept road. High above the moors the stars glittered and shone. They brought to mind the memory of the comet. Somewhere up there Kahoutek was in orbit, its life span anything from ten to fifty thousand years. Somewhere, by someone, its influence would be felt. Today she had seen the comet and at the same time had met the black-browed stranger who was to take over Ravensholme. It seemed to Tory in that moment that his coming too was going to influence and change all their lives.

CHAPTER TWO

THE village school consisted of eighteen children in all. Once there had been sixty, but now the 'eleven plus' children were whisked away by bus to the market town of Kirk Newton, nine miles away, leaving the under-elevens to be taught by Miss Ewing, the headmistress, and Tory, her assistant. This morning, after Tory had rung the bell, the children scampered in from the windy playground, and soon they were settled down and all was quiet save for the low hum of voices as they repeated after her the lessons she had set.

It would be sad if the school closed and the village was deserted of its children each day. The North Riding, more than most of the country, had kept its way of life unchanged, the manors and big estates remaining untouched by the growth of industry farther south. Small farms as well as large ones were owned by the same families for hundreds of years, and if this fact tended to an anachronistically feudal outlook, it also made for a community closely linked by the ties of land, rather than the possession of money. Tory's own grandfather, though only a hill farmer, was yet accepted by greater and wealthier landowners because Websters had lived and worked at Wether Bell for generations.

Sometimes her grandfather talked of selling the sheep.

'I'll not be able to do this job much longer, Tory,' he said once. 'Can't get around same as I did. Sam was talking to me the other day—he's saved money and his wife came into a bit when her uncle, Harry Bastow that kept the Drovers, died two years ago. Sam's not more'n forty—he could make a good thing of it for himself.'

Tory started aghast.

'But—Wether Bell? You couldn't live anywhere else but here, Gramps. You couldn't leave Wether Bell Farm.'

'I don't intend to. Sam would run the sheep from his cottage, it's but a few miles down the road and he's planning to enlarge and modernise the place. Get a grant, he reckons.' He smiled wryly. 'I shall stay on here until they carry me out feet first. Then the place'll be yours, Tory, to do as you wish with. You'd best marry a sheep farmer.'

'I wish I knew an eligible one,' Tory answered with a lightness she was far from feeling.

Now as she sat at her desk, gazing over the small heads, brown and black and golden and auburn, bent dutifully over their books, she wished she could put the clock back and keep Scarsfell and all the countryside as it had always been. She thought of Foxridge, up on the fells. Once it had held sixteen families, now a handful of people lived in the few remaining cottages, while Whistone, an even more remote community, was abandoned, for the winters up there and its inaccessibility had driven the people down to the dale.

It was midday break and the children were shouting and racing about when Tommy Dawson ran up to Tory, to say breathlessly, 'It's yer feller, miss. He's out there askin' to speak to you.'

Tory ignored the reference to her 'feller' and said with dignity, 'Thank you, Tommy. I'll see who is there.'

'It's yon Mister Brierley!' Tommy shouted after her so that all the playground could hear.

Tory, her cheeks pink, walked to the gate and there was Ralph standing by his car. He said quickly, 'I hope this isn't an awkward time, but I've been up to Batts Farm and I was too near to miss the chance of having a word with you. It seems weeks since we met.' He took her arm and opened the door of the car. 'Sit in here for a few minutes— we can talk.'

Tory gave a backward glance to the children, aware of a few curious stares and even one or two figures jumping up and down to catch a further glimpse of her 'feller', and then she slid into the car.

'Just for a minute, Ralph.' She turned to look at him. 'How are you?'

He shrugged.

'Sticking it out as best as I can. I wanted to come and see you and tell you what happened, but I've been tied up with trying to settle everything. There's a lot to do, as you can imagine.' He frowned, staring straight ahead down the empty road. 'Uncle Harold left me Bramwick, and a couple of thousand pounds. That's all.'

'He left you Bramwick? That—that was generous, Ralph. It's a beautiful old house.'

'So what?' Ralph turned his head and she saw his blue eyes were hot and angry. 'We lived there practically rent-free, as you know, so I'm not much better off. Except that I can sell the place, if I want to, and get some cash that way. But my mother has to have a home—and Carole, until she marries.'

'Yes.' Tory was silent, remembering that Ralph's father had come to live at Bramwick after the worsted mill he owned had failed several years ago. Some people said it failed because of Doris Brierley's extravagance; that she had forced her husband to take more out of the business than he had ploughed back and, in the competitive age of man-made fibres, he had not had the necessary capital to install new machinery and so had gone under. His health broke under the strain and Harold Brierley, Robert's brother, lent him the house in the dale across the river from Ravensholme in which to live. He had died within two years, but Mrs. Brierley and Ralph and Carole had stayed on, Ralph to leave college and come to work as his uncle's agent while Carole took a secretarial course and got a job with a firm of architects in York.

She said slowly, 'And—and everything else has gone to your cousin?'

'Yes, damn him. I'm sorry, Tory, but I find the fact hard to take. It's altered the whole course of my life.'

'Are you going to work for him—help run the estate, I mean?'

'For the time being. He wants me to—hasn't the faintest idea of how to carry on. Of all things, his job was—' He broke off at the sound of the school bell and the sight of Miss Ewing standing at the door of the school house ringing it.

Tory put her hand on the door.

'I'll have to go, Ralph, I'm sorry—'

'Shall we have dinner together? What about Friday evening—seven o'clock at the Bell? We can really talk.'

'Yes, I'd love that. Thank you, Ralph. I'll be there—the Bell at Kirk Newton at seven on Friday.'

He bent forward and kissed her quickly.

'Darling, bless you. See you then.' He pushed open the car door and she slid out and waving, dashed across the road into the school.

Tommy Dawson was there waiting, his round red face one wide grin of mischief.

'Told yer it was yer feller, miss.'

'That's enough, Tommy. Hurry into class,' Tory said in her best schoolmarm manner.

She was so happy to have seen Ralph. It had been two, nearly three weeks since that evening he had called at the farm. Perhaps things would work out with him and his cousin. Bramwick was his now, he could live there or sell it. It was a charming old place, originally a farmhouse built of stone and later converted for a tenant of Mr. Brierley's before he had let his brother live there.

Things might be better for him now. With a house of his own and the salary that he had been paid by his uncle and which now obviously Julian Brierley would continue to pay, he would be independent. If he—if *they* married, Tory thought the house was big enough to make a separate establishment for Ralph's mother. Would she be agreeable to that? Tory's heart sank a little as she thought of Mrs. Brierley, who was charming enough to her in a cool composed way but who somehow always gave Tory the feeling that she set her sights for Ralph considerably higher than a sheep farmer's granddaughter.

Ralph thought that not inheriting his uncle's house and estate was a bar to their marriage, but to Tory it seemed rather the opposite. Now he would not be so rich or so grand it would be easier. They would be able to work through their difficulties together and one day they would be married and live happily ever after.

Meanwhile, there was Friday evening to look forward to.

It rained for the rest of the week, a persistent drizzle with cloudwrack lying low on the hills, but on the Friday, when Tory drove down to Kirk Newton, the rain ceased temporarily and there were shafts of yellow light in the western sky. She had left straight after school closed as she hoped to do some necessary shopping before meeting Ralph at the hotel, and she was glad that she had done so when she saw the state of the road. At the best of times it was narrow, winding and precipitous, and today, with the surface ground into muddy runnels, the Mini was slipping and sliding all over the place. She dropped into a lower gear, for the brake didn't seem to be holding as it should and was thankful that she had managed to do so, for the next moment, when she put her foot down, there was no response and the car went bumping on unchecked.

She pulled at the handbrake, but with no result. Tory had a frightening feeling of helplessness, for the car was running away, its speed held only by the low gear. On either side of the road was a narrow grass verge and then solid stone walls. She dragged at the steering wheel, trying to swing the car on to the grass without turning it over or running into the wall. The grass was thick and tussocky—when at last she mounted the verge it checked her speed but sent the car rocking dangerously from side to side. Somehow she held it steady, felt it slowing again and, in one desperate attempt, ran for a few seconds level with the wall, and then, with a tearing scraping crash, brought it to a standstill nose up against the grey stone.

For a moment she was so shaken she could do nothing more than switch off the engine and flop, head down, arms across the steering wheel, while her thudding heart slowly quietened and she got her breath back.

She heard a loud bark, the scratching of paws against the car, and looking up she saw huge white teeth, a lolling red tongue and grinning brown mask. A voice said, 'Down, Jason. Down,' and someone tried to open the door for her. With shaking fingers Tory unfastened the catch and almost fell out of the car. Two hands came out to steady her, the same voice said, 'I saw you careering down the road and then heard that almighty crash. Are you all right—you're not hurt, are you? I thought for a moment you'd passed out.'

'I—I'm all right, th-thank you.' Tory pushed the hair back from her face. She looked up and saw dark eyes and level dark brows and a frowning dark face, and said blankly, 'Oh.'

The man stared down at her.

'Hello. You're the comet girl.' He was still holding her, his arm firm and steady about her waist. 'Come and sit over here—you look rather green,' and he led her to a stile built in the stone wall. He lowered her so that she was sitting on one of the steps, her back against the wall. The dog, a young and boisterous mastiff, bounded up to lick her hands and was reprimanded again with a stern 'Down Jason, down!' and subsided on to the grass with a panting jaw and wagging tail.

The man walked over to the car to give it a cursory examination and Tory closed her eyes against the peculiar feeling of weakness that threatened to overcome her. When she opened them he was standing beside her. He said, 'I'm afraid the car's a write-off. Were you going anywhere important?'

'I—I'm meeting someone in Kirk Newton, but—but not until seven.'

'Then I suggest, if you feel able to do so, you walk back with me to my house where you can telephone the AA or a garage who will see after your car, then when you've had a drink or something I'll run you to Kirk Newton.'

'Th-thank you.'

'Do you want me to fetch anything from the car?'

'Just my shoulder-bag—it's on the seat.'

He came back with it and said, 'I'm afraid we have to go over this wall. I'll go first and help you.'

She stood up, aware of a curious trembling at the knees, but somehow she climbed up the steps. She slid her legs over to go down, but the man, taller than the tall wall reached out to her and said, 'Let me lift you down,' and before she realised it Tory was swept up into his arms and for a moment was held close against a broad shoulder, her cheeks almost brushing the one so near her own, before being deposited gently on to the ground while one hand remained under her elbow to steady her.

'All right?'

'Yes, th-thank you.'

'Good.' He whistled the dog, who came bounding up to

them to go careering along the path ahead. 'It's not far through the wood to Ravensholme.'

'I know.'

She was aware of his quick sideways glance.

'You know? You know the house? And the Brierley family?'

'Yes.'

'I see. Then I suppose you know who I am?'

'I know you're Ralph's cousin.'

'I'm Julian Rivers. And you?'

'I'm Victoria Webster.'

'Victoria? That's an old-fashioned name.'

'They call me Tory for short.' She was wondering why his surname should be Rivers, but she hesitated to ask. She said rather breathlessly, aware of the long loose stride it was difficult to keep up with, 'Do you think—we could walk a—a little slower?'

'I'm sorry. Here, hang on to me,' and he pulled her arm through his. 'We'll take it easy.'

It was dusk in the woods, dark with overhanging trees and damp from the recent rain. It was the strangest feeling in the world to be walking along the muddy leaf-strewn path arm-in-arm with Ralph's cousin. What was she doing here like this? And yet she was grateful for the strong arm supporting her and knew that without Julian River's aid she would never have managed what seemed an endless walk.

The woods came right up to Ravensholme, surrounding its stone splendour with massive beeches and great oaks; casting dark shadows across grass-grown terraces and weed-filled flower beds. The house had a melancholy aspect, not dispersed when Tory was led into the wide hall with its linenfold panelling and dark oil paintings in heavy gilt frames. For a moment Julian Rivers hesitated, looking about him with a frowning face.

'I'm sorry there's no one at home but me. My aunt—' he shrugged—'I've hardly got used to calling her that yet—has gone to York for the day and my cousin isn't home yet. There's some sort of daily staff who sleep out. It's not a cheerful or welcoming place at the best of times, I'm afraid. Did you visit here when my father was alive?'

'Hardly at all. He—he seldom entertained.' She looked up at him. 'I—I was very sorry to hear of his death.'

He lifted broad shoulders in what could have been a shrug. His expression was grim rather than sorrowful.

'Thank you. But my grief is limited. I never knew him, never saw or spoke to him in my life.'

'That seems dreadfully sad.'

'I suppose it is. But as I was never even aware of his existence, believing him to have been killed in an accident, from what my grandparents told me, it would be hypocritical to assume a pose of mourning.' He turned, as if dismissing the subject. 'You'd like to telephone about your car? There's a phone in here,' and he pushed open a door leading into a book-filled room.

'Thank you.' Feeling somewhat rebuffed, Tory walked across to the desk in the window and sat down in a big carved armchair beside it, glad to rest for a few moments. What a strange man Julian Rivers was—abrupt, almost harsh in manner at times, yet he had been kind enough a little while ago. Oh well, it was nothing to do with her what sort of man he was, and opening her shoulder-bag she checked the number of the garage at Kirk Newton. When she had finished telephoning she went back to the hall to find Julian Rivers waiting for her.

'Finished? I thought you'd like a drink before we got to Kirk Newton. The room over here is more cheerful than this gloomy mausoleum of a hall—' and he led the way into a small den-like place where a fire cast a glow on faded red wallpaper and shabby velvet chairs. 'Please sit down. What would you like—a warming whisky—gin? Or a sherry?'

'A sherry, thank you.' Tory put out a hand to stroke Jason's broad brown head. 'What a beautiful dog. He's not very old, is he?'

'Five months. I've only had him ten days, but he's great company.' His mouth curled sardonically. 'Better than the humans in this house, I assure you. *They* only tolerate me.'

Tory didn't know how to answer that remark, so she was silent, staring down at the glass of golden liquid in her hand.

'You say you haven't been to Ravensholme very often,' he went on. 'Does that mean you don't know the Brierley family well?'

She said carefully,

'I didn't know your—your father. I know Mrs. Brierley and I was at school with Carole. And I know Ralph.'

The eyes so heavily lashed they looked black instead of hazel narrowed to regard her.

'Do you know him well—or very well?'

She hesitated. 'Very well. As—as a matter of fact it's Ralph I'm meeting in Kirk Newton. We're having dinner together.'

'I see.' He drained his glass and stood up to refill it. Over his shoulder he said cryptically, 'So you're on his side.'

'His side?'

'Oh, come. If you're such friends you must know that Ralph was expecting to inherit Ravensholme and my father's estate. It's been a bitter blow to him that I should have done so and he very naturally resents me and doesn't make much effort to hide his feelings. Our relationship is strained, to say the least of it.'

'No one knew Mr. Brierley *had* a son. Ralph was—was led to believe he would be the heir. It's natural, I suppose, that he should feel a—a little disappointed.'

Julian Rivers gave an abrupt laugh.

'That's putting it mildly! He's damned resentful. And his mother and sister haven't exactly welcomed me with open arms. I find it very uncomfortable living with a group of people who can scarcely stand the sight of me, and I shall be relieved when they return to their own home. I can't very well tell them to go.'

'You—you intend to stay here—to live at Ravensholme?'

'Certainly. Is there any reason why I shouldn't?'

Tory felt uncomfortable under his cool sardonic gaze.

'N-no. Except that—I mean, won't you be lonely here on your own?'

'I didn't say I was going to be on my own.'

She was momentarily startled.

'Are you married, then?'

'No. You ask a lot of questions. Shall I start? Are you in love with my cousin Ralph?'

She said stiffly, 'I've known him nearly all my life.'

'That's no answer.' He held his hand out. 'Another sherry?'

'No, thank you. I—I think I ought to be leaving. Please

don't trouble to take me all the way to Kirk Newton. I can telephone for a taxi.'

'It's no trouble. A welcome change, in fact. Wait here and I'll get the car.'

Tory was no more at ease when he had gone than when he had been present. Had Ralph shown his animosity so clearly—his chagrin at losing his inheritance? What would happen if he and Julian could not work together? There was the estate to run and unless Julian was experienced in such matters it would continue to be Ralph's job. Yet how could that be if the two cousins were at loggerheads? And Mrs. Brierley. She was cool and unfriendly too? And Carole?

The car was outside on the gravelled drive—the high old-fashioned Daimler, in which Mr. Brierley had driven round the countryside. Julian Rivers caught her glance and lifted a black eyebrow.

'Prehistoric, isn't it? I'm planning to change to a later model. My late father was either an eccentric or a miser, or perhaps he was both. One thing's for sure—he wasn't a *poor* man, so he didn't keep a car like this through necessity.' He closed the door and climbed into the driving seat beside her. It was dark now and the headlights cast a bright beam between the long avenue of trees which led to the road. They drove in silence for a while and then Julian said, glancing through the windscreen at the star-filled sky, 'By the way, did your grandfather see the comet that night?'

'No. He was very disappointed. He'd been watching out for it for so long. Astronomy is his hobby.'

He gave her a sideways glance.

'Odd, isn't it? That you and I should see it together. I wonder if it's a sign of something.'

'Why should it be?'

'Anyone who sees a comet is supposed to be influenced by it. Didn't you know that?'

'It's just superstition.' She spoke sharply, yet her voice carried no conviction.

'I am superstitious. Aren't you?'

'No.' She stared straight ahead aware that he was watching her. 'And I don't think you're a very credulous person either.'

'You're wrong there. Stage people are very superstitious.'

'Stage people?' She turned her head to look at him.

'I'm an actor.'

'An actor?' She could do nothing but repeat his words.

'You make it sound like a hangman. I assure you, it's quite a respectable profession.'

'But you're giving it up—you're going to stay at Ravensholme, you say.'

'And become one of the landed gentry? Yes. I never expected anything like this to happen to me, but now it has I'm going to make the most of it. I've got so far in the acting profession, and I've had a certain amount of success, but I've not attained stardom. Maybe with a lucky break I might have done so. I don't know. But I'm thirty-two and I've lived in a suitcase most of my life. Now I'm prepared to settle down, and with or without Ralph's help I intend to learn how to run the estate and sink roots in the place from which my forebears came.' His mouth twisted wryly. 'If that's not too grandiose a way of putting it.'

She was silent, thinking over his words, and then she said slowly, 'Is Rivers your stage name?'

'The English adaptation is. My grandparents' name was Rivière and when I was six, after my mother died, my name was changed by deed poll from Brierley to Rivière. When I went on the stage I anglicised it. It's a long story, but some time we'll get together and I'll tell you the details. If you'd like to hear, that is.'

'I—I would.' She knew that this was true. This strange man interested her in a way she couldn't account for.

They were driving over the bridge now, the river ran, swift and foam-flecked, below them, the lights of Kirk Newton lay ahead.

'The Bell, you said? I'm not sure which way that is—do I turn right by the church here?'

'Yes—the hotel is on the other side of the Market Place. Thank you very much for bringing me all this way. I— would you—would you come in and meet Ralph—have a drink with us?'

He smiled grimly.

'And spoil your evening? I don't think so, thanks all the same.' He leaned over to push open the door for her and she felt his thick black hair brush her chin and was aware of the warmth and strength of the powerful body near her own. His eyes, darkly intent, held her glance before she slid quickly on to the road.

'Goodnight.'

For some unaccountable reason Tory was breathless and her voice wasn't quite steady as she said, 'G-goodnight,' and turned to go through the swing doors of the hotel.

'And he brought you here in the Daimler? Well, I suppose he more or less had to. But don't get too thick with the fellow, Tory. We don't want to make him feel he's welcome here, because he damn well isn't.'

They were seated in the oak-beamed dining room of the Bell eating Tournedos chasseur, for Ralph had extravagant tastes.

'There's no question of my getting "thick", as you put it, but, Ralph—' Tory hesitated, staring down at the plate in front of her as she tried to find the right words. 'He's here to stay—he said so. And he wants to learn how to run the estate. How are you going to get along together if—if you don't get over the antagonism you feel for him? You'll be at loggerheads all the time.' She looked up and met his frowning glance and went bravely on, 'It—it isn't your cousin's *fault* he inherited the estate. He didn't do anything to bring it about—it's just the luck of the game.'

'My bad luck, you mean. It's no use, Tory. The whole thing is so galling I can scarcely be polite to Julian. Perhaps it's childish, but that's the way I feel. I can't help it.'

'But what's going to happen—will you be able to work with him?'

Ralph sighed.

'I shall have to try—unless I can get another job as an estate manager. That won't be easy. Let's talk about something else, Tory. You know you've just about ruined our dinner together.'

'I'm sorry.' She put her hand out and touched his fingers. 'Sorry in every way. I think it's very hard on you, Ralph, and I do understand how you feel. It wasn't fair or kind of your uncle to make such a will, and yet Julian is his son. What else could he do?'

'If only we'd known of his existence, then I'd have been

prepared to accept second best. I wouldn't have had my hopes raised in this way. Look, we're at it again, Tory. Let's forget it just for this evening. Are you going to Madeline Langford's party on the fifteenth?'

'I don't think so. I hardly know her, though I sometimes see her out riding and she nods and smiles. She's very striking-looking.'

'Yes. A bit horsey for my taste, handsome rather than pretty, you'd say. Her father's a bit of a rough diamond, but I understand he's loaded. He's spent a packet on Lindley Grange—and built all new stabling for Madeline's horses. She's going to run a small stud there.'

'You seem to know a lot about them.'

He smiled. 'I get around. But don't worry, angel, you're my girl. You know that.'

She said slowly, almost wistfully, 'I like to think so.'

'There's no one else. There never will be.' His fingers tightened round her. 'If only things were different! We'd have some sort of future—we could make plans. As it is— well, don't let's start on all that again, but you know as well as I do why things are at a deadlock.'

'Yes.' She was quiet, thinking that if Julian Rivers had not inherited his father's estate Ralph would have asked her to marry him. His coming here had altered everything, their very lives. For a moment she felt some of Ralph's antagonism for him.

Then reason prevailed. As she had said just now to Ralph, it wasn't his cousin's fault that this had happened. And Julian couldn't be expected to hand everything back to Ralph. Ralph, like herself, would have to make the best of things and adapt to changed circumstances.

She longed to say, 'We could get married. I have a job— you have one running the Ravensholme estate, or if you wanted to, you could try for another place. You have a house of your own, Bramwick. We could make provision for your mother there. And Carole is independent, soon she'll marry,' but the words remained unspoken. Even in these days of Women's Lib, Tory couldn't make the running. It was for Ralph to say these things.

A week went by—two weeks. At Wether Bell Farm there were blanket-lined baskets in front of the range and before the sitting room fire and tiny new-born lambs brought in by Sam Dyer came slowly back to life in the warmth. Troy sniffed them in kindly fashion and Topaz gazed benignly down at them out of blinking green eyes and sometimes licked them gently with a rough tongue. Mr. Webster fussed over them, as did Tory. It was part of the spring ritual.

The sleety rain was blown away at last and March winds swept the sky, chasing sun and cloud across fell and dale. The trees lost their bareness and were dusted with a faint fresh green and the great ridges rolled skywards, changing from purple to gold in the wake of the sunlight.

Tory, coming out of school in the fresh spring afternoon, heard the clatter of hooves from behind her and turned with a strange sense of expectation. Two riders were coming along the fell road from High Burton. The man waved his crop and she waited for them to approach. Some of the children had gathered about her and from among them Tommy Dawson piped up with, 'It's yer feller, miss. An' he's with that Miss Langford.'

'Thank you, Tommy. I can see who it is for myself.'

''E's ridin' a smashin' 'oss,' another boy said. 'Wish I had one like it,' and he clicked his tongue encouragingly. 'G'id up there—g'id up!'

Ralph reined in, and tipped the crop to his cap.

'Hello, Tory. You know Madeline Langford, don't you? Madeline, this is Tory Webster.'

Tory smiled up at the girl on the big grey. 'Hello.'

'Ralph's very kindly helping me exercise one of my horses. Jasper was so fresh he went off like a rocket when we got up on the moors. I don't think I could have held him.'

The bolder of the children reached out to pat the horses, Tommy Dawson among them. Madeline Langford tapped a cautionary crop. 'Careful, please. This one's nervous.'

'I think you'd better all be off home now,' Tory said. 'Goodbye, children.'

They scattered away shouting over their shoulders, ''Bye, miss. 'Bye, miss. See you termorrow, miss.'

The horses tossed their heads and pawed nervously, then subsided to calmness again as the last shrill voice faded away.

Madeline Langford smiled.

'What a job, handling that lot! I'll settle for horses any day.'

'I'm used to them. And we're only a small school.'

The sun gilded the bright gold hair under the black riding hat and showed up a clear pink and white skin. Slanting blue eyes smiled down at Tory.

'I know you by sight, but I'm so glad to be introduced to you properly. I wanted to ask you to the party I'm giving on March the fifteenth. Do come. Ralph is coming, and his sister, and I'm sure lots of other people you know.'

'It's very kind of you. I should like to.'

'Good. I'll put an invitation in the post. Isn't it a super day? After all the rain.' The grey horse fidgeted and Madeline smiled and added, 'We'd better get on—see you on the fifteenth, Tory,' and she lifted the reins and moved away.

Ralph held his horse in long enough to say, 'I'm delighted you're coming to Madeline's party. But I'll be in touch and we'll meet before then. 'Bye, Tory sweet,' before cantering down the road.

Tory stared after them with a queer mixture of feelings. It was kind of Madeline to invite her—she seemed a friendly girl, and she was very attractive in a fresh open-air way. How well did Ralph know her? They appeared to be on the best of terms.

'I'm not jealous,' Tory admonished herself. Of course not.

Just oddly depressed. As if seeing Ralph and Madeline riding together like this made her feel it was something they were used to doing together. She felt lost and lonely and a little neglected.

In the school house Miss Ewing was tidying up, after the children.

'I'll do that.' Tory took the duster and chalk from her and started to clean the blackboard. Miss Ewing, tall and thin and grey-haired, went over to her desk and took something out of it.

'How is your grandfather?' she asked. 'Is he getting about more easily?'

'Yes, thank you. But his leg is still very stiff and I think it's painful at times.'

'Bound to be. These things take time—and he isn't a young man.'

'No.' Tory put the duster down. 'He talks of giving up the farm—the sheep, I mean. As it is, Sam is doing most of the work. He has a nephew who helps, but he's still at school in Kirk Newton.'

'What will you do when this place closes? You'll want to find another post—but what about your grandfather?'

'Is the school really going to close?'

'I'm afraid so. I had a letter from the Council—you'd better read it. They're making plans for closure next year— at the end of the summer term.'

Tory took the letter and read it through. It was couched in formal terms and conveyed little.

'There will be an enquiry, of course,' Miss Ewing said. 'It's a Church school, as you know, and the Church provides money for the upkeep, although it's run by the County Council. The Board of Governors have to be consulted before any final decision is arrived at.'

'Some of the parents will want to fight it,' Tory said.

'Yes, I expect so. But others will want the children to go to the bigger, more modern school. Heaven knows I don't want to give up here, but sometimes I think it's inevitable. The village is growing smaller every year—soon there won't even be the fifteen children we have now to attend.'

'Everything's changing,' Tory said slowly. 'I wish it wouldn't.'

Miss Ewing smiled, her long bony face softening as she looked at Tory.

'Most young people welcome changes. They don't want life to stay the same. Do you?'

'In a way, yes. I mean, I wish Grandfather could farm Wether Bell for ever and never grow old. And—and Scarsfell stay the same—the same people and children—no one to go away.' She added, thinking of Madeline and of Julian, 'Or come here.'

'Now you're asking the impossible, Tory. People come and go all the time, and places alter. Some die and others develop. Where would progress be otherwise?' Miss Ewing shook her head. 'You know, this is all wrong. *You* should be saying this and I should be protesting, instead of the other way round.'

Tory smiled. 'I must be an anachronism—'

But as she drove home in the recently repaired Mini she thought that her grumbles were not entirely due to the threat of the school closure but caused through the arrival of newcomers into what had been a small enclosed world for so long.

Ralph arranged to pick Tory up on the evening of Madeline's party and also to take her home again, which pleased Mr. Webster.

'Don't want you drivin' back over these moors at two o'clock in the morning on your own,' he said.

'What makes you suppose it will be such a late party? It's only a supper and dance. Like Cinderella, I'll be home at midnight.'

Tory had bought a new dress for the occasion, long and flowered but not too frilly. The colours were turquoise and cyclamen, the turquoise deepening her eyes to sea green and the cyclamen in startling but effective contrast to her red gold hair. Tonight she wore it loose over her shoulders and she had brushed it until it sparkled with light.

Her grandfather stared bemused at her.

'Why, Tory lass, I've never seen you look so bonny. You're your grandmother all over again, with your red hair and bright eyes.' He shook his head. 'There was no one to hold a candle to her when she was young and dressed in her best.' He put out his hand. 'You'll be the belle of the ball.'

She put her hand in his rough one.

'You say that to all the girls, Gramps.'

'Nay, I mean a thing when I say it—you know that! Is that a knock at the door?'

'That'll be Ralph already.'

Ralph came in looking handsomer than ever tonight in a new dark blue dinner jacket which set off his fair good looks and blue eyes. He smiled down at Tory and said, 'You look gorgeous, a real dolly. Doesn't she, Mr. Webster?'

'Aye, she's pretty fetchin'. Will you take a drink before you go, Ralph?'

'That's very kind of you. Just a small one, to give us all the party spirit.'

Outside by the car Ralph put his arms round Tory and gave her the kiss he had refrained from doing in front of Mr. Webster.

'Darling, you look so lovely. And you smell heavenly—umm!'

She kissed him back and for a moment time hung suspended and she was happy beyond words to be in Ralph's arms and to have this wonderful evening ahead of them.

He released her gently and opened the car door.

'Hop in. We mustn't be late,' and in a few minutes they were on their way.

Lindley Grange had once been part of Lindley Abbey which lay a few miles farther down the river and was now in ruins. It was a grey stone house with a beautifully gabled roof and tall chimneys. Extensive paddocks surrounded it and the gardens ran down to the Scar river which flowed, swift and deep, from the waters of the high fells around it.

Tonight the house was ablaze with light and cars were jam-packed along the gravelled drive. Tory was interested to see the place since its recent renovations, for she had visited it in the past when the owners, an elderly couple without children, had invited her to tea with her grandmother.

She would scarcely have recognzied it. The hall was now velvet papered to set off several fine oil paintings and two massive eighteenth-century lions *rouennais*. The enormous drawing room which had once been old-fashioned and chintzy was resplendent with low modern furniture and eight-foot settees in soft cream leather—people were everywhere, sitting, standing, talking, laughing. Madeline was waiting to greet her guests as they arrived, a tall figure in a gold and white dress which set off her shining fair hair. Her father, a short thickset man who scarcely reached to her shoulder, was standing at her side and he shook hands with Tory and Ralph and said, in his deep gruff voice, 'Nice to have you with us. Go through and get yourselves some drinks.'

Hired waiters in white jackets were moving round with trays of glasses—double doors led through to an even larger room, cleared of furniture and with a polished floor ready for dancing later.

'How long has Mr. Langford been a widower?' Tory asked as Ralph handed her a glass of sparkling golden liquid.

'Three years, I think. Losing his wife is one of the reasons he moved up here.'

'And Madeline is the only child?'

'Yes. He dotes on her.' He broke off as someone approached them and Tory looked up to see Dr. Spicer, and with him, Mrs. Brierley. 'Hello, here's Mother. Carole's somewhere—Lester brought them in his car.'

It was obviously going to be a party for the entire neighbourhood.

Mrs. Brierley, her fair hair scarcely touched with grey and her light eyes deepened in colour by the delphinium-blue dress she was wearing, looked queenly elegant as she smiled at Tory and said, 'How nice to see you, Tory. You look charming, my dear.'

As ever Mrs. Brierley made the right gestures, but somehow her manner and glance lacked the warmth of her words.

'Thank you. I—what a grand party Mr. Langford is giving. Everyone seems to be here.'

'It's Madeline's birthday—a special occasion. Didn't you know?'

Tory shook her head.

'No. Did you know, Ralph?'

'Yes, I thought I told you?'

'I would have brought her a present—some small thing as a remembrance.'

Ralph shrugged.

'She wouldn't expect it. We sent something, as we know her fairly well—Mother saw to it. Here's Carole—and Lester.'

Carole came up, her small heart-shaped face all smiles for Tory. She was a small pretty girl with brown hair and golden-brown eyes.

'Tory! Super to see you—it's been *ages*. How are you—you look fabulous. Doesn't she, Lester? I love you in those colours. Isn't this house gorgeous? You'd never know it from the fuddy-duddy old place it was when the Parkinsons lived here.'

'It's certainly very striking—what I've seen of it.'

'Upstairs is out of this world—four-poster beds and rich old Spanish furniture. Fantastic! You ought to see it.'

It was obvious that Carole had seen it. And Ralph. They knew Madeline so well they had sent her a birthday present.

Lester Fawley, who was thin and dark and an ardent admirer of Carole, interrupted Tory's train of thought to say, 'The whole thing was planned for them by a firm of London designer-decorators—it must have cost the earth.'

'Lester, please! Who wants to know what anything costs? How typical of a chartered accountant to reduce everything to pounds and pence,' Carole exclaimed. 'Oh, look, there's Molly Brewer and Derek. I must speak to them,' and she was gone, a vivid darting figure in her scarlet chiffon dress. Lester stared wistfully after her while Mrs. Brierley with a murmured excuse moved on with Dr. Spicer, leaving Tory and Ralph with Lester.

'You need another drink, Lester, to cheer you up,' Ralph said, signalling to a passing waiter.

Someone came and spoke to Ralph and he turned with Lester to answer. Tory, still sipping her first glass of wine, looked slowly round the room. She knew a number of the people here, but not as many as she would have expected; apparently the Langfords had invited guests from away. Some would be staying here, no doubt, in the old house which had undergone such a metamorphosis.

A voice from behind her said, 'Hello, Tory,' and she swung round so abruptly the wine danced over the rim of her glass.

She was surprised, startled even, to see him here, as tall, and somehow despite his slight smile, as intimidating as ever.

'H-hello.'

He was in a dinner jacket with a decorously frilled shirt. He stood head and shoulders above the other guests—black-brown hair curling into the nape of his neck, level black brows above the hazel eyes that sparkled golden flecks under the bright lights.

'You didn't expect to see me here? I can't think why not. As heir to the Ravensholme estate I'm beginning to discover I am *persona grata* everywhere.' He lowered his voice.

'I'm pleased to say not everyone suffers from my cousin's prejudices.'

She glanced nervously over her shoulder at Ralph, still deep in conversation.

'I—I didn't realise you knew Madeline.'

'Our acquaintance is deepening. She's about to sell me one of her horses, or perhaps two.'

Ralph turned at the sound of his voice and for a moment he stared blankly at Julian. Then he said shortly, 'Oh, hello. You know Lester Fawley?'

'I don't think so. How d'you do.' The two men shook hands.

'And this is Harry Clegg.'

From the other room music sounded and people were drifting through to dance. Ralph took Tory's glass from her hand and said, 'Come on. See you later, Lester,' and with a brief nod to the other two men he swept her away before she could speak.

Dancing slowly round among the few couples who had essayed the floor, he said frowningly, 'Julian gets on my nerves. He turns up everywhere these days. Of course Madeline had to invite him this evening—she couldn't very well do otherwise as she knows Mother and Carole and we're all at Ravensholme. But it's a bind, having him breathing down our necks.'

'When are you going back to Bramwick?'

He shrugged.

'Pretty soon, I suppose. It's been kindness on Mother's part to stay on and see the house is run for him. Not that he seems particularly grateful.'

'Things aren't any better between you, then?'

'Not really. He wants to know everything about everything. Won't make a decision until he's been into every detail. He should leave it all to me.'

'But if he wants to learn about running the estate—?' Tory began.

'He won't do that in five minutes. He's no experience of farming, of land matters, of tenancies. Do you know what he was before he came here?—an *actor*. Can you beat it? One minute he's in some second rate theatre declaiming Shakespeare or something and the next he's trying to run a three-thousand-acre estate. Well, he won't be able to do much without my help.'

He jerked his head back in an angry manner. 'Don't let's ruin Madeline's party talking about Julian the same way you ruined our evening out together the other week.'

'Oh, Ralph, I didn't! I didn't mean to—I'm sorry. It's only that I—I want things to go right for you. I won't say another word.'

Ralph smiled, his frowning face transformed.

'Promise?'

'I promise.'

'Good. Now we can begin to enjoy ourselves.'

The evening whirled by. Tory danced with Ralph and with Lester and other men she knew. Soon it was the supper dance. A buffet meal had been laid out on long flower bedecked tables in what had once been the billiard room and small tables placed along the walls and in the big glass-domed conservatory beyond.

Tory glanced round to see where Ralph was, thinking he would be coming to claim her as his partner. She caught sight of Madeline. She was talking to Julian. They made a striking couple, Madeline golden fair in her golden and white gauze dress and Julian tall and dark, a sombre but arresting figure standing close beside her. He bent his head and tall though she was, she still had to look up at him as she smiled and said something.

Carole's voice said at her shoulder, 'Isn't he a dish? Ralph's got this feud thing going, but it's not for me. Julian's definitely got sex appeal. I could fall for him.'

Tory turned to look at her.

'What about Lester?'

'Oh, Lester. He just dogs my footsteps. Devoted but dull. Now Julian's something different—thrillingly magnetic and *all* man.' Carole rolled her eyes. 'Po-ow! Don't you agree?'

Tory hesitated, not knowing what to say. Carole didn't wait for an answer but rattled on gaily, 'I know what it is—you're too involved with Ralph to notice.'

That wasn't strictly true. She had noticed. She had been very much aware from the beginning of Julian's compelling personality.

'He is—unusual,' was all she could find to say.

'The understatement of the year.' Carole gazed wistfully in Julian's direction. 'D'you suppose he's asking Madeline for the supper dance—some girls have all the luck. Of course, as hostess and birthday girl she has the pick. Oh, there's Ralph talking to her now. He's a bit dog-in-the-manger, he won't like Julian muscling in. And here comes Lester. He booked this dance early on. See you, Tory,' and with a wave of her hand she turned away.

Tory stood irresolute as the music started up again and people moved on to the floor for the supper dance. Ralph was still talking to Madeline—she smiled at him and nodded. Julian had disappeared.

Harry Clegg was advancing purposefully towards her, and while Tory waited, still hesitating, he reached her side and said somewhat breathlessly, for he was a short thickset man with the powerful shoulders of a Rugby player,

'Tory, Ralph sent me to deputise for him—it seems Madeline thought he'd booked the supper dance. So will you have this with me?'

Before Tory could answer she felt a hand on her arm and heard Julian say from close behind her.

'I'm sorry, but Tory's my partner for this. Aren't you, Tory?'

She looked up at him, felt the strange spell of the dark gaze, heavy-lidded yet piercing, saw the smile curving his deep cut mouth. She glanced quickly back to Harry whom Ralph had sent with so cursory a message and her chin went up almost defiantly.

'Thank you very much, Harry, but—but as Ralph's not free I—I shall be partnering Julian. I'm sorry.'

Harry looked disappointed but gave a philosophical shrug.

'That's all right, then. Not to worry,' and he turned away.

Julian's hand slid down her arm to catch her fingers in his. His other arm came about her waist.

'Not before time. I've been waiting to dance with you all evening.'

Tory was determined not to be beguiled by compliments. She said coolly, 'That's not true. You didn't ask me before.'

'What? And be killed in the crush? Or be invited to a duel by Ralph?'

As usual he was mocking her. It wasn't as though she

wanted to dance with him. Why had she, when Harry, whom she knew well and who was a friend of Ralph's, had asked her? Was it a gesture against Ralph, because she was hurt at his partnering Madeline and she knew that her dancing with Julian, instead of Harry, would annoy him? What a trivial reason, she thought, and refused to admit to herself that somehow when Julian had come to stand beside her and looked at her in that intent way she had been unable to refuse his invitation.

He was looking at her now, a cool scrutiny that flicked over face and hair and dress.

'Relax,' he said in his drawling way. 'You spoil yourself frowning like that. I'd no idea you had such gorgeous red hair—it's really something with that dress. Have you the temperament that goes with it, I wonder? Or just the temper?'

The music had changed—now they were dancing two feet away from one another, each making their own rhythms. Despite Julian's height and powerful build, he moved lithely and with grace, which surprised Tory, until she realised that this was due to his stage training.

She looked away from him and saw, not far from them, Ralph dancing with Madeline. He met Tory's glance and his quick smile changed to a frown as he saw with whom she was dancing. Tory smiled back, aware of the compunction that had followed a childish impulse to toss her head.

Now the music brought her close to Julian again. His arm tightened about her waist as he swung her round to the slow tempo of a waltz. It was dreamy, hypnotic; the lights had dimmed, someone was singing into a mike,

> 'Come close, where you belong,
> Let's hear our secret song,'

Her cheek was against Julian's shoulder, she felt his breath on her hair, they seemed to be dancing on a cloud. When the music ended in an arpeggio of notes on the electric guitar she wasn't sure whether it was relief or regret that she felt.

Julian retained her hand in his and said, 'Over here, I think,' and led the way towards the conservatory.

The setting was fantastically attractive, the glass walls

interspersed with *treillage* up which vines and clematis climbed in profusion. The furniture was white-painted wickerwork and Chinese red rattan, elaborately curved and shaped. Flowers were everywhere, in pots and urns and tubs, great paper lanterns hung from the domed roof to shed a soft golden glow over everything.

Tables were already filling up—people calling and waving to one another. Julian lifted a hand in casual salute to someone and the next moment Tory found herself sitting at a table with four people whom she had never met before.

Julian introduced her quickly, 'Dolly Graham, Captain Graham, Marion Chester and Derek Beaton—Tory Webster.'

They were cheerful and smiling and all had come from some distance away. It turned out that Captain Graham was the tenant of one of Julian's farms and had known his uncle well. With food collected from the buffet and with champagne served by the white-coated waiters it was soon a very merry party indeed. There was no sign of Ralph or Madeline—obviously they were sitting in the other room with Mr. Langford and Mrs. Brierley and Carole and Lester. Tory wished that she could have been with them, but she had to admit that if Julian and Ralph had been together in the same party things would not have gone with such zest.

After supper, in the big bedroom upstairs temporarily turned into a powder room, Carole was repairing her make-up before a dressing table mirror. She turned at sight of Tory and said, 'You dog, sneaking off with Julian like that! How did you manage it?'

Tory shrugged.

'It seems there was a mix-up of partners—Ralph had invited Madeline for the supper dance. So when Julian asked me—' she left the sentence unfinished.

Carole smiled, outlining her cupid's bow of a mouth with bright red lipstick to match her dress.

'You mean *she* invited *him*. I'd better warn you, Madeline has taken a fancy to Ralph. She's always ringing him up—about the horses, or the dogs, or the pheasants or whatever.'

'Is she? Tory tried to sound casual. 'Well, she's very attractive.'

'The most attractive thing about her is her money. Look at this place—it's been absolutely transformed, and it must have cost a bomb.' Carole saw that despite Tory's seeming indifference her expression was wistful. She put out a small hand. 'Not to worry, sweetie. You know you're the light of my darling brother's life. Always have been.' She patted Tory's arm consolingly and moved away from the mirror as another girl came to smooth her hair before it.

Downstairs, Ralph was waiting for Tory; he slid her hand through his arm in proprietorial manner, and said, 'What on earth possessed you to dance with Julian? I sent Harry over to you.'

'That was kind of you,' Tory answered coolly, 'but as you were—booked yourself, I felt free to choose my own partner. Harry isn't much of a dancer.'

'And Julian is? But you didn't know that. You took him on just to annoy me.'

'Ralph, please. Don't shout.'

He lowered his voice to say tersely, 'I'm not shouting. I'm just saying it seemed a bit pointed of you to dance with Julian. You know how I feel about him.'

Tory softened. She could never remain annoyed with Ralph for long.

'You're not by any chance jealous?'

'Of course not.' He met her teasing glance and smiled reluctantly.

'Well, perhaps I am a little.'

She said slowly, 'I think I was too—over Madeline. I took it for granted we would have supper together.'

'Darling, we would have done, after I'd danced with her, but you cleared off with Julian. Otherwise we'd have all been together—Mr. Langford, Mother and Carole and Lester—and Harry, if you'd danced with him.' He frowned. 'I don't know how it came about.'

Tory wondered if Madeline had manoeuvred things without Ralph being aware. Anyway, it was over and done with. She smiled, 'It was just a mix-up—it doesn't matter.'

He smiled back, 'What matters is that we're dancing this one together—and the next—and the next.'

Tory shook her head ruefully, 'I rather think I'm spoken for—I promised Bill Wainwright a dance after supper and one with Charles Hyslop.'

There was nothing to mar the rest of the evening, and

everyone voted it the best party ever. There was hot soup and bacon and eggs at one o'clock in the morning and by the time Ralph was driving Tory over the wide windswept moors her grandfather's prediction of the time of her return was more or less correct.

'School breaks up next week,' Tory said, as the car came to a stop outside Wether Bell Farm. 'Jane has asked me to stay for a few days during the Easter holiday and she wonders if you would like to come over for a night or two while I'm there.'

Jane was Tory's cousin who was married to a doctor and lived in Whitby.

Ralph frowned.

'Ye gods, is it Easter already? When do you go to Jane's?'

'The Wednesday after Easter. I shall stay until Monday, I expect.'

He hesitated, then he said: 'I don't think I'll be able to manage it. I seem to be very tied up at the moment. Please thank Jane for me and explain to her. Maybe I'll be able to get over for a day.'

'It's a long way there and back—I wish you could stay a night,' Tory said wistfully.

Ralph shook his head.

'Not much hope, I'm afraid. But I'll let you know if I can.' He bent his fair head to hers. 'Goodnight, Tory darling. It's been a super evening, hasn't it?'

'Super.' For a long moment she stayed in his arms and returned his kiss, and then because she knew her grandfather would be awake listening for her she pulled herself free and said, 'I'd better go—Gramps will be waiting.'

'The old watchdog? He keeps a firm eye on you, doesn't he?'

'Not really. I have all the freedom I want—it's just that he—worries a bit if I'm very late. Or rather early—do you know it's tomorrow—or rather today.' Slowly, reluctantly, she slid out of the car, Ralph holding on to her hand until the last moment. 'Thank you for bringing me home. Goodbye, Ralph.'

''Bye, darling.'

She stood a moment in the darkness after he had gone wondering at the curious sense of flatness, as if everything had not turned out quite right. 'Super evening,' Ralph had said, and she had echoed his words. If that meant music and laughter and delicious food and champagne to drink then super described it. And she and Ralph had been together and he had brought her safely home and kissed her with his usual love and affection.

Never more than that. But what should there be? What more did she want? A demonstration of great passion? She wouldn't be able to cope. She *loved* Ralph and he loved her, and everything was just as it should be. And yet, as she turned into the house, she seemed to hear the music of the waltz echoing on the quiet air and she spun round, her feet skimming the ground and a strange tingling sense of excitement possessing her as if once again she was dancing with Julian.

She came to her senses with a shock and stood, breathless, her hand against her throat, thinking. 'What's got into me? I must be mad—whirling round in the darkness as if I was still at the party! Tory Webster,' she admonished, 'you've had too much champagne. It's gone to your head and you're not yourself. If Grandfather had looked out of the window and seen you just now—' she started to laugh and then stopped abruptly, and nothing was very funny any more and the sense of what—disappointment? regret?—*longing* was with her again, and she hurried away from it into the house.

The day after school broke up Tory went to Sam Dyer's house with a message for Bessie. Sam's cottage lay a mile down the road nearer to the village and it was such a fine spring morning she was glad to walk and take Troy with her. Bessie was busy washing. She scorned all modern aids and used an old-fashioned wringer for the sheets that were already blowing on the line.

She insisted on making Tory a cup of tea and plied her with slices of the feather-light Sally Lunn which was Bessie's specialty. Troy had a piece too, sitting drooling at them, pink tongue hanging out expectantly.

Tory walked home slowly up the hill, thinking that when the sun shone and the sky was blue and the moors were blue, violet blue instead of purple or brown, there was no more beautiful place than Yorkshire. Larks were singing overhead—piercingly sweet, the very sound of a spring morning. Small brown butterflies flitted above the fresh green grass.

From behind her came a car's warning toot—she called to Troy, who slunk in close beside her. The car coming up behind her tooted again and slowed to a standstill. Tory turned her head, not recognising the sleek dark green lines, then saw that it was Julian sitting in the front seat above which the hood had been rolled neatly back.

He lifted a hand in greeting. 'Good morning.'

'Hello.'

'How d'you like it? An improvement on the Daimler, don't you think?'

Tory's glance took in the gleaming bodywork and shining chromium, the long low bonnet.

'Definitely.'

'I'm just trying her out. Going over to see a tenant farmer the other side of Rylstone.'' He lifted a questioning eyebrow. 'Like to come with me and see how she goes?'

'I—thank you, but I—I have to get back to the farm.'

'Let me give you a lift up there.'

'It's no way to walk. And there's Troy here.'

'What's the matter, don't you trust me? I won't abduct you.' Julian leaned over and opened the door. 'Hop in. The dog too.'

Troy took up most of the floor space—Tory found herself pressed more closely against Julian than she could have wished. The car seemed to leap forward as if jet-propelled and almost before she had got her breath back they were at the gate of the farm.

'Thank you.' She slid out. 'Come on, Troy.'

Julian was gazing round.

'So this is where you live? *Very* Brontë-ish. Is your grandfather at home—I'd enjoy meeting him.'

'I—' Without seeming rude it was impossible to refuse. 'If you're not in a hurry—' she shrugged. 'Please come in.'

'Thanks. I'm in no hurry—I've all the time in the world.' He slid his long legs to the ground and followed her down the track.

Mr. Webster was in the yard, hobbling round on his stick.

His eyes narrowed to gaze at Julian and Tory quickly introduced him.

'I'm happy to meet you. I knew your father, I won't say well, but over a long period of time. Come on in to the house where we can have a bit of a chat.'

'That's very kind of you.'

In a few minutes Julian was seated in one of the leather armchairs with a glass of beer in his hand while Mr. Webster sat across the hearth from him. Tory, with a murmured excuse, went into the kitchen to start preparations for lunch, determined not to play the hostess or encourage Julian to stay too long.

When after a time she returned to the sitting room it was to find Julian on the point of departure.

'I've told Julian if he'd like to stay we can find him something to eat, but he says he has to get on,' her grandfather said. 'He's coming up another time to look at my telescopes and have a talk about the stars.'

'Yes, I shall look forward to that,' Julian answered. For a moment his glance met Tory's before he added casually, 'I wondered if Tory would like to run over to Hepworth's farm with me—there's a lot I'd like to know about the countryside round here that perhaps she could tell me, but she wasn't sure she was free to come.'

Mr. Webster looked at her.

"Why, you'd enjoy it, Tory. You know every dale and fell between here and Rylstone. What's to stop you going? I can get my own lunch, you know that. If you want something to eat yourselves, there's the Packhorse Inn where you can get a ploughman's lunch or a sandwich.'

'A splendid idea,' said Julian. He cocked an eyebrow. 'What about it, Tory?'

Why did she always seem to be in two minds when she was with Julian? Wanting him to say goodbye and go and yet feeling it would somehow be fun to go with him?

He saw her hesitation and said firmly, 'That's settled, then.' He put his hand out. 'Goodbye, Mr. Webster. I've very much enjoyed meeting you and I'll look forward to coming again. And you must visit me at Ravensholme.'

Tory collected her windbreaker for warmth in the open

car and against the winds that blew round Rylstone Fell
before walking out to the car.

As they drove away Julian turned his head to say, 'Do
you know Hepworth Farm where I'm going to?'

'I know where it is.'

'I'm visiting all my tenants in turn. This is the last one—
it must be a remote spot if it's in the middle of these moors.'

'It isn't, actually. There's a lower road to Rylstone—the
one that runs at the back of Ravensholme. It passes near to
Rylstone Ghyll, where there's a famous waterfall. Hepworth
Farm is off the lower road, but you can get to it by taking
a road to the right farther along this one.'

'There you are, you see, you know it all. That's why I
asked you to come.' He gave her a slow sideways glance.
'Well, partly.'

Something in his look confused her momentarily. She
glanced away to the fells, their grey edges scarred and
broken where the scree fell away down the hillside. Rock
and boulders rose above the stone walls that ran in endless
crazy patternings to the dale floor while round them for
miles stretched the moors, a waste of purple blue heather
and cotton grass.

When she didn't answer he said, 'Are you thinking I
conned you into coming? Perhaps I did. You're not a very
forthcoming girl, are you, Tory? I thought we were by way
of being friends.'

'It takes time to make friends,' Tory said more primly
than she felt.

'Does it? Can't there be instant friends, like falling instantly
in love?'

'I—don't know. I've never done either.'

'But you're in love with Ralph. Or think you are.'

'I don't *think,* I know I am. We've been friends all our
lives, and that's the best basis—for loving someone.'

He shook his head.

'I don't agree. People should be lovers first and friends
afterwards. It doesn't work so well in reverse—the affair
never gets properly off the ground.'

She turned her head to stare at him.

'I've never heard such—such a wild statement. You can't
be serious.'

'I'm perfectly serious. Oh, don't get me wrong. I'm not suggesting people should pop into bed first and discover afterwards whether they prefer two or three lumps of sugar in their tea, or prefer Bach to the Beatles. I meant that there must first of all be a powerful overriding physical attraction. That's the most important thing—the reality of any love affair between a man and a woman, and the basis of passion. Without it any so-called romance is a watered-down substitute.'

She said coldly, 'Theatrical people exaggerate—it's part of their stock in trade. If you speak from personal experience your view of things is probably coloured by the life you've led. I think you said you'd never sunk roots anywhere? I suppose all your love affairs had to be instant because they were taken on the wing, so to speak.'

One black eyebrow rose sardonically.

'You've a sharp tongue—the hazard of a redhead. I don't think about *all* my love affairs—they weren't that numerous, but most enjoyable while they lasted.'

She longed to lash out at him again. Something about him, his arrogance, his mockery, angered her in a way she had never known before. She felt provoked beyond reason. How dared he pass any criticism of Ralph and herself, even if the criticism was implied and not stated? What did a man like this know about loving—he had probably never *loved* anyone in his life but just gone from affair to affair. She wished fervently that she had never let herself be talked into coming out with him like this.

He must have read her thoughts, for he said quietly, in the deep-toned voice that against her utmost determination beguiled her, 'Don't look so cross. I didn't mean to annoy you. I'm sorry. Let's be—if not friends, yet, at least amicable acquaintances. We have a bond in common—we saw the comet together, and how many other people round here have done that?'

Tory looked at him from under her lashes, thinking that there was something formidable about him, some quality that whispered—'beware'. He wasn't a man you could ignore or defeat easily. He was dangerous.

Dangerous? She felt her heart beat quicken and thought, 'But why should he be dangerous to me?' No, she meant he would be dangerous to someone like Ralph, perhaps, or to anyone who opposed him. That was it.

She said slowly, 'All right. But let's talk generalities—we don't know one another well enough to discuss personal matters.'

He smiled crookedly. 'That's a pity. I was about to tell you the story of my life. You said once you'd like to hear it. Perhaps later, when you've forgiven me?' He broke off and the car slowed down. 'Here's a turning on the right—is that the one I'm to take?'

'Yes. It's rather steep and narrow—only a side road.'

He braked again and drove carefully between the high stone walls until, after a few miles, they reached the lower Rylstone road and the moors were left behind. Soon they came to a low stone-built farmhouse and in a few moments Julian was introducing Tory and himself to the farmer and his wife.

Mr. Hepworth, a tall bulky man with a high colour, knew Tory's grandfather, so conversation went easily, and then, while Julian went off to discuss farm matters with Mr. Hepworth, his wife entertained Tory. Another bond in common was found when Mrs. Hepworth discovered that two of her grandchildren had attended Scarsfell school.

In the end they were persuaded to stay to the midday meal, for, as Mrs. Hepworth said, she cooked daily for five or six people and two more were easily fitted in. It was three o'clock when at last they said goodbye and drove away.

'Thank you for coming with me,' said Julian. 'You get along so well with these people—you're part of their world.' He stared straight ahead at the empty road. ''Since I came here I've felt very much a ''stranger in a strange land'', perhaps because no one at Ravensholme wanted or welcomed me. But since I've been round the estate and met so many of the tenants and cottagers I begin to feel I belong. They knew my father and so they accept me, because I'm his son.' He smiled wryly. 'The only thing is, I wish my name had stayed Brierley—I'm tempted to change it back again.'

Tory was feeling calmer again, more relaxed. She said slowly, 'Why did your grandparents change it?'

He looked sideways at her.

'Do you really want to know?'

She nodded.

'Yes. Yes, please tell me.'

He braked and drove the car on to the grass verge.

'It's a long story, but I'll try and make it as brief as I can.'

CHAPTER THREE

'I THINK I told you, I never knew my father. I suppose he saw me as an infant. My mother was very young, just nineteen. My father was twelve years older than she was. It must have been an incongruous marriage from the start, for from what I've gathered my mother had led a very sheltered life, apart from the shock and upheaval of being taken to Canada from the convent school in Paris where she was being educated. She was born late in life to my grandparents. I remember them as being a sad, withdrawn elderly couple, for their lives had been disrupted by leaving France. Naturally, they centred on my mother, who was the focus of their lives.'

'Were—were your parents very much in love?' Tory asked hesitantly.

He shrugged.

'They must have been, for they had to brave my grandparents' strong opposition to the marriage. The last thing in the world they wanted was for their cherished only daughter to marry a man of another nationality and upbringing. Apparently my mother and father were introduced at some charity do and my father fell immediately in love with her. She was very beautiful—I remember her, and I have photographs too that show how lovely she was, young and delicate-looking with smooth dark hair and enormous hazel brown eyes.' He paused, as if deep in remembrance.

'She must have been courageous, to withstand her parents' disapproval and marry your father,' Tory said gently.

'Yes. And though at first sight it might seem strange that two such different people should fall so deeply in love with one another, when you consider it, it's natural enough. My mother was enclosed in an old people's world, for my grandparents' circle was elderly, narrow and very French. She must have been hungry for gaiety and laughter, and she met my father, who though several years older than she, was an air pilot. He was part of the glamorous élite, of young active life. She was invited to the concert and dances, and my father, thousands of miles from his Yorkshire world and probably homesick, fell overwhelmingly in love with her.'

'But how did her parents become reconciled to the marriage?'

'They never were. My mother threatened to run away, in fact, I have an idea she did and lived with my father, so, in the end, they agreed to the marriage. I was born the following year, and soon afterwards my father returned to England. My mother remained in Canada and went to live with her parents. He begged her to follow him to England, but she wouldn't do so. Her mother's health was failing, her father leaned on her for help and support. They couldn't face another upheaval and go with her to England, so she stayed behind in Quebec to be with them.

Tory looked round at Julian's sombre and frowning face.

'That was awful—absolute self-sacrifice. How could it have happened, when they'd been so much in love?

'I don't know. I suppose my grandparents' influence was very strong, once my father had gone away. You must remember my parents had only lived together for a short while. She didn't have a chance, and my father, who from all accounts was a rigid, unbending sort of character, decided she had chosen her parents instead of him, and closed his heart against her and lived alone for the rest of his life. There was no question of a divorce, but he never wanted to see or hear of my mother or myself again. It was as if we'd never existed.'

'You say your mother died when you were young—then did your grandparents bring you up?'

'Yes. She was not very strong and I think, although she was such an affectionate and dutiful daughter, the failure of her marriage broke her heart. She died when I was six and it was then my name was changed to that of my grandparents. They wanted to bring me up as a Frenchman, and to a certain extent they succeeded. They were poor people— most of their money and possessions were lost in the war, but they were proud of their name and their lineage. When

I was nineteen my grandmother died, she had been ill for a long time, and within a year my grandfather died too, I think because he couldn't face life without her. I was at college. There was enough money left for me to finish my education—I had done an Arts Course and I won a grant to the Banff School of Drama and became an actor.' He smiled wryly. 'I don't know what my grandparents would have thought—they wanted me to become a teacher or a lawyer.'

Tory was silent, thinking of the strange twist of fate that had brought Julian to Yorkshire. Of the lonely, unhappy man who had lived at Ravensholme and never spoken to anyone of his wife and son, and then, at the end, remembered Julian, and left him his entire estate.

'I wish you could have seen him before he died. Your father, I mean. It seems very sad that he thought about you in the end and yet never even spoke of you.'

Julian sighed. 'You know what they say—as people live so shall they die. And that's what my father did—lived without knowing his son and died that way too.'

'Has it made you—unhappy?'

He shook his head.

'Not really. You see, I thought he was dead—my grandparents as good as told me he was killed, perhaps because they didn't want me to go looking for him. I hardly knew my mother, and although I was very fond of my grandparents and grateful to them for their love and care of me, I can't say we were really close. They were too reserved and strict in their ways.' He looked round at her, his dark glance ironic. 'I've been a loner for the best part of my life—I'm used to it.'

'I was brought up by my grandparents, just like you,' Tory said slowly. 'Doesn't that seem strange? But we were very united . . . I loved them dearly. My parents were killed in a train smash and my grandfather and grandmother took me to live with them—I was five years old at the time. My grandmother died a few years ago, but we were great friends, just as Gramps and I are now.'

'You've been lucky in that, Tory, although you so sadly lost your parents. Perhaps that's why you seem such a happy balanced sort of person.' He smiled slightly. 'Apart from a quick temper.'

'You provoked me.'

'I didn't intend to.' He put a hand out and laid it for a moment briefly on her own. 'Now we know more about one another shall we be friends? We've a lot in common.'

She sat very still. The touch of his fingers seemed to send a current of warmth flowing through her—it was as if he had turned on a switch. She was shaken, and because she was afraid that he might notice the sudden shiver of awareness she sat without speaking or moving.

He lifted his hand back to the steering wheel.

'Well? Are you considering the possibility?'

Tory swallowed and said in as casual a manner as she could assume, 'I—I suppose we can be.'

'You might even succeed in softening up Ralph,' he added a trifle grimly.

'If Ralph knew more of your circumstances he would understand you better.'

'Thanks, but I don't intend to put in any special pleas for sympathy. I meant that if you and I are friends, Ralph, being so close to you, *might* become more amicable. It's difficult working with him when he remains so antagonistic towards me. I need his help, and there ought to be room for both of us at Ravensholme.'

He started up the car and they set off again along the empty road.

'Very tempting,' Julian said, and increased the car's speed. In a matter of seconds they were zooming along at eighty, the wind whistling past them, streaming Tory's hair back from her face. The sense of speed exhilarated her, she felt excited and alive, as if she were on her way to some thrilling destination. The speedometer touched ninety—she had never gone so fast in her life before. Then slowly, imperceptibly, Julian eased the car off as the long open stretch of road began to narrow. He turned to look at her.

'Enjoy that?'

She nodded, breathlessly. 'It was super.'

'Just the place to try her out. No traffic, no sheep, nothing.'

The sense of intoxication was still with her. She looked at Julian and saw that he was watching her, his eyes dark and intent on her face. For a moment their glance held and it seemed to Tory as if something passed between them, a silent communication for which there were no words. It confused her. She forced herself to look away and to break the strange spell she said quickly, 'Oh there's Ravensholme down there.'

He looked to where she gestured.

'I can only see trees.'

'That's Ravensholme woods—the house lies somewhere in the middle.'

'I didn't realise we were so near. Where does this road come out?'

They were back to normalities. Tory almost sighed with relief.

'It comes out at the crossroads, where the school is.' She nearly said, 'Where we first met—that night I saw you on horseback.'

He seemed to read her thoughts.

'I remember. It's where we met—the night we saw the comet together.'

'Yes.'

'I've often thought about it. It was an incredible sight, wasn't it?'

She nodded and said again, 'Yes.'

They reached the crossroads, and as Julian hesitated she said, 'Turn right here—it's almost a U-turn. Now we're back on the Scarsfell road.'

'I remember. Your grandfather's farm is a few miles up the hill.'

'Six to be exact.'

'And not a house between here and your farm. Don't you ever feel lonely—cut off?'

'No. We're used to it. Sometimes, in a bad winter, it's a bit much. The road becomes impassable until the snow-plough digs us out. Grandfather was once marooned for three months, but that was a long time ago. I remember as a child being cut off for a few weeks by bad weather. It was strange—the entire farm enclosed in a world of snow. A lot of the sheep died—'

'It sounds as bad as Canada,' said Julian. 'Hello, there *is* a house after all between you and the village.'

'Sam Dyer, Grandfather's shepherd, lives there, with his wife and family and his unmarried sister.'

Julian turned his head to look at her.

'I've enjoyed today. Will you come out with me again— perhaps you could show me some of those beauty spots. What about that waterfall you mentioned?'

Tory hesitated, not sure whether she was glad or sorry that she had an excuse to refuse.

'I—I'm going away for a few days, to stay with a cousin who lives at Whitby.'

'Well, perhaps when you get back?'

'Perhaps.'

He said no more and soon they were back at Wether Bell Farm. Tory didn't invite him in but said, 'Goodbye, and thank you. I—I enjoyed going in your super new car.'

'Goodbye, Tory.' For a moment he stared down at her, a silent, sombre stare, and then, abruptly, he got back into the car and with a brief wave of the hand drove away.

As she went into the house she was remembering their talk together, the things he had told her about himself. He was a strange man, a strange mixture of casual friendliness and off-putting arrogance. As he had said, he had been a loner all his life. It had been a sad life in many ways, with, seemingly, little of the warmth and closeness that had made her own so happy, despite the loss of her parents. Who had loved him, and whom had he loved? The women of his affairs, the ones which had proved 'most enjoyable while they lasted'?

Tory felt a spasm of resentment replace the sense of sympathy. She needn't waste her time being *sorry* for him, he was more than capable of getting on with his own life and *enjoying* himself. He probably assumed a different role with every girl, and knew just how to win admiration and attention wherever he went. He was that sort of man. Oh yes, she admitted his attractiveness, the dark magnetism that surrounded him like an aura. But she was proof against it. She was in love with Ralph, and someone like Julian could never make any real impact on her.

Tory's cousin Jane was only a few years older than herself and the mother of two lively infants, Bobby and Betsy.

Geoffrey, her husband, was a hard-working young doctor attached to the local hospital. He welcomed Tory warmly, but she saw little of him during her few days' visit, for he was busy most of the time. However, she thoroughly enjoyed being with Jane and spoiling her small godchild Betsy and playing ball games with Bobby, and she and Jane and the children went for drives and picnics in Tory's Mini and clambered up and down the steep streets of the harbour and explored the old town again.

Ralph did not telephone or write. He was obviously tied up with the affairs of Ravensholme, and after all, she was away from Scarsfell for less than a week so she could hardly expect to hear from him, Tory explained to herself.

Jane was keenly interested in the affairs of Ravensholme.

'How absolutely thrilling—the discovery of the long-lost heir and all that. It must have caused quite a furore in the neighbourhood, but of course, it's bad luck on Ralph. I'm sorry for him. And for you, Tory, because if he'd inherited his uncle's estate it would have made all the difference to you both. But you say he's nice, this Julian?'

Nice? Had she said that? Hardly the word to describe Julian. Rather, dynamic, forceful, smouldering. Unforgettable.

She said slowly, 'He's—striking-looking and he—he can be charming.'

Jane gave her a quick look.

'He sounds a dish.'

Tory was reluctant to talk about him. She made a pretext of rescuing Betsy from some hazard and the subject was forgotten.

Two days later she drove back to Scarsfell. On the way up to the farm she called at the school house to leave a small gift for Miss Ewing, a plant from Jane's garden that Miss Ewing was anxious to grow.

'How kind of you to remember,' Miss Ewing said as she unwrapped the moss-moistened cutting of Caryopteris Mastacanthus. 'I do hope it will thrive in my garden—we get so much wind up here.'

'No more than at Whitby,' Tory said consolingly.

'Ah, but there's not the frost there—the sea tempers it,' said Miss Ewing. She glanced at Tory. 'I don't suppose you've heard the news—everyone is very upset about it, and blaming the new owner of Ravensholme for allowing such a thing.'

'Allowing what?'

'It's a scandal, really. Old Mr. Brierley fought so hard to keep this sort of thing at bay. What do you think, Tory? Those fields near the bridge—the ones that slope down to the river have been sold. They're to be developed as a caravan site.'

Tory gaped. There was no other word with which to describe the way her jaw dropped and her eyes opened.

'I—I don't believe it!'

'My dear, it's true. It seems the negotiations have been going on for some time and last week it was confirmed as a fact, permission has been granted and the contract signed and sealed. Of course, it's going to ruin the dale.'

Tory went on staring while a furious anger began to ferment in her. How could Julian do such a thing?—go against all the restrictions and taboos his father had put up against development in Scarsdale. He must know how the people around him felt and realise that they wanted to keep it unspoiled and unchanged.

She found her voice at last and said, chokingly, 'It's dreadful! There'll be cars everywhere—picnic parties—ice cream stalls. Is it to be a big site?'

'I have no idea. The fields cover several acres.'

'We must fight it. Everyone must protest—appeal or whatever one does.'

'Yes, that's the only way. Even if the project is still allowed a watching brief will ensure the site is developed discreetly.'

Tory was too upset to stay talking—she wanted to get back to Wether Bell Farm and see what her grandfather thought about the shattering news. She said goodbye to Miss Ewing and drove quickly away. She longed to go to Ravensholme and see Julian, tell him what she thought of him and his wretched plan to ruin the dale. And, as if she had conjured him up out of her thoughts, when she turned to go through the gates of the farm she saw his sleek green car coming slowly up the rutted track to the road.

She braked and reversed, then got out so that when he drew up she was standing on the road facing him.

He cut the engine and slid long legs over the side of the car.

'Hello, Tory. This is a nice surprise. I've just been to call on your grandfather—brought him a book I thought he'd be interested in. I didn't know you were coming back today—I—' He broke off, suddenly aware of her angry stare, her set expression. 'Is anything the matter?'

The words poured out of her in a spate of indignation.

'Everything's the matter! I've just heard what's happened—what frightful thing you're planning to do to the dale. How *could* you? How could you agree to such a thing? I thought you liked it here—you said the countryside was beautiful, unspoilt. And now—you've given permission for something your father fought all his life to prevent. A caravan site down by the river—those lovely fields will be cluttered up with weekenders and holidaymakers. I suppose you couldn't resist the *money*—it's typical of—of someone who's never had a real home of his own. You can't possibly understand how people feel who live in a place all their lives and love it and want to keep it unchanged.'

She came to a trembling stop and Julian's voice, clipped and cold, sliced through the silence that followed.

'Have you quite finished?'

She met his narrowed dark gaze and said, with defiantly tilted chin, 'F—for the moment.'

'You're very quick to go into the attack. I suggest that next time you want to censure someone you first verify your facts.'

She stared. 'It's true, isn't it? That—that the fields have been sold for use as a caravan site?'

He inclined his head stiffly.

'Perfectly true. But you haven't given me any benefit of the doubt, have you? Or stopped to consider that there may be other reasons why this sale has occurred not entirely due to what you regard as my dishonourable dealings. However, I've no intention of explaining myself—' and turning on his heel he went back to the car and dropped into the front seat.

Tory stared after him, a queer uncertainty cooling her

anger. What did he mean, she hadn't given him any benefit of the doubt? The fields were sold, weren't they? He had just admitted it. And who could have done that if not the owner of the land?

The car streaked away down the empty road. She was left alone with a remembrance of Julian's cold glance and even colder voice. As if *she* were guilty and not him.

CHAPTER FOUR

IN a way, Tory thought, turning things over in her mind later that day, it had been disappointment as much as anger that had caused her to attack Julian in the way she did. Somehow she had expected him to be different, to *care* about Scarsdale and not enter into money-making schemes to develop part of the countryside. The day they had visited Hepworth's farm she felt she had begun to know him, to understand him better. And then this had happened and he seemed like a different person.

She talked the matter over with her grandfather, who had already heard the news about the caravan site from Sam. He shook his head sadly. 'It was never Harold Brierley's intention for his heirs to sell land, of that I'm sure. He'd have given up Ravensholme, I reckon, before he'd have made money out of developing the dale. He looked on it as a sacred trust, to keep it as it's been for four hundred years or more. I wonder what young Ralph thinks about it.'

'I shall know tomorrow. He left a note at the school house and said he would call to take me out for a meal.'

Mr. Webster nodded, his shrewd glance on Tory.

'You'll enjoy that.'

'Yes, I haven't seen him for two weeks.'

Ralph when he arrived the following evening seemed preoccupied. He kissed Tory absentmindedly and said, 'D'you mind if I don't come in? I want to get back to Bramwick.'

Tory was startled.

'Bramwick? But I thought—have you left Ravensholme, then?'

'Yes. I'll tell you about it as we drive along. Mother's expecting us to supper. Is that all right with you?'

'Yes. Yes, of course. Thank you. When—when did you go back?'

'To Bramwick? Last Tuesday—all in a flap, I can tell you.' A frown clouded Ralph's handsome face. 'Cousin Julian practically threw us out—or at least, threw me out. Of course, Mother and Carole had to leave too.'

She started round at him.

'You're—joking! He—he didn't really throw you out?'

'All but. The fact is, we had a blazing row.' He turned his head and met her bewildered glance. 'I suppose you've heard about the proposed caravan site near the river?' and when she nodded and said quickly, 'Yes, I think it's frightful,' he interrupted to say, 'Hold on! I negotiated that deal. And it's not the end of the world, as some people seem to think.'

She could only stare at him in deepening dismay.

'Ralph—no!' and then, slowly, 'You mean you—you sold the land on Julian's behalf?'

He shook his head.

'It was sold before he came here—when it belonged to Uncle Harold.'

'But he would never sell *any* of it—everyone knows how he refused all offers.'

Ralph glanced sideways at her.

'Look, Tory, my uncle was a reactionary. He hated any sort of change—progress. He was absolutely hidebound and would never listen to other people or take advice. We were at loggerheads the whole time. When he was ill I had power of attorney—I was able to sign documents in his name. I agreed, on his behalf, to sell the Sawley fields.'

'How could you?' she gasped, as she had said to Julian. 'How *could* you sell the land like that? Is that what you call progress?'

Ralph's mouth set. He said without looking at her, 'I don't know what *you're* carping at. It's Ravensholme land and doesn't affect you or anywhere near you. A few caravans in a couple of fields. They'll be hidden by walls and trees.'

'But why? Why sell the land in the first place—Scarsdale doesn't need a caravan site. I think it's madness!' She was aware that she and Ralph were quarrelling and bit her lip to keep back the angry words that threatened.

'To begin with the estate can do with the money. No one

seems to consider the handsome profit I've made. Julian ought to be grateful to me instead of blowing his top, like you've done.'

A chill came over her as she remembered the way she had spoken to Julian the day before.

'He—wasn't pleased about it?'

Ralph laughed abruptly.

'Pleased? On the contrary, he was thoroughly nasty about it. He said he should have been told about it, but it wouldn't have made any difference, because the papers were signed before he came to Ravensholme. We had some words, and the outcome was that Mother and I were glad to return to Bramwick.'

Tory sighed despairingly, 'Oh Ralph, I wish I'd known.'

'Known what? About my selling the land on Uncle Harold's behalf? What difference would that have made?'

She meant she wished she had not been so violent in her outburst to Julian. She said slowly, 'What will happen now?'

He shrugged.

'Things will simmer down. Julian's annoyed because he feels he's the boss man and tries to run the estate himself. But he can't, because he doesn't know how to.' Ralph smiled confidently. 'He can't do without my help and he knows it. Forget it, Tory.' He glanced sideways at her. 'And don't say much in front of Mother, she's naturally upset about leaving Ravensholme in such a hurry. Carole too. I can't think why, except that she's got rather a thing about Julian.'

They had arrived at Bramwick. The house, long and low and built of stone and mellowed brick, was on the south side of the river, nearer to the small town of Kirk Newton than Lindley Grange. It was a pretty house, not large but with a beautiful old walled garden, so sheltered that peach and apricot trees grew and fruited against the warm brick.

Inside it was furnished with charm and distinction, for Mrs. Brierley had managed to salvage, despite the failure of her husband's business, some of the luxurious fittings from their former home which included gorgeous Persian rugs and antique pieces of great value, as well as expensive damask curtains and a handsome velvet Knole suite. Tory, looking at it all, thought with a sinking heart that the house itself might belong to Ralph now, but it was very much Mrs. Brierley's home. She could not imagine Ralph's mother sharing it with anyone, much less giving it up to any daughter-in-law.

Mrs. Brierley welcomed her rather wearily, saying, 'We've had an exhausting few days settling in here again. I expect Ralph has told you that Julian took a high-handed attitude with him over this silly land business.' She shrugged slim shoulders. 'Still, I'm happy to be home again. And it's a consolation to think we have those nice Langfords as our nearest neighbours. Mr. Langford has been *so* kind, offering to send one of his men over to tidy up the garden, and Madeline is a charming girl.' She looked directly at Tory as she added, 'Don't you agree?'

'She—she's very attractive.'

Mrs. Brierley nodded complacently.

'We think so. Now, Tory, will you sit here? I'm afraid it's only a cold supper, but I know you don't mind—you're quite one of the family, being so friendly with Carole. And with Ralph, too, of course. Almost like brother and sister after so long an association.'

The remark was made pleasantly enough, but it carried an undercurrent of warning. As if Mrs. Brierley said in code, 'Ralph is not for you.'

The evening, already marred by the shock of learning that Ralph had sold his uncle's land without the latter's knowledge, was now shadowed by Mrs. Brierley's unspoken challenge.

Tory longed to be alone with Ralph, to be assured that he loved her. If he had not said so in precise words he had implied it in every other way. She was always 'his lovely Tory', the 'dearest girl he knew'; he spent his spare time with her, it was a recognised thing that they belonged together.

Tory sat quiet and unsure of herself, while Carole was openly restless. Not long after supper Mrs. Brierley yawned delicately and said, 'You must excuse me, Tory, but I really think I shall go to bed. Goodnight, my dear.'

When the door closed behind her Carole flung back into her chair, tossing her curly brown hair back to say petulantly, 'It's so *boring* here. I wish we were back at Ravensholme. Julian was teaching me to play billiards.' She sighed, her eyes half closing. 'When he put his arm round me to show me how to hold the cue properly I got goose pimples.'

'Oh, shut up about Julian,' Ralph said with sharp and brotherly candour. 'We're not interested.'

'Aren't you? What a pity. I suppose you want me to disappear so you can get together with Tory. Well, I'm not going to. I intend to sit here and watch TV.'

'Thrilling for you. Come on Tory. Let's go out and have a drink somewhere.'

Tory hesitated. 'I—I'm quite happy to watch television for a bit. I shall have to leave soon.'

On the way back to Wether Bell Farm Ralph said, 'What's the matter, Tory? You're not yourself this evening.'

She couldn't tell him that his mother's words had upset her, or that she was worried about his involvement with the sale of the caravan site.

'Aren't I? I'm sorry.'

'I believe you're bearing me a grudge over this land business. But you might as well accept the fact that the dale's going to change, sooner or later. The County Council are bent on building a new bridge over the Scar. Uncle Harold refused to sell them the land, but someone else will.'

'Not—not Julian?'

'I don't know. Possibly. He's only fed up with me because the deal was made before he turned up and it went through without his say-so.'

She said slowly, 'But it was without your uncle's sanction too. Didn't you feel it was—wrong to permit it, knowing he would have refused if he realised what was happening?'

'Ethically speaking, yes, but practically speaking, no. Uncle Harold wasn't going to get better, in fact he was sinking away with every day that passed. I had to act for him, and I did, disposing of some useless fields for a profitable sum of money. The money hasn't come to me, you know. It's gone into the Ravensholme coffers. I admit that at the time I thought I was going to inherit the estate, so to a certain extent I acted in my own interests. But Julian reaped the benefit, apart from the commission I earned on the sale.'

'Commission?'

'Well, of course, I got something out of it, for heaven's

sake. Don't look so disapproving about it, Tory. You don't understand these matters.'

Tory bit her lip, shaken by Ralph's account of things.

'I don't think I do.'

Much as she loved him the doubts and uncertainties were still there, even when he put his arms about her to kiss her goodnight and though she kissed him back it was as if an invisible curtain hung between them, hiding their real selves from one another.

The fine weather held and Tory, walking Troy along the moorland road, heard the cuckoo calling in the dale below while overhead curlews dipped and mewed and the fell ponies stampeded ahead of her in a spring fever of high spirits.

Mr. Webster finished reading the book Julian had brought him and handed it to Tory saying, 'It might interest you. It's an old history of the dale he found in his father's library. Do you know, a hundred years or more ago the linen industry was strong round here and folks 'ud see rows and rows of white sheets stretched out in the fields bleaching in the sun.' He shook his head. 'I'd have liked to have seen that. And there's a chapter on the forest horn they used to sound so travellers ont' tops would hear it and find their ways safe down to the dale.'

'I'll read it.'

'You do that. And then you'd best return it to Julian or it might get lost hanging about.'

Tory read the book over the weekend and found it a fascinating chronicle of the North Riding. Yorkshire had everything, she thought; noble castles and ancient abbeys, great houses still inhabited, towers and peles, Norman churches with painted roofs and Jacobean pens, hidden valleys and small secluded villages, and always the moors, sometimes wild and forbidding, open to the four winds and at other times, beguiling in the beauty of yellow gorse and sweet-scented ling and beckoning blue distances.

She braced herself to take the book back to Julian. They had not met since the day she returned from Whitby and he had left her in so angry a mood. She owed him an apology and knew that if the opportunity presented itself, she would somehow have to put it into words.

When she arrived at Ravensholme it was to find a posse of workmen both in and outside the house, and as she hesitated outside the open front door, seeing the sheeted hall floor inside and planks balanced precariously between pairs of steps one of the painters nodded to her and called, 'Dos'ta' want to see t' boss? 'E's back there somewhere.'

Tory hesitated.

'Thank you, I—perhaps I'd better go round to the other door.'

'Nay, we'll not drop paint on thee—come in this way. 'Old on, Bert, young lass is walkin' through. I'd give a shout if I was you, miss.'

Tory was saved the necessity to do anything so bold by the advent of Jason, who came bounding out through the green baize door which shut off the hall from the back quarters. He rushed up to Tory in boisterous greeting followed by Julian who said, sternly, 'Down, Jason. Down, boy!' The dark glance he gave Tory was as stern as his command to Jason. 'Hello, Tory. Did you want to see me?'

'Yes—I—Grandfather asked me to return this book to you. He—he enjoyed it very much and would like to say thank you for lending it to him.'

'It was a pleasure.' The dark eyes, cool and remote, seemed to belie the politeness of his words. A spatter of paint fell like snow through the air. 'You'd better come this way,' and he strode to the baize door and held it open for her.

She went through, careful to avoid any contact with the intimidating figure above her. The passageway led past a butler's pantry to a big empty kitchen, silent except for the purposeful hum of a shining new dish-washer.

Tory hesitated, not knowing how to begin, aware that Julian was waiting for her to take her leave and depart.

'You—you're busy. The—painters, I mean.'

'Yes. I'm having the place cleaned up. It badly needs it. Apparently my father let everything slide when he was ill. I hope to get on with things now I'm on my own here.' His mouth curled sardonically as he added, 'I suppose you know my aunt and my cousins have returned to their own house?'

'Yes.' His dark face was aloof, he stared at some spot high above her head. She said slowly and with difficulty, 'I—I owe you an apology for the way I spoke to you the other week—the things I said. Ralph told me that he arranged the sale of the caravan site—that it was all fixed before you arrived at Ravensholme.'

His glance came back to her but there was no softening of the expression.

'Yes. A great pity. I would have prevented it if I'd been here at the time.' He shrugged. 'Too late, I'm afraid. But it's made a breach between Ralph and myself. Not so much because he took such an action—but because he gave no intimation of what had occurred until he presented me with the *fait accompli*. I don't feel he's to be trusted.'

She coloured at the contemptuous tone of his voice.

'You're being unjust to Ralph.'

'I don't think so. But you're bound to be biased in his favour, naturally. However, I think you should take warning from this and realise that Ralph will always act in his own interests and nothing and—' he paused and added with curt emphasis, '*no one* will be allowed to stand in his way.'

She said sharply, in angry defence of Ralph, 'Don't you think you're being rather dramatic? *Nothing to stand in his way*. You make him sound like some villain in an old-fashioned melodrama. I suppose that's your theatrical training.'

His jaw set. A muscle twitched in his lean brown cheek as he said coldly, 'Possibly. But the slight exaggeration doesn't detract from the truth of my statement. I just hope you won't have to find out for yourself the hard way. I appreciate your coming here to apologise. Now, if you'll excuse me, I have several things to attend to,' and he moved to the door.

His brusque voice shook her. Without looking at him Tory walked quickly to the door which he now held open for her. From some Olympian height above her head he said, 'Sure you can find your way? Goodbye.'

'Goodbye.' She hurried round to the front drive where the Mini was parked. Her cheeks were burning—she touched them with her hand as if to cool the fire of anger—or was it humiliation that flushed them? He was a most hateful man, harsh and arrogant. No wonder Ralph found it almost impossible to work with him. He would give no quarter to anyone who opposed or angered him.

She had made the effort and gone out of her way to apologise to him, and what had he done? Thrown the words back in her teeth. Well, that was that. She would take good care to keep well out of his way in future.

Halfway down the tree-lined drive she had to slow at the approach of someone on horseback, a rider with a horse on one leading rein and a small white pony on another. It was Madeline, fair and pink-faced, her golden hair caught back in a chignon beneath the black riding hat.

She pulled up and raised a gloved hand to say, 'Hello. What are you doing here? Ralph's gone back to Bramwick, you know.'

'Yes, thank you, I do know. I—I've been to return a book Julian lent my grandfather.'

'You're still on holiday, then? When does school start up again?'

'Next week.' Tory looked at the pony, wondering if Madeline was taking it to Ravensholme and if so why, and seeing her questioning glance Madeline smiled and said, 'This is Moppet. Julian's buying him for some child who's coming to stay. The mare too.' She leaned over and patted the bay's sleek neck. 'Isn't she gorgeous?'

'Gorgeous,' Tory echoed. A child? So Julian was having visitors to stay. Well, it wasn't surprising, but she hoped he would be more amenable to his guests than he had been to her. Resolutely she put the remembrance of his sombre dark face from her and said briskly:

'I'd better be on my way.' She waited for Madeline to move off before starting up the car again, then drove thankfully away from Ravensholme.

On every side there was criticism of Julian for selling the land for the projected caravan site. Tory was torn between her loyalty to Ralph and, despite her feeling of animosity towards Julian, a sense of injustice done to the latter. She compromised by indicating whenever she became involved in a discussion about it that she thought the matter had been arranged during Mr. Brierley's lifetime, but this most people found hard to believe.

'Nay, t'owd feller 'ud never do that. He was allus for keepin' the dale same as it's allus bin,' was said by more than one local inhabitant, and the general opinion was that the new heir was responsible for the sale. It didn't make for friendly feeling and Tory couldn't help wondering if Julian was aware of the sense of animosity that surrounded him.

Another week went by and still she had not seen Ralph, and then, unexpectedly, she met Julian again.

She was shopping in Kirk Newton one Saturday morning. The town was busy, the small market crowded with sturdy brown-faced men, sticks over their arms and dogs at their heels, deep in conversations that concerned huggs and gimmers and tups and lamb crops and wool clips. There were black and white calves in a pen—a small boy leaned over the rail to watch them. One young bullock, larger and bolder than the rest, lifted his curly head with the short thickset horns just beginning to show through and bellowed loudly.

The small boy fell back and stumbled to the ground. As Tory put her hand out to lift him up, she realised that he was lame, with one leg slightly shorter than the other and in an iron. She bent her head to him.

'Are you all right?'

'Yes, th-thank you.' He was small, pale-faced and about six years of age. He had dark hair and dark eyes. He dusted the back of grey shorts with a wary glance towards the pen against which the bullock now rubbed his head.

'He won't hurt you,' Tory said reassuringly. 'He's a bit frightened of all the people here and I daresay he's a bit homesick.'

'Y-yes.' The brown eyes, enormous in the thin face, stared up at her. 'I like him really.'

'I like him too. He's very handsome.' She glanced round and asked, 'You're not on your own here, are you?'

He looked over his shoulder.

'No. I'm with Mummy and—' he broke off. 'Oh, there she is.' He waved energetically. 'Mum, I'm here! I'm over here with these bulls!'

A girl was pushing her way towards them through the

jostle of drovers and countrymen and when she reached him she said in a relieved voice, 'Peter, where on earth did you get to? You mustn't wander too far from us, we can't see you in this crowd.' She glanced enquiringly at Tory and Tory said, 'Your son and I have just become acquainted.'

'I fell down and she picked me up,' Peter said. 'At least I didn't really fall, I sort of slid off the railing because a big bull ran roaring at me.'

'Oh, Peter, he *didn't*!' Smoke blue eyes, slanting and black-lashed, looked at Tory for confirmation and imperceptibly Tory shook her head, smiling in reassurance. The girl nodded. She had cloudy dark hair swept back from a wide forehead and smoke blue eyes under arched dark brows. The high cheekbones curved down to a mobile smiling mouth, and her whole expression was vivid and alive. She was quite the most beautiful girl Tory had ever seen.

She slid an arm about her son's shoulders.

'I believe you're exaggerating just a little bit? But I'm glad you were rescued.' She smiled at Tory. 'Thank you. I—my name's Damaris Lawton.' She paused, as if expecting Tory to say something before adding, 'And this is my son, Peter, as you've discovered.'

'I'm Tory Webster,' Tory began and then stopped abruptly, for wending his way through the throng, head and shoulders above the people about him, came Julian.

Damaris Lawton saw him too, and she waved gaily and when he came up to her said, 'Did you think we were lost? This is Tory Webster and she very kindly helped Peter, when he fell down.'

Julian inclined his head stiffly.

'We already know one another. Hello, Tory.'

'Hello.'

There was a short silence during which Damaris glanced curiously from one unsmiling face to the other. She said lightly, 'Well, have we had enough roaring bulls for the moment? Let's go to the hotel and have a drink. Come with us, Miss Webster.'

'I—thank you, but I—I haven't very much time.'

'Oh, what a pity. D'you live in Kirk Newton?'

'No, at Scarsfell.'

Damaris Lawton frowned.

'Scarsfell? Not Scarsdale, where Ravensholme is?'

'No—up on the moors above the dale.'

'We haven't been up to the moors yet, but Peter wants to see them.' She smiled again, her whole face lit with a radiance that charmed and beguiled. 'I've been reading *The Secret Garden* to him.'

'It's a marvellous book. The children love it.'

Damaris glanced quickly at her. 'The children?'

'Tory's a schoolteacher,' Julian said shortly. 'At Scarsfell.'

'Oh. Oh, that's interesting.' Damaris's glance went to Julian's aloof dark face, but she didn't enlarge on the remark.

Tory, uncomfortably aware of Julian's abrupt manner, said, 'I must go.' She put her hand out. 'Goodbye, Peter. Perhaps I shall see you up on the moors one day. Goodbye, Mrs. Lawton.' She glanced quickly in Julian's direction but did not meet his eyes. 'Goodbye.'

'Goodbye, Tory,' said Damaris. 'I hope we meet again. And it's Miss, not Mrs. Lawton.'

Tory was too surprised to answer. She said again, 'Goodbye', and as she walked quickly in the direction of the car park she was in a confusion of thought. How stern and unforthcoming Julian had been! Not that it mattered, but it wasn't very pleasant to feel he disliked her so much. And Damaris Lawton? She was obviously the visitor Julian had been expecting, and Peter must be the boy for whom he had bought Madeline Langford's pony.

Damaris wasn't married. Then where and who was Peter's father?

Ralph came to see Tory the next day and the sun shone again, both literally and metaphorically. It was the first day in May, a morning of lark song and sunshine, the moors bright with broom flower and yellow gorse. Small blue butterflies darted above the grass and brown honeybees foraged busily among the harebells. Tory, wearing jeans and a cotton check shirt, her red hair tied back in a ponytail, felt happiness bubble up inside her as she walked with Ralph, Troy loping slowly along behind them. It was like old times, to be out together on such a perfect day.

He glanced sideways at her and smiled, catching her hand in his, the sunlight glinting on his fair head, clean-cut features smooth and brown above the grey polo-necked sweater he was wearing.

'Grand isn't it? I haven't walked up here for a long time—not since last summer. When you came back to live here, Tory.'

'Yes.' It had been wonderful, those first weeks of getting to know one another all over again. Not just as childhood friends but in a deepening relationship that had begun the day Ralph kissed her. It was then she fell in love with him, and she had never been in love before; there had been boy-friends, dates, but nothing serious. There hadn't been much time for dalliance because she was at college studying and she wanted to work hard and get her degree for her grand-father's sake.

As if reading her thoughts he said, 'We were happy, weren't we?' His mouth twisted thinly. 'Living in our fools' paradise.'

'Why do you say that?'

'Well, wasn't it? I lived in the hope that one day Ravens-holme would belong to me, and then—Julian arrived on the scene and the bottom dropped out of my world. Nothing's been the same since.'

'No.' It was true. Julian's coming had thrown everything out of balance, everything seemed to be changed.

'I suppose you've heard the news? That he's got a girl-friend living with him. Now I know why he turned us out in such a hurry—he wanted to have her to himself.' Ralph smiled frostily. 'Well, not quite to himself, there's this child around. Everyone says he must be Julian's son.'

'You—we shouldn't listen to gossip,' Tory protested, thinking of Damaris's lovely face and the small boy with his thin legs and painful limp.

'Julian shouldn't make himself into a sitting target for scandal. He's asking for it. She's not married, you know.'

'I know. Actually, I've met her.' Tory went on to explain the incident in the cattle market. She said slowly, at the finish, 'Perhaps they want to get married and can't—perhaps there's some snag.'

'Such as? They're both single, unless—well, of course, Julian *could* have a wife tucked away somewhere.'

'Do—do you think so? He never talks in that way.'

'Why should he? Neither you nor I are on intimate terms with him. Madeline says the boy is very like him. She's been to the house once or twice in connection with the pony she sold Julian—and the mare he bought which the girlfriend rides.'

The clouds, huge and white, chasing across the sun cast a shadow over the moor, dimming blue to brown, and gold to grey so that the landscape looked suddenly cold and colourless.

'Do you see much of Madeline?'

'Quite a bit. The old man's always coming over on some pretext or other.' Ralph grinned. 'I think he's rather taken with Mama. He's a widower and very wealthy—it would certainly solve a lot of problems if she decided to marry again.' He screwed his eyes up. 'That would make Madeline my stepsister—umm?'

'Would you—like that?'

'Madeline as a stepsister, do you mean, or Mr. Langford as my stepfather?' He shrugged. 'I don't care either way.'

The clouds were gone, racing across the fell towards Great Scar, and all around them the world sparkled in sunshine again. Tory felt her heart lighten. If Mrs. Brierley remarried then Ralph would feel free of responsibility of his mother. He could marry and bring a wife back to Bramwick.

'Are you and Julian getting along any better?' she asked. He shook his head.

'Decidedly not. He's got it in for me about the caravan site, and he can be a difficult devil. I wonder sometimes how long I shall be working there.'

Tory turned her head to stare at him in dismay.

'But, Ralph, you couldn't leave Ravensholme. Where would you go—what would you do?'

'I suppose I could get another agent's job—perhaps in Scotland. Or I might emigrate.'

'Ralph!' She felt she was on a perpetual see-saw, one moment happy and thinking of the future and the next dashed into uncertainty.

'You could come with me—teachers are at a premium. We'd have a great future.

'I couldn't—there's Grandfather to think of—' she began to say, when he shook her hand angrily and said:

'For God's sake, you don't think I'm serious, do you? I've no intention of clearing out to suit Cousin Julian. Whatever happens—whether I continue to work for him or not I've no intention of leaving Scarsdale. My roots are here— a damn sight deeper struck than his are. I shall find something to suit me, you can take my word for that.'

Tory let out a long sigh.

'I couldn't bear it if you went away. I should miss you terribly.'

'Darling.' He stopped and put his arms about her and kissed her, there and then, standing on the moorland path with only the placid sheep cropping the turves and the larks overhead to see them.

Ralph stayed to Sunday lunch and left before tea, saying he had to get back to Bramwick. Tory was in a happy mood, reassured to hear that no matter what happened he would not leave Scarsdale and cheered by the faint possibility of Mrs. Brierley's remarriage. Despite the friction between Ralph and Julian, which was unfortunate, Tory couldn't help being more hopeful for the future.

One afternoon a few days later she was driving back from school when the heavens opened and the rain came down in blinding suddenness. She had seen the cloud building up over Great Scar but had hoped to reach home before the storm came. With the windscreen wiper working overtime she drove carefully up the hill towards the farm, and as the road levelled off before the dip down to Wether Bell she saw a party of horse riders coming towards her and recognised Madeline on her smart grey with Damaris riding beside her on a brown horse, while behind them came Julian on his black horse, and Peter riding the white pony on a leading rein. The rain was beating down on them, and because it was obvious Peter could only go at walking pace, the four of them were getting soaked to the skin.

She slowed the car and put her head out to say, 'Hello. Please don't go on in this but come back to the farm with me and take shelter—there's room in the barn for the horses.'

Madeline, the rain running off her riding hat on to her pink cheeks, lifted the riding crop in her hand.

'Oh, may we? Wonderful!' She swung her horse round, followed by Damaris who smiled warmly at Tory, and, with a signal to Julian to come after them, they trotted behind the car down the track to the farmyard.

Julian was already off his horse lifting Peter down. He said to Damaris, 'Take Peter in the house. Madeline and I will see to the horses.' For a moment his glance met Tory's and he said abruptly, 'Thanks, Tory,' before turning away to lead his horse to the shelter of the barn.

Inside the farmhouse Tory found dry sweaters for Damaris, Madeline and Peter, but she shook her head ruefully at Julian.

'I'm sorry—nothing of Grandfather's would fit you, but if you give me your jacket I'll put it by the range to dry while I make tea for us all.'

The sitting room seemed to be overflowing with people—she was relieved that her grandfather had gone in the Land-rover with Sam to a sheep sale at High Burton. Madeline, her fair hair loose over the shoulders of the green sweater Tory had lent her, cast a cursory glance at the worn leather chairs, the homely rag rug and copies of *Farmers' Weekly* and *The Stockbreeder* sliding untidily across a side table, But Damaris, as she sat down to rub Peter's wet hair, smiled and said, 'What gorgeous old beams—they must be hundreds of years old. And that inglenook fireplace and those thick walls. It's a gem of a house, Tory.'

'Thank you. Excuse me—I think the kettle's boiling,' and Tory hurried out to the kitchen. She was busy buttering scones when she heard a step behind her and turning, saw Julian standing there.

'Thank you for giving us refuge. We certainly needed it.'

'You could have come to the farm and sheltered, even if no one had been here.'

'I should have hesitated to do that.'

'It's part of the fell tradition. We help one another at all times.'

'I'll remember in future.' He seemed to hesitate, then he said, 'I wanted to talk to you, Tory. To ask you something.'

She deliberately finished buttering the last scone and turned, the plate in her hand, before answering.

'Yes?'

He took the plate from her and against her will, as if

mesmerised, Tory was forced to look up and meet his gaze. How could any man have such dark smouldering eyes? Or was it the tangle of lashes that gave them such intensity? Just as she had been made to look at him, now she could not look away when she wanted to. For a seemingly endless moment their glances held. When at last he spoke it was to say, surprisingly, 'It's about Peter. I wondered if he'd be able to attend the school where you teach.'

'Come to—to Scarsfell School? I—you'd have to see Miss Ewing about that. It's got nothing to do with me.'

'But you'd be teaching him, wouldn't you? I wanted to ask you to help him all you can. He's lost a lot of time from schooling, you know he was ill with polio a year ago?'

'No, I didn't. I thought perhaps he'd met with an accident. I—I'm sorry.'

'Yes, it's bad luck. He's much better, but it's a slow business. He's learning to ride the pony I bought from Madeline and that helps him a lot. He'll be able to ride up to the school from the house.'

'He's—he's going to live at Ravensholme?'

'Yes, I want him to stay with me.'

She had a curious sinking feeling, as if the news depressed her. Was it an awareness that the interest Julian took in the boy must mean he had some special connection with him? That perhaps rumour was right and Peter was his son? But what does that matter—it's got nothing to do with me, Tory told herself.

She looked at him. He was wearing a cream shirt tucked into fawn cavalry twills and without his jacket his shoulders looked very broad above his narrow waist. His hair, worn long but well cut into the shapely head, was brown-black and his skin smoothly tanned by wind and sun. She couldn't deny his attractiveness, the combination of formidable masculinity with an unexpected grace.

But you are my enemy, she thought. Mine and Ralph's. Everything you do cuts across our lives in one way or another and nothing has been the same since you came here.

Yet he asked a favour of her she couldn't refuse. And so she nodded slowly and said, 'If Peter comes to—to the school, of course I'll do my best for him.'

'Thank you. I'll ring up Miss Ewing and make an ap-

pointment to see her.' He smiled with a twist of his mouth.
'As it so happens, I'm one of the Governors of the school,
a sort of heriditary job. But I wanted specially to appeal to
you, Tory, for help.'

She didn't answer but turned to lift the teapot from the
table.

'I'll take this in—tea's made.'

He followed her into the sitting room where she proceeded
to hand out cups of tea and pass bread and butter and scones
and jam round. As she did so she couldn't help her glance
moving first to Peter's face and then to Julian's, as if against
her wish, she looked for a likeness in each. Peter had brown
eyes, as Julian had hazel ones, and both had dark brown
hair. That was all. He no more resembled Julian than he
did his mother.

The rain had stopped and the sky was brightening as
patches of blue began to appear.

'It was only a summer storm,' said Madeline, fastening
up her hair and sliding her arms into the sleeves of her
hacking jacket.

'Thank you for your hospitality,' Damaris said warmly.
'We've enjoyed it very much, haven't we, Peter?'

Peter, sitting on the floor between Troy and Topaz, strok-
ing first the great black head and then the golden one,
nodded.

'It's super here. Can I come again, please?'

'May I?' corrected his mother. 'And may we?' she added
smiling to Tory.

'Of course. Any time.'

Damaris's beautiful eyes shadowed suddenly.

'Oh dear. I won't be here much longer.' She looked across
to Julian. 'We must have our picnic soon, and Tory must
come on it. And you, Madeline, of course. Julian's promised
to take us to a place called Rylstone Ghyll where there's a
waterfall,' she went on in explanation to Tory. 'I expect
you know it?'

'It was Tory who told me about it,' Julian broke in to
say.

'Oh, lovely. Then let's make a date now. It must be at
a weekend because Tory works, so how about a week on
Saturday? It should be good weather by then.'

The date was settled and Tory said goodbye to her unexpected guests. As Madeline led her horse out of the barn she said to Tory, 'Ralph must come. When I see him I'll ask him, shall I?'

'Yes—yes, please do,' Tory answered, somewhat taken aback by Madeline's proprietorial manner. 'You—live so near I expect you often see him.'

'Fairly often. Mrs. Brierley's a charmer, isn't she? As a matter of fact she and Ralph came up to see us yesterday evening to meet some friends who were staying with us.'

'How—how nice,' was all Tory could say, remembering that Ralph had been unable to stay for tea because he had to get back to Bramwick. And now I know the reason, she thought with a pang. Then, quickly, to reassure herself, 'But it's on Mr. Langford's account they went—because he admires Ralph's mother. Not because Ralph particularly wanted to go.'

Or did he?

It was successfully arranged that Peter should attend the village school and be under Tory's supervision. She was already attached to the little boy and she made a point of introducing him, on his first morning, to Tommy Dawson, knowing that the tough but kindhearted character was the one to smooth Peter's path with the other children. And so it proved. Tommy quickly took Peter under his wing and made sure that his precise little voice and delicate ways were not made a subject of teasing among the lively Yorkshire boys who attended Scarsfell School.

Peter in turn gave them rides on Moppet, for most mornings he rode through the woods to the village, accompanied by Damaris, except on the days Julian brought him by car.

Through their encounters at school Tory got to know Damaris better, and she discovered that she was on the stage and had also appeared in several films.

'But I've been out of it for a year,' she told Tory. ''Since Peter's illness. Now he's so much better Julian insists that Peter shall stay with him for a time to give me a chance to get back to work. I start rehearsals for a new play next week. It opens in Brighton at the end of June and goes on to Oxford and Birmingham and then—' she smiled holding up two crossed fingers, 'London and a long run, we hope.'

'I remember now,' said Tory. 'When you told me your name that first day we met it rang a bell. I saw you in a film—a costume thing, about Cornwall and smugglers.'

Damaris laughed.

'Oh, that! Best forgotten.' She shook her head. 'But it made good money for us all.'

Tory couldn't help feeling curious about her. She was beautiful and warm-hearted and entirely natural in approach and manner. Why wasn't she married to Peter's father, whomever he was? If it was Julian, then surely he was in love with Damaris, for how could any man not be? And Damaris, was she in love with Julian? It was obvious that a close bond lay between them.

Tory waited to hear from Ralph that he was coming on the picnic the following Saturday, but no word came from him. It was planned that Julian would bring Peter and two of his school friends in his car, as it was too far for Peter to ride on the pony. Tory was to meet them all at the Rylstone crossroads in her car, with three more children from the school. Everyone was to bring a contribution of food and Julian was responsible for the coffee and drinks.

Saturday dawned warm and fine and by eleven o'clock when Tory drove down in her Mini to meet Brian Gosforth and Barry Kempter and his twin sister, Millie Kempter, the sun was shining and the blue sky without a cloud.

The children scrambled into the car with excited greetings and a moment or two later Julian drove up with Damaris and Peter and Tommy Dawson and another boy; Jason too was one of the party and came bounding out of the car in boisterous greeting.

'Carole is coming too,' Julian said. 'Lester's bringing her—they'll join us at the Ghyll.' He hesitated and added, 'Ralph's also coming—but of course, you know that. And Madeline.'

'Madeline said she was going to ask him,' Tory answered as casually as possible. 'We shall be quite a big party. I'll go first, shall I, as I know the way?' and she put the Mini in gear and drove off with unexpected speed.

She had gone some way, scarcely heeding the children's voices, their chatter and various remarks before she began to slow down. They were going on a picnic, not a race, she told herself. What was there to get so steamed up about? Hadn't she known all along that Madeline was going to invite Ralph to the picnic? They were probably coming with Lester and Carole, and what could be a more natural arrangement than that?

But when they arrived at the Ghyll, and left the cars at the top of the lane so as to walk down to the waterfall and pool, it was to find Madeline and Ralph were there already, having ridden up one of the bridle paths that led from the dale to the Ghyll.

'It was glorious,' Madeline enthused. 'So green and peaceful—and it smelt heavenly, didn't it, Ralph?'

Ralph nodded as he crossed over to Tory.

'Yes, super. Hello, Tory. You guessed I was coming, didn't you?'

'Yes—Madeline told me she was going to ask you along.' She couldn't help her voice sounding stiff.

'We could have come with Lester, but Madeline likes to use the horses whenever she can, and she offered me a mount.' Ralph's manner was apologetic, but instead of being appeased by his explanation Tory felt perversely annoyed and had to struggle hard to keep any trace of resentment out of her voice as she said:

'Of course. It's much nicer to ride—Julian thought about it but decided it was too much for Peter.' She turned away. 'I must put this food with the other stuff.'

'I'll take it.' Ralph put his hand over for the basket, but when he carried it over to the other food which Damaris was helping to unpack Tory did not follow him, but walked over to Barry and Millie and taking their packages from them, said, 'Go and explore, and keep an eye on Peter, won't you?'

The twins nodded solemnly, then dashed away in search of Peter and Tommy.

Rylsone Ghyll was a famous beauty spot, but at this time of year there were few holidaymakers, so the party had the glade to themselves. Narrow pathways beckoned enticingly between the trees and in the clearings great drifts of bluebells scented the air, while above, below and all around them came the sound of tumbling streams and rushing waterfalls. The children couldn't wait, but dashed ahead to where the rocky cliffs formed a pool, deep and glass green in colour from the reflection of the hanging trees above.

Damaris hurried past Tory with a warning, 'Peter must take care not to slip—he's not used to anything like this.'

'He'll be all right,' Tory gestured to where Tommy Dawson stood, one small strong hand holding Peter's while on Peter's other side stood Stanley Dean, one of Tommy's cronies, clutching at Peter's arm, while Jason sniffed and ran to and fro.

Damaris sighed with relief and slacked her pace.

'They are good to him—I've noticed it before.'

Beyond the pool the water boiled and swirled, hurrying between fallen boulders as if anxious to escape down the hillside to the river far below. Spray sparkled in the air, rainbow-coloured—the children ran about with hands outstretched as if to catch it in their fingers.

'What a lovely spot,' said Damaris. She turned as Julian came up behind them. 'Isn't it beautiful here?—a perfect place for a picnic. I'm glad Tory told you about it.'

'She knows all this countryside. You—once showed me a little of it, didn't you, Tory?'

She met his dark, unsmiling glance fixed intently on her as if forcing her to remember the time they had gone to Hepworth Farm. They had talked together that day and got to know one another. They had not been friendly since.

'I expect you've discovered a lot of places for yourself since then,' she said abruptly.

'Not many. By the way, Carole and Lester have arrived.'

She was glad of the excuse to leave him and Damaris.

'I'll go and say hello,' and turning, she walked quickly back up the path.

No one could say the picnic wasn't a success. The weather stayed fine, the food was excellent and ample, Julian brought two bottles of wine to drink, as well as coffee and lemonade for the children, and everyone seemed gay and happy. Everyone, that was, but Tory. To Tory it was a travesty of an enjoyable time.

'I'm odd girl out,' she thought, watching everyone pair off. Damaris and Julian sat together on a rock discussing the theatre. Lester walked away with Carole who appeared, for the moment, to have taken him back in favour. And

Ralph? Ralph and Madeline went to see after the horses and were gone for over an hour, for Madeline thought the horses should be exercised along the level ground at the top of the wood.

That left Tory with the children. The children were used to her, they ran to and fro with their discoveries. 'Look, miss, a frog! Harry caught him in't grass.' 'Here, miss, I've found this moss—shall I take it back to grow summat in it?' Peter, tired after such undue activity sat close beside Tory and rested his head against her arm in sleepy fashion and said, 'I shall ride Moppet here one day. Will you come with me?'

She smoothed back the lock of dark hair which fell over his pale forehead and said, 'Yes, it would be nice, wouldn't it?' and tried to forget that as far as she was concerned it had been a failure of a day.

At last it was time to pack up the paper cups and plates and remnants of food and organise the children to help clear the litter. Ralph was back, and Tory saw him look in her direction and knew he was coming to find her. She felt she couldn't bear it, couldn't listen to any more polite excuses about Madeline, so she walked away until the trees hid her from sight. Several times she glanced over her shoulder in case he was following her, but evidently she had successfully hidden her escape route and he had gone back to the others, unable to find her.

She slowed her pace, thinking she mustn't lose her way in the woods. She listened and heard the sound of the waterfall and turning, walked in that direction, knowing the rushing stream would lead her back up the hill to the pool and so to the picnickers.

It was cool and dark in the Ghyll, the sunlight muted now and the rainbow spray dimmed. Some birds twittered nearby, she could hear the faraway echo of the children's laughter. It was time to go back.

A twig crackled behind her and she swung round expecting to find that Ralph had followed her after all. But it was Julian who came up and stood beside her on the wet brown rock overlooking the pool, Jason at his heels.

'So you're here. I'm the spearhead of a search party.'

Tory didn't answer, but stared into the pool's bottle green depth.

He said abruptly, 'Are you moping because of Ralph? Snap out of it, Tory, or you're going to get hurt. Can't you see what's happening in that direction?'

Anger bubbled up in her.

'Why don't you mind your own business? It's got nothing to do with you.'

'It has in a way. Ralph missed his inheritance through me and now Madeline is in pursuit of him. She's attractive, determined and has money, so Ralph feels he still has a chance to hit the jackpot.'

She swung round on him.

'That's a horrible thing to say! But typical of you. You're so—so cynical you think the worst of everybody. I'm not going to stay here and listen to you denigrating Ralph,' and she tried to push past him.

He caught hold of her wrist and held it so tightly she was unable to move along the narrow ledge they were standing on.

'I said before you'd a temper to match your red hair which is positively standing on end and your eyes blaze green as a spitting cat's. I like you this way—you really come to life when you're angry. I had an idea you were like this under that neat schoolmistressy Miss Webster facade.' His dark eyes narrowed as he stared down at her. 'It would be interesting to see how you'd react if I kissed you,' and his arm reached out to draw her to him.

Tory, on a wild impulse of rage, struggled to free herself, and unable to do so, raised her hand to give Julian a stinging blow on the cheek. He flinched back involuntarily, but the grip on her wrist didn't weaken. Tory, desperate, twisted and fought against his hold, and as she did so, managing to pull back a few steps away from him, her foot slipped on the slimy surface of the rock and she felt herself go over the edge into the pool.

For one dizzy frightening moment she swung there, held only from falling into the deep dark waters below by Julian's vice-like grip on her wrist. The pain was excruciating, it was like an iron cable cutting into her flesh. She heard Julian gasp.

'For God's sake, hold on, Tory. Here,' and, looking up she saw he was kneeling above her and stretching out his other hand towards her. She managed to clutch at it and slowly, achingly, he pulled her inch by inch to safety. His arms closed tightly round her, he held her fast while, trembling from the alarming suddenness of the accident, Tory leaned against him, struggling to get her breath back.

'That was a near thing. I'm sorry,' he said, 'it was all my fault. But I didn't expect you to react quite so violently.'

His voice was wry-sounding. She looked up and met his dark gaze and saw the reddening mark on his face where she had hit him. She said shakily, 'I—it was my fault too. I'm sorry.'

'Shall we seal a pact of mutual forgiveness?' he said, and slowly bent his black head and put his mouth against hers and kissed her.

There was thunder in her ears, the pounding echo of the waterfall as it rushed down the hillside into the pool. Or was it her heart beating with such turbulence and power? Julian's kiss, close and warm and passionate, seared through her like a flame, she felt a shaming response and her lips opened beneath his of their own volition. Her arms were about his neck, her bruised wrist rested in the thickness of his dark hair. Everything and everyone was forgotten and she was transported.

Slowly sanity and the remembrance of Ralph, of Damaris, came back to her and somehow she managed to free herself from Julian's arms. For a moment she stood without speaking, pushing the wave of hair from her hot forehead, then she said in a low voice, 'You—you shouldn't have done that.'

'I couldn't help it.' He shook his head, his eyes, darkly intense. 'You're obstinate and exasperating, but very lovely.' The glimmer of a smile touched his lips. 'Especially when you lose your temper.' He saw that she was rubbing her wrist, and took her hand in his and the smile faded. 'That's a rotten bruise. I'm sorry, Tory.' He passed a finger over the discoloured skin and she felt a quiver go through her. 'I had to grab you hard or you'd have gone over into the pool. Not that you'd have drowned—I'd have got you out all right. But you could have hurt yourself badly on the rocks.'

She said without looking at him,

'We—we both bear the scars of our encounter, but I'd like to forget about it, if you don't mind.' She was thinking of Damaris as well as Ralph. If Julian was in love with Damaris, he had no right to have kissed her like that just now. And she should never have returned that kiss.

He said slowly, 'Can you?' Then abruptly, 'All right, let's go.' He whistled to Jason who came leaping out of the bushes.

Tory moved away on legs that felt as limp as foam rubber. Her heart was still beating in that strangely tumultuous way. As if, she thought, as if she'd never been kissed in her life before.

CHAPTER FIVE

THERE was immediate consternation at Tory's dishevelled appearance. Her dress was dark with dust and slime from the rocks, and her hose, for the day had not been warm enough to go bare-legged, were torn into holes. Her face was dirty and her hair untidy and she had lost one of her sandals.

'What on earth happened?' Ralph demanded frowningly, as he put an arm about her shoulder and stared down into her pale strained face.

'I—I slipped near the pool and nearly fell in. Julian managed to grab me, but the rocks tore my things as he pulled me up again.'

'You should have waited for me—I came after you when I saw you going off into the wood, but you were gone in a minute.' He looked across at Julian. 'What happened to *you*?'

Julian's hand touched the mark on his face.

'Oh this? I hit my face on some rock.'

'You both look the worse for wear. Come and sit down over here, Tory. You look a bit shaken.'

Yes, she was shaken. But not just because she had almost fallen into the pool. Julian's kiss had been a traumatic experience and she was still feeling the effects of it. She felt even worse when Damaris came over and said, sympathetically, 'Poor Tory, it must have been frightening. I don't want to sound unkind, but thank goodness it wasn't one of the children.'

'Yes, thank goodness.' The children had gathered in a little circle and were staring with curiosity at her. Tommy Dawson stuck out his underlip and said belligerently:

'Bet I wouldn't 'ave fell in. Not 'less I'd wanted to. I can swim anyway, so it wouldn't have mattered if I had.

Shall I go and find your shoe, miss?' He half turned to run off, but Tory put a restraining hand out and said quickly:

'No, Tommy, thanks all the same. It's fallen in the pool and you wouldn't be able to get it.'

'Bet I could.' He looked at Brian Gosforth and said, 'Bet you couldn't.'

'Bet I could.' Brian struck out at him and the two boys fell on the grass wrestling with one another.

'Its time to go,' said Julian, 'before we all come to blows.' His glance met Tory's for a brief moment and a faint smile edged his grim mouth. He put a hand on the back of each boy's shirt collar. 'Come on chaps. The party's over,' and with Brian and Tommy on either side of him he walked to where the cars were parked, Jason running along beside them.

Ralph took Tory's arm.

'We haven't seen much of one another today.'

She said quietly, 'That's not my fault. You've been—occupied.' She nearly said 'with other people', but that would have sounded petty.

'So have you. Surrounded by those kids and then going off with Julian like that.'

She turned to look at him.

'I didn't go off with him, as you put it. He happened to come to the waterfall when I was there.'

'Did you push him—or did he push you?'

His remark was so unexpected that she could only stare blankly at him, and before she could answer Ralph laughed abruptly,

'My dear girl, it stood out a mile. The air was electric with the fact that there'd been some sort of a row. You'd obviously smacked him down. Did he make a pass at you?'

She couldn't bring herself to admit the truth. Nor could she put the entire blame on Julian, for hadn't she stayed in his arms instead of struggling free at once, and hadn't she returned his kiss?

'We—we had—an argument,' she replied, for after all that was how it had started.

'*That* I can understand,' Ralph said grimly. They had reached the top of the lane where the cars were parked and

the horses tethered. Madeline was waiting, her cool blue
glance surveying them as they came into sight.

'The horses are getting fidgety,' she said. 'Are you ready
to go, Ralph?'

He nodded.

'Yes.' He turned to Tory. 'Goodbye, sweetie. Shall we
meet on Thursday evening? I'll come to the farm.' He bent
his fair head and kissed her briefly. 'Bye, Tory.'

She watched him ride off and limped sandalless to the
Mini where the Kempter twins and Brian were waiting for
her. As she unlocked the door Damaris came up to her.

'I'd better say goodbye, Tory. I'm off to London on
Monday, you know.' She smiled her lovely caressing smile.
'Look after Peter for me, won't you?'

'Yes, of course. I—I'm sorry you're going away, but I
do hope the play's a great success.'

'So do I. Otherwise I'll be back here in no time.' She
looked round at Julian, who had come to stand beside her,
'Julian will put me in the picture. He's a good correspon-
dent.' She slid her hand through his arm and smiled up at
him. 'Wish you were going with me?'

'In some ways. That first night excitement—nothing quite
like it, is there? But I'm committed to this place now, you
know that. Otherwise I'd be on the train with you.'

'You promised to come and see the play. Don't forget.'

'I won't.' He looked at Tory. 'Are you going now? I'll
see you at the school, I expect, when I bring Peter.'

'Yes.' She gestured to the children, 'Hop in,' and sliding
into the car after them said through the open window,
'Goodbye, Damaris. I—I hope we shall meet again.'

'Sure to. 'Bye, Tory.' Damaris waved as the car moved
forward and Tory waved back, her salute meant as a leavetaking of Julian too.

That was that. The picnic was over and she was determined in future to avoid all unnecessary contact with Julian.
It only led to trouble and scenes. She didn't want a repetition
of what had happened by the waterfall. It was too unnerving,
and unsettling.

She frowned as she drove along the road to the village,
the chatter of the children beside her and in the back seat
a noisy accompaniment to her thoughts. Why did she use

the word *unsettling?* As if Julian's kiss had in some way undermined her emotions, and thrown her relationship with Ralph out of kilter? It was nothing to do with Julian that she should suddenly feel unhappy and uncertain about Ralph. Madeline was the cause of that, for she seemed bent on a take-over of him.

Tory sighed. She wanted to put the clock back and have everything the same as it was before these strangers came to the dale.

On Thursday evening Ralph came to supper and afterwards they walked on the moor with Troy. It was a beautiful May evening, but Ralph was so quiet and withdrawn that a cloud seemed to fall over Tory, shutting out the sunlight that gilded the fells, and softened distances into a golden haze.

At last she forced herself to ask, 'Is anything wrong, Ralph?'

He shrugged. 'The usual thing. I'm in Julian's bad books again.'

'What about?'

He frowned, his blue eyes narrowing angrily.

'Oh, various matters. Chiefly about this bridge business. He's been approached by the Council again to sell some land near the river so they can build a second bridge. I've mentioned it before to you, haven't I? Anyway, I'm in favor of it and Julian isn't, so we had a bit of a set to this morning.'

'I don't think it's a very good idea. It will bring more traffic through the dale,' Tory said slowly.

'That's inevitable, whatever we do. I've got news for you, sweetie—the automobile is here to stay. So take your choice. More cars piling up in congestion to cross that ancient hump-backed affair we drive over now or *two* bridges, one of them wide and two-laned and an easy flow of traffic.'

'But we don't *need* motorists dashing over a double lane bridge—if they want to get on in a hurry let them go somewhere, use the motorways or something. The dale should stay the slow peaceful place it's always been.'

'You're on his side, then?—has he been getting at you?'

'Of course not. It's the way I feel.' She looked at him. 'I can't understand how you can want or approve of changes that spoil things.'

'I approve of progress.'

'That's sometimes another word for desecration.'

'Look, you don't even *live* on the dale,' Ralph said sharply. 'You live up on these fells, miles from everywhere. If someone like Madeline who lives down there doesn't object why should you?'

'Oh, *Madeline!*' Tory cried, with, despite herself, the edge of temper in her voice. 'I suppose if Madeline approves it's bound to be all right. You forget that she and her father are newcomers—they don't *belong* to Scarsdale.'

'They will in time.'

Tory bit back the angry words that threatened to spill over. She took a deep breath and after a long moment said quietly:

'Don't let's quarrel, Ralph. There's been enough trouble falling out with—with other people. You and I should stick together.'

She looked at him, waiting for his set angry face to soften in a smile, for him to turn and put out his hand and say, 'Of course we should,' but he stared straight ahead, his mouth a thin line. When he spoke his voice was cold.

'I'm not quarrelling with you, Tory, but why is it that I am always the one to be put in the wrong? It's bad enough having Julian always picking on me, criticising everything I do, without *you* starting. I'm in favor of the new bridge and if I had any say in the matter the land would be sold to the Council so they could go ahead with it. And I can tell you this. A lot of people in Kirk Newton are for the project—it will bring business to the town and the shopkeepers will benefit.'

She couldn't answer for a moment because she was frightened she would say the wrong thing. In the end all she could say was, 'I see.'

'I hope you do.' He half turned. 'Shall we go back now?'

'Yes.'

They walked back over the moor in silence, the differences between them unsettled. The sun had gone down behind High Burton, the landscape lay in deepening shadow. Tory was unhappy and she had never felt so cut off from Ralph in all their times together. Troy padded wearily behind them, his big black head drooping, and when at last they reached the farm Ralph said abruptly, 'I'd better get back to Bramwick. Say goodnight to your grandfather for me.'

She put a hand out to him in a helpless gesture.

'Ralph, don't be—I'm sorry, I—' her voice trailed off because he wasn't looking at her but had put his hand on the car door to open it. He slid into the driving seat and gave her a brief glance.

'I'll be in touch, Tory. 'Bye for now.'

She stood back as he reversed the car.

'Goodbye.'

He was gone, and she was left standing in the summer dusk feeling empty and sad and very alone.

Thank goodness for school, Tory thought in the week that followed and the week after that and the week after that. Thank goodness for the children and the attention they needed and the demanding job that was hers. There wasn't much time in which to brood over Ralph and the fact that they had parted on an unresolved quarrel. And yet she *did* worry and wonder when she would hear from him or when he would come again to Wether Bell Farm.

She saw Julian on the occasions he brought Peter to school, either by car or riding on his pony. They exchanged polite greetings and that was all. And if at times Tory remembered the day of the picnic and their encounter by the waterfall and Julian's somehow unforgettable kiss she immediately battened down such thoughts as unaccountable weakness and traitorous to Ralph. She was always relieved when Alberto, the small dark Spaniard whom Julian had now engaged, along with Alberto's wife Elena, to help run the Ravensholme household, accompanied Peter to the school. He would walk beside Moppet or ride the old hunter which had belonged to Mr. Brierley, and Moppet would trot alongside him.

Sometimes Tory felt as if she were living in a void, waiting for something to happen that would bring everything back into focus. And then something did happen, but not in the way she would have wished.

It was after school one afternoon that she discovered Peter had left the treasured new watch that had been given to him on his recent birthday in the wash room. The children had gone and Tory debated whether to ask Miss Ewing if she

would telephone through to Ravensholme and tell someone
that the watch had been found, then she decided that she
might as well drive down to the house before going back
to the farm. She could then give Peter the watch or leave
it with Julian.

It had been showery, a day of rain and rainbows, with
great beams of sunlight lighting up the countryside, warming
the bracken to rose gold, and flushing the distant hills with
colour before disappearing again behind sullen clouds. Rainbow after rainbow arched the sky, or perhaps it was the
same one, first brightening, then fading in the changing
light. Tory thought, as she had thought before that up here
in this high country, the weather was never the same for
two days running.

She turned through the gates of Ravensholme and in a
few minutes reached the house. The wide drive had been
freshly gravelled, the shrubberies and borders tidied and
weeded and the house newly painted. A great improvement,
Tory decided as she slid out of the car. She went up the
steps and pulled at the heavy hanging chain and wondered,
with something that was half dread and half expectancy, if
Julian himself would come to the door.

It opened and a tall thin young man with brown untidy
hair and horn-rimmed glasses stood looking at her.

'Good afternoon. If you want to see Mr. Rivers, I'm
afraid he's out.'

'It's all right—I—I came to return something that belongs
to Peter.' She held the watch carefully wrapped in tissue
paper, out to him. 'Is he in—so I could give this to him?
He left it behind at school today. It's his wrist watch.'

'I'm afraid he's out too.' He had a shy but pleasant smile.
'Would you like to come in and wait?'

Tory shook her head.

'No. No, I won't do that. Perhaps you'd be kind enough
to give the watch to Peter.' She turned, hesitated and then
added: 'Is Ralph—is Mr. Brierley still here or has he already
left for home?'

The young man frowned.

'He's not here at all, actually. I mean, he's not working
on the estate any more. I've come in his place—as Mr.
Rivers' agent. My name's Lewis Morton.'

Tory could only stare in complete astonishment. Ralph gone? And no one had told her. Neither Ralph nor Julian. She frowned, trying to think when she had last seen Julian. A week ago—ten days? Yes, all last week Alberto had brought Peter to school. But how had this happened, and why? She felt a sinking of the heart as the full meaning of Lewis Morton's presence before her registered.

Ralph was no longer connected with Ravensholme, but did that mean he had left of his own accord or had Julian got rid of him?

She wanted to ask a dozen questions, but Lewis Morton was staring at her in a bewildered way as if he wondered at her odd manner and long silence.

'I'm sorry, I didn't realise he—Mr. Brierley had left,' she said. 'Thank you. I—' she put the watch in his hand. 'Please give this to Peter. Goodbye,' and she turned and almost ran down the steps.

Why? she thought. And why didn't Ralph tell me? She felt indignation boil up inside her. It's Julian's fault. He's responsible—I know it. He sent Ralph away. Ralph would never leave of his own accord. Poor Ralph, how worried he will be. What will he do now?

On impulse she turned left at the bridge instead of taking the right-hand road and going back up the hill. A little farther along she turned left again and was soon at Bramwick. She wanted so much to see Ralph, to find out what had happened and tell him how sorry she was and how much she sympathised with him.

In the garden, stooping over the roses, was Mrs. Brierley. She looked up at the sound of the car and stared for a moment, then recognising Tory, she waved and walked towards the Mini. As Tory braked and slid out of the driving seat Mrs. Brierley said smilingly, 'Hello, Tory. What a pleasant surprise.'

'Hello, Mrs. Brierley.' She stopped, wondering what to say, how to go on. Mrs. Brierley waited calmly, the basket of roses in one hand, the secateurs in the other, her cool blue eyes on Tory's hot agitated face.

'I—I've come from Ravensholme. I—I've only just heard about Ralph leaving his job there. I'm so sorry about it— I wanted to talk to him.'

'My dear, what a shame. Ralph's out at the moment. I'm sure he'd have liked to have seen you and told you all about it.' The blue eyes narrowed to Tory. 'Of course, I thought you already knew what had happened. Won't you come in and have some tea? I was going to make myself a cup.'

The last thing in the world Tory wanted was a tête-à-tête with Mrs. Brierly. She had come so hurriedly and so eagerly to find Ralph and commiserate, and now felt dashed.

'Please don't trouble—I—I have to get back to the farm soon anyway—it was just that—I was so near I thought I'd call and see Ralph—' Her voice trailed away under Mrs. Brierley's cool gaze.

'Are you sure? Ralph will be sorry to miss you, I know. At the moment he's over at Lindley Grange, helping Madeline with the horses. Something for him to do, you know. The break with Julian has been a great shock to him, as you can imagine—a shock to us all. But poor Ralph found his cousin *very* difficult—he just couldn't work there any longer.' She sighed and then added, more cheerfully, 'But I'm sure he'll tell you all about it when he sees you.'

'Yes—yes, I know he will.' Tory stood irresolute, then said politely, 'How is Carole? I haven't seen her since we all went on the picnic.'

'She's well—always coming and going somewhere. I'm afraid she's finished with Lester—he was very upset about it, but if Carole is not in love with him it's kinder in the end to make the break.' Mrs. Brierley shrugged slim shoulders. 'So many of these boy and girl affairs drag on uselessly—and people drift into marriage and then are not at all happy. I'm glad that Carole has had the sense to end her involvement with Lester if she has had a change of heart.'

There was no answer to that, or to the undercurrent of meaning that seemed to run beneath Mrs. Brierley's words, as if she would have liked to substitute Ralph's name for Carole's.

Now I'm imagining things, Tory thought. Mrs. Brierley doesn't mean any such thing. I'm suspicious and—yes I admit it, *jealous,* because Ralph is with Madeline again.

'I—I must go. Please tell Ralph how sorry I am about what has happened and tell him I hope to see him again

soon. Goodbye, Mrs. Brierley.' She turned to add, 'Your—
your garden looks lovely.'

'Thank you. We've had a lot of help in it lately—Mr.
Langford's gardener is such a hard-working old man. Goodbye, Tory my dear. Be sure to remember me to your grandfather.'

'Yes, I will.'

Tory was submerged under a cloud of depression as she
drove up the steep winding hill towards Scarsfell. So that
was it. Ralph and Madeline. That was why he hadn't been
near her, or telephoned. He had been spending his time at
Lindley Grange, working there, helping with the horses,
Mrs. Brierly had said.

She turned the bend in the road and saw the tall figure
on the tall black horse walking slowly along the grass verge.
Julian. She felt heartache, anger and indignation fuse together in an explosion of rage, and she braked sharply and
came to a standstill at the same moment that Julian reined
in beside her.

For a long moment they stared at one another, then Tory
said slowly, through gritted teeth,

'I've been to Ravensholme—to return Peter's watch, he
left behind at school, and I met Lewis Morton.'

One black eyebrow rose up, the deep-cut mouth curled
sardonically.

'Oh yes?'

'You never told me that Ralph had given up his post as
agent to the estate. Or did you dismiss him?'

'Hasn't Ralph told you the details? I should have thought
that would be the first thing he'd run to do.'

His coolness infuriated her, and the sting in his words
only added to her resentment. Because it hurt; it hurt very
much that Ralph hadn't confided in her.

'I—I think you've been vindictive over Ralph. Taking
someone else in his place like that. How can he help you
as much as Ralph would have done who's worked at Ravensholme half his life?'

'What I do and what I don't do is my own business. But
I don't mind telling you this. Ralph could be of the greatest
possible help if he'd *wanted* to be, but he never has done.
He resents my inheritance of Ravensholme too much to work

as a partner. He's gone underground, done things without my knowledge or agreement, and generally undermined any plans I might have for the good of the estate. I don't pretend to have Ralph's professional know-how, but I'm determined on one point—the preservation and conservation of the entire Ravensholme property. I want to follow my father's wishes in that direction and I don't intend to sell one foot of the land to alter Scarsdale in any way, if I can prevent it.

'As for Lewis Morton—I agree he hasn't Ralph's practical experience, but he's a graduate in Agriculture and will be of great use with the office work and in supplying technical information. That's what I need—I can learn the rest.'

Tory met his stern implacable glance and for a moment felt rebuffed. Towering above the car on his tall horse he looked both formidable and dangerous, a man it wouldn't be easy to get the better of. The son of his father, she thought, remembering the stern misanthrope who had ruled Ravensholme. Julian wasn't in the least misanthropic, but he possessed the same unyielding streak in his nature as old Mr. Brierley, the same vein of Yorkshire granite.

When she made no answer Julian said coolly, 'Anything else you want to know?'

Her chin went up.

'You've just about said it all.' She put her hand on the ignition to start the car and drive away when, from behind her she heard the clatter of hooves and saw the pony Moppet come cantering up the hill, the figure of a man crouched in the saddle. It was Alberto.

He called excitedly and waved as he approached them.

'Señor—Señor Bree-lee! *Despáchese! Sigame!* Is the leetle Señor—is hurt. *Sigame!*'

Julian swung his horse round and said a few words quickly in Spanish. Alberto nodded his cropped black head, gesticulating wildly, and Julian turned back to Tory and said briefly:

'Peter's met with an accident—he fell in the stable yard and, from what Alberto says, he's broken his arm,' and without another word, he trotted the horse a few yards down the road, then, backing it, jumped the stone wall and disappeared into the Ravensholme woods. Alberto stared after him before setting off down the road obviously to go through the gate set in the wall some way down, as Moppet was too small for him to jump.

It had all happened so suddenly that for a moment Tory was bewildered. She sat in the car, wondering what best to do. She wanted to go and see after Peter, to help in any way she could. Yet following her encounter with Julian just now it was the last thing in the world she felt inclined to do. Then she remembered Damaris smiling at her and saying, 'Look after Peter for me, won't you?' and she knew she had to go to Ravensholme no matter what Julian said or did when she got there. Quickly she reversed the car on to the grass verge and drove down the road after Alberto.

In a matter of minutes she was back on the river road, the Mini eating up the three miles to Ravensholme with the speed of a sports car. Soon the house came into sight and Tory braked on the gravel and dashed out of the car and up the steps to the door. It stood half open and before she could knock she heard voices and excited chatter in Spanish. Walking through the foyer, she saw three people gathered about Peter who was half sitting, half lying on the big carved settle in the hall.

She addressed Julian's broad back.

'I'm sorry—I had to come and see how Peter was.'

He turned and saw her and for a moment gave her a long hard stare, then he said briefly, 'He's broken his wrist—it looks like a Colles' fracture. I've tried to get Dr. Spicer, but he's at the hospital, so I'm taking Peter there straight away. They'll give him an X-ray.'

Tory fell on her knees beside the small boy and smoothed back the dark hair from his pale tear-stained face with a gentle hand.

'Poor pet, what a horrid thing to happen!' She laid a finger on his arm and said, 'We'll put this in a sling—you'll look like a wounded soldier.'

'Alberto's gone to find some wood for a splint,' said Julian.

Tory examined Peter's hand which was tilted to the thumb side, a swelling already forming up the forearm.

'A splint may not be necessary. A thick pad of cotton wool soaked in cold water will do if he's going to the hospital

at once. And a large handkerchief or scarf to make a sling.'
She looked round at the anxious-faced Spanish woman. 'If
you could make Peter a cup of tea with plenty of sugar and
find him another cardigan or coat to keep him warm against
shock, it would be a great help.'

The woman stared and shook her head; Julian said something in Spanish to her, and when she nodded and hurried
away, he added: 'Elena doesn't speak or understand much
English yet.' He laid his hand lightly on Peter's shoulder.
'Feeling better, old boy?'

Peter nodded, his lower lip caught between his teeth. He
bent his head towards Tory and rested it against her cheek
as if finding comfort in her presence, and she stroked his
hair and, turning her face, pressed a kiss against his forehead. Glancing up to ask a question of Julian, she found
him watching her, and felt a momentary tension, aware
again of the quarrel between them.

She asked with a calm steadiness, 'How did the accident
happen?'

'Peter fell on the cobbles in the stable yard— he had been
riding with me and gone back on his own. Alberto was there
to help him off, but Peter's been managing to dismount on
his own lately. The stones were slippery after the rain and
his bad leg didn't support him—he fell on his wrist in an
effort to save himself.'

'It was lucky Alberto was able to find you so quickly.'

'Peter told him I would be coming down the Scarsfell
road.'

At that moment Alberto appeared with the wet cotton
wool and a heavy silk scarf, and by the time Tory, helped
by Julian, had wrapped the injured wrist in the pad and put
Peter's arm in an improvised sling Elena came hurrying in
with a tray of tea. Peter sipped some of the warm well-
sweetened liquid and then Julian lifted him carefully up and
carried him out to the car, which he had brought to the front
door.

Peter put a pleading hand out.

'Tory's coming too? I want Tory to come.'

Julian gave Tory a brief glance.

'Will you come with us?'

'Of course. I'd like to if I may.' She opened the car door,

'Is it better if we sit at the back—there's more room and I can support Peter so he won't be bumped about.'

'Yes, that would be best.' His mouth twisted in what could have been a smile. 'You're very much in charge, aren't you?'

'I'm sorry, I didn't mean to—to—give orders. I—it's just that I've done First Aid—mishaps like this are an occupational hazard of a teacher's job.'

'I'm glad you're so competent.' He lifted Peter in beside her and she put an arm about him.

'All right, pet?'

'Yes. Yes, thank you, Tory.'

This wasn't the time to insist on the Miss Webster aspect of things.

'Lean back against me. I'll steady you at the bends so you don't knock your arm.'

Soon they were at the Kirk Newton hospital and in a short time after that Peter had had his wrist X-rayed and put in a cast by one of the doctors in attendance. Then they were driving back to Ravensholme and Tory was helping Peter into bed.

'Will you come and see me tomorrow, Tory?' he implored as she settled him against the pillows. 'Mummy can't come just yet, you see, because of the new play.'

'I'm sure she would do if she knew you wanted her, but perhaps you can be very brave and not ask her to come.'

He nodded wanly.

'Uncle Julian says we mustn't worry her or she won't be able to carry on and it's awf'lly important that she does well.' He shook his head. 'I wish she *could* come. But you'll come instead, won't you, Tory?'

'Of course, darling. I'll come tomorrow after school. And when you're feeling a bit better Tommy'll come to see you perhaps, and Brian. You'd like that, wouldn't you? But don't worry, you'll be back at Scarsfell very soon.'

Julian appeared in the doorway, a glass of water in his hand.

'This is for the tablets Peter's to take,' he added. 'Make you sleep, old fellow, and stop your arm aching.'

Peter sighed.

'My arm does ache—it sorts of jumps inside.'

'I know. But you'll feel better in the morning. Open up.'
He dropped the tablets on to Peter's tongue and held the
glass to his lips. 'There. I'll be around—sitting here in the
room with you after I've seen Tory off. Say goodnight to
her.'

''Night, Tory.'' One thin arm came out to clasp her neck
as Tory bent over him and she gave him a gentle hug in
return.

'Sleep well, dear. Bless you.'

She went out of the room followed by Julian who had
drawn the curtains to shut out the evening sunlight. When
they reached the hall he said briefly, 'Thanks.'

She hesitated.

'Will it be all right if—if I come to see Peter tomorrow?
Would you mind? He asked me to. He—he's missing his
mother at a time like this.'

'And you're the substitute? Just as well—it will be all to
the good if Damaris doesn't come haring back here, which
she would do at the drop of a hat unless I make it very clear
Peter's O.K. and being properly looked after.'

His voice was clipped, almost curt. How much does he
care? Tory thought, thinking of Peter's *'Uncle Julian'* and
wondering if the title was a euphemism or not.

'I'm sure Peter will be himself in a day or two,' she said
in a voice almost as abrupt as Julian's.

He shrugged.

'Come and go as often as you wish—until he's back at
school. Feel free to do so, and don't bother to see if I'm at
home or not.'

She got the message. She was to keep out of his way and
not worry him, and that suited her just fine, because she
certainly didn't want to have any more contact with him
than was necessary. She would visit Ravensholme solely
on Peter's account.

She said shortly, 'Thank you. Goodbye,' and hurried
down the steps to the waiting car.

As she drove back to Wether Bell her thoughts returned
to Ralph again. She wished so much she had been able to
see him when she called at Bramwick and she wondered if
when he got her message he would come to the farm. How
worrying and upsetting it was. What would Ralph do now?

Of course he could get another job as land agent, but it might mean him leaving the North Riding—even Yorkshire. She hated to think of that.

Her grandfather was as surprised to hear the news as Tory had been. He shook his head and sighed.

'It's a pity them two couldn't have worked together in double harness. Reckon they're oil and water. I'm sorry for Ralph—but maybe he's had things a bit too much his own way and couldn't give in.'

'It's not Ralph who won't give way, it—it's Julian. He's so—so domineering and autocratic—at least, over everything to do with Ravensholme. He won't listen to reason.'

Mr. Webster, drew on his pipe.

'Aye, well, 'appen he gets things a bit out of proportion seeing as he's a landowner for the first time in his life. The place means a lot to him, Tory, I'm sure of that. From what he told me and from things you've said he never properly belonged anywhere before, did he? Kind of a rolling stone. Now he's part of Ravensholme and all that goes with it. Stands to reason he's not going to play second fiddle to anyone over the running of it.'

'But to—to have got rid of Ralph and taken on this Lewis Morton person—it was a mean and horrible thing to do!'

'Now, Tory lass, you don't know for sure he *did* get rid of Ralph, as you put it. It could have been by mutual agreement, with Ralph wanting to go as much as Julian wanted to shift him out'n way. Ralph's been unsettled these past weeks, you know that. A change might not be such a bad thing for him.'

'I don't want him to go away.'

Mr. Webster stared into the low burning fire and puffed at his pipe.

'If young Ralph's as fond of you as you are of him it won't make any difference whether he's at Scarsdale or Singapore. You'll be together in the end.'

'Yes.' Why couldn't she feel sure of that? Why did she have this dire feeling that somehow she and Ralph were drifting apart? 'I'll get supper for us.'

'Don't put yourself about for me—I'm not that hungry.'

Tory looked back from the doorway and was suddenly aware that tonight her grandfather looked tireder than usual.

In the dim firelight his face was thinner and more lined. She said lightly because he hated her to fuss over him, 'How's the leg? Has it been aching much today?'

He glanced up, his eyes wary under the grizzled grey eyebrows.

'It's been a bit stiff—maybe I've been walking more'n usual.'

'Why don't you ride Jock—it would save you a lot?' Jock was the grey cob that Tory sometimes rode over the moors and which her grandfather also used behind a small pony cart.

'I go out on him sometimes, but I like to get round among the sheep when I can, and walkin's best for that. But if this leg doesn't mend better than it has done I shall begin to wonder how much longer I'm going to be able to carry on.'

Tory stared at him in dismay. She wanted to cry out. 'Gramps, don't! Don't talk like that. Don't ever grow old.' She turned away before she should make some tactless remark and hurried into the kitchen.

As she sliced the beef galantine she had made the day before and washed and dried lettuce and tomatoes with which to make a salad she realised, for the first time, how tired she was herself. It had been a whirlwind few hours since she had left school that afternoon, for she had driven to Ravensholme and then to Bramwick, then back to Ravensholme, she had gone with Julian to the hospital at Kirk Newton and returned to Ravensholme and, eventually, driven home to the farm. And still it was only half past eight in the evening! So much had happened, it seemed incredible.

One comfort, she was so tired that when she went to bed that night she fell asleep immediately, instead of lying awake and worrying about Ralph and the uncertain future, as she might otherwise have done.

At school the next day the children were all sorry to hear of Peter's accident and some of his friends begged to be able to take time out to write letters to him. Tory agreed to deliver them when she visited Peter after school later in the day.

'Tell 'im I'll bring me hamster when I come to see him,' Tommy Dawson said. ''E can keep it for a day, if he likes,' he added magnanimously.

'Well, I'm not too sure about that,' said Tory. 'It might not be a good thing with Jason around—he's a very boisterous dog.'

Tommy frowned.

'Aye. Well, 'appen I'll just take it along and let Peter 'ave a stroke of it.'

'That would be best,' Tory agreed.

School finished for the day, the children went pelting down the road and Tory stayed a few moments to talk with Miss Ewing before leaving. She said goodbye and went to find the Mini. It was a warm, still afternoon; on the skyline a farmer and his dog stood in silhouette and a file of sheep moved slowly along the narrow tracks below them. For a moment she watched, thinking how peaceful the scene was, how timeless. The small grey houses tucked against the hillside, their windows facing into the warm south sun, their back gardens rising to the fells. Far below, at river level, the farms were toy size, the sheep and cattle moving dots in the meadows.

So it had always been, so it would always be. Wars were fought, revolutions came and went, people lived and loved and died and still the slow unchanging life of the fell country went on. Why must anyone ever try to alter it? she demanded of no one in particular as she slid into the driving seat and reversed the car on to the road. She had just turned down the Kirk Newton road when she heard someone shout her name and glancing over her shoulder she saw Ralph coming towards her. She braked sharply and stopped the car by the roadside, and immediately his hand was on the door and he was saying at the open window, 'I was waiting for you along the road to the farm. I saw you backing out and turning this way. Aren't you going to the farm?'

'No—no, I—' she hesitated, and he slid into the car beside her and said,

'It doesn't matter. Mother told me you called at Bramwick yesterday.' He put his hand out to cover hers lying on the steering wheel. 'I'm sorry I've been non-existent just lately, but I hadn't the heart to come and tell you all my troubles. You know I'm out on my ear from Ravensholme, don't you?'

'Yes—I met Lewis Morton—and then your mother told

me. I'm terribly sorry, Ralph. I think it—it was unforgivable of Julian.'

'I had to leave—there was no alternative, though it was actually more or less of my own accord. I didn't wait for the push but told Julian I couldn't stick the job with him breathing down my neck.'

She said again, 'I'm so sorry. What—what are you going to do?'

He dropped his hand from hers.

'I haven't made up my mind. There are one or two things in the offing.' He stared moodily down the hill. 'But the future's pretty bleak.'

'Oh Ralph!'

For a moment they sat in silence. Then Ralph said slowly, 'It's bound to make a difference to—us, Tory.' He hesitated and added, still without looking at her, 'I—I don't want you to count on me too much. If we don't meet as—as often as we did, I hope you'll understand.'

Tory blinked hard, as if by seeing more clearly she would be better able to take in Ralph's words. Not meet as often? Not count on him too much? What was he trying to say to her—that he didn't love her after all?

She felt curiously cold and a sort of blankness came over her. She couldn't think of anything to say but just went on staring through the windscreen at the empty road and the trees that leaned all one way from the cruel winds that blew in autumn and winter.

Ralph said almost anxiously,

'You do understand, don't you? We had a good thing going between us, but as things are I—I just don't want to be committed.'

Tory turned her head and somehow found her voice.

'You never were committed—you know that. And—and I do understand. Of course you want to be—be free in every way.'

She heard him sigh as if with relief.

'That's it. I mean . . . as things are at the moment. If Uncle Harold had left me Ravensholme everything would be different—I could make plans—'

If, Tory thought. If Julian hadn't come into their lives—*if* you loved me enough.

'You see, I might be going away, might be going anywhere,' he said again. 'I—I want to feel free to do so.'

'Of course,' Tory said very calmly, as if she were discussing some quite ordinary everyday matter instead of the slow destruction of all her hopes and dreams. 'That's understandable.' She bit her lip to steady the tremor that suddenly shook her. 'We've always been—friends, Ralph. We— we always will be. I hope with all my heart things will come right for you.'

'Thanks, Tory. You're a wonderful girl—I knew you'd take it like this and understand. Mother said you would. She said that, in the circumstances, I should be absolutely straight with you and not—not—' He hesitated, and Tory said, with a sharp and unexpected bitterness:

'Not lead me up the garden? Or string me along? No, your mother wouldn't use slang like that. She'd say, "Be kind to Tory and don't let her misunderstand you." I suppose I should be grateful to her for her consideration, but I wish you'd been open with me on your own account.'

'Don't be like that. Mother meant well, and I was going to talk things over with you anyway.'

Tory was already regretting her undignified outburst. She didn't want to part from Ralph in anger.

'I'm sorry,' she said tiredly. 'I'm glad you've been honest with me. It—it makes things easier.'

As if anything, any words could make what had happened between them easier. Whichever way he did it, it hurt just the same. To be told a long and close relationship was over, to be given the brush-off.

'Does it?' Ralph's voice quickened with relief. 'No hard feelings, then?'

She shook her head.

'None.'

'We had some good times together.'

'Yes.'

She sensed his glance on her averted face, and fought to remain calm and self-controlled.

'I'll say goodbye, then. For the moment, I mean. Of course we'll be bumping into one another from time to time. Unless I go away, but if I do I'll let you know, Tory.'

'Yes, you must do that.' She forced herself to turn her

head and meet his anxious look. 'Goodbye, Ralph, and good luck.'

'Bless you.' For a moment his lips touched hers and then he pushed open the car door and jumping out strode up the road to where he had left his car.

She sat very still and upright. Her tightly clasped hands felt icy cold despite the warm June day. She heard the toot of a horn as Ralph's car flashed by and then it was gone, down the hill and back to Bramwick. And still Tory went on sitting and staring blankly at a landscape she didn't see, while she tried to make sense of her thoughts and realise that Ralph had gone out of her life for good.

No use sitting here for ever, a drained empty-hearted zombie. She was supposed to be going to visit Peter, but she couldn't bear the thought of seeing Julian. It was all Julian's fault. If he had not inherited Ravensholme instead of Ralph, Ralph would have asked her to marry him. He had as good as said so to her once. They could have been so happy. For a moment she felt she hated Julian. An echo of her grandfather's words came to her. 'If Ralph's as fond of you as you are of him it won't make any difference whether he's at Scarsdale or Singapore. You'll be together in the end.'

Then Ralph hadn't loved her enough. Was that it? Or were the circumstances of fate too much for him?

She switched on the ignition and started up the car. She *must* go and see Peter, and just hope that Julian would be as anxious to avoid her as she was to avoid him. She couldn't let Peter down.

Fortunately, when Tory arrived at Ravensholme there was no sign of Julian. Elena took her up to Peter's room. He was staying in bed for the day so as to rest, for the fall had shaken him up and jarred his bad leg. His eager welcome restored Tory's drooping spirits a little and she stayed to have tea with him and read Tommy and Brian's and some of the other boys' letters aloud. She told him about Tommy's hamster and promised that Tommy should come to see him and bring his pet with him.

Afterwards she read one of his favourite stories to him, and then, fearing that Julian might put in an appearance before she left, she said goodbye to Peter and went downstairs.

The hall was fresh with the new paint; a big jar of blue and yellow lupins and starry pink pyrethrums stood on a carved oak chest, the rug lying on the tiled floor below it echoing the colours of the flowers. Everywhere there was evidence of care and attention.

She was going towards the front door when she heard steps behind her and swung round, dreading to see Julian. It was Lewis Morton, a tall figure in dark blue shirt and dark blue jeans. For a moment he stared at her through the thick-rimmed glasses, then he smiled shyly and said, 'Hello. We've met before, I think. Were you looking for Julian? He's out, I'm afraid.'

Tory shook her head thankfully.

'No. I came to visit Peter—I'm just leaving.'

'Poor little chap, he's had a rotten time of it. First his leg and now this injury to his wrist. But he's a brave soul and seems to be making the best of things.'

'Yes.' They had come out on to the steps. The garden was bright in the afternoon sunshine, the great beech trees a shining green, the oaks dense with foliage. The flower beds had been weeded and planted out with floribunda roses, the overgrown shrubs pruned and tidied. The whole place wore a very different aspect from when old Mr. Brierley had lived at Ravensholme. Tory could not help commenting on it.

'Someone's been hard at work here—it was very neglected before.'

'So I believe. Julian's got a new gardener, and Alberto helps quite a lot round the place. The terrace has all been re-paved—have you seen it?' and at her shake of the head Lewis gestured, 'Come and have a look—' and led the way round the side of the house before Tory could say no.

The broken stones had been lifted and replaced, the chipped balustrade repaired. A new rose entwined green fingers between the pillars; thyme, low-growing pinks and tansy had been planted in spaces left between the stones. Below the terrace where shrubs and trees had once grown unrestrained, a clearing had been made and the view opened up so that now Tory could see across the park to where cattle and sheep grazed to the dale and the shining Scar river wound through the meadows.

She said involuntarily, 'Oh, it's lovely. I'd no idea—'

'It is nice, isn't it? I don't know what it was like before, of course, but everyone tells me it's an incredible improvement. Julian's full of ideas for the place, but he won't have anything drastically altered. He just wants to bring the whole estate back to life.'

'Yes.' It was only to be expected. He had inherited the estate and wanted to put it to rights. For Damaris to live there with him? For someone, most certainly. Hadn't he said right at the beginning of their acquaintance that he wasn't going to live alone at Ravensholme?

She turned.

'I must go.' They walked back to the front of the house.

'Thank you for showing me the terrace. Goodbye.'

'I expect we'll meet again before long,' Lewis said, and opened the car door for her. She slid in and started up the engine and drove away before there was any chance of an encounter with Julian. Today, of all days, when she had parted from Ralph, was the one time in the world she couldn't have borne to have spoken to him.

CHAPTER SIX

It was July. Soon school would break up. The meadows, one day flower-filled, scented with crimson clover and creamy meadowsweet, were the next day lying mown beneath the hay-cutter, and in swathes of drying blossom and grass.

Every day Tory thought about Ralph and every day she felt lonelier, and emptier. She realised, for the first time, how much she had come to count on him; even when a week or more had passed and they hadn't met or made contact, still there was the looking forward, the dreaming and hoping. Now that was gone. Whatever had been between them was over.

She kept as busy as she could; school work and end-of-term exams; the farm and the extra work at haymaking. Somehow time went by. Tory went to see Peter several times, taking Tommy and Brian on more than one occasion. She encountered Julian, but only briefly; he talked to the boys and took them to the stables to see the horses and ride Moppet round the fields, but he was as aloof with Tory as she with him. Except one day when, calling to see Peter on her own, she met him in the hall as she was leaving. He gave her an abrupt greeting, then stopped to stare down at her, his dark eyes narrowing under the formidable black brows.

'What's the matter? You look a bit wan. Too much teaching?'

She shrugged, looking away from his close gaze.

'Something like that. This—this hot weather's rather tiring.'

'You've lost weight, and it doesn't suit you. Redheads need curves.'

Her chin tilted defensively.

'Thanks, I'll remember that.' She made to go past him, but he put a hand out to check her.

'You're not worried about anything, are you? How is your grandfather keeping?'

She hesitated.

'Well enough. He—he seems rather tired too.'

'I'd come and see him again, but I'm not sure of my welcome.'

She looked directly at him.

'You're as welcome to come and visit my grandfather as I am to visit Peter here.'

His mouth twisted in its usual sardonic fashion.

'Meaning they're duty, not social calls?'

'I don't come to see Peter as a duty—I'm very fond of him.'

'Yes, I think you are. And I like your grandfather—he's a great character.' He let go of her arm. 'Give him my best regards and tell him I'll come and see him.'

'I'm sure he'll be pleased.' She walked past him, saying over her shoulder, 'Goodbye.'

Julian kept his word and called to see Mr. Webster, but one morning, when Tory was at the school. Another time he called during the afternoon, but she had stayed late to correct some examination papers, so missed seeing him, for which she was grateful.

Then, the week before the term ended, she came out of school to see the familiar green sports car parked on the road outside and someone waving to her, and recognised Damaris.

She crossed over as Damaris slid out of the front seat.

'Hello, Tory. We hoped we'd catch you. I'm up on a flying visit to see Peter and I wanted to thank you for all your kindness to him.'

'It was a pleasure. How thrilled he'll be to see you.' Tory's voice was warm, for she could not help being drawn to Damaris. She looked across at Julian who had got out of the car and nodded a greeting to him before turning back to Damaris. 'How is the play going?'

'Like a bomb. We've had rave reviews—did you see them?—and it's booked up weeks ahead. If it really settled down to anything like a long run I'll be able to have Peter in town with me.' She put a hand on Tory's arm. 'You've been angelic to him.' She looked round, her beautiful eyes soft and warm as they rested on Julian. 'Julian's told me all about you—he's been a darling too to Peter, but then he always is.' She looked back at Tory. 'Wasn't it the horridest thing to happen to the poor lamb—and he's been so brave. Julian should have sent for me at once, but he waited to see how things went because of the new play. I just have to trust him always to do what's best for both of us.'

'I understand that—and Peter did too. He was most sensible about everything.'

Damaris shook her head.

'He always is, bless him. Tory, do come back and have a drink with us—I want to talk to you and I'm going back first thing in the morning—Julian's taking me in his car and staying on in London to see the play.'

Tory hesitated, and Julian added his request.

'Come back for a little while—you know Peter will like to see you too.'

'He has his mother now,' Tory answered, but she found herself agreeing to go back to Ravensholme with the two of them, and in a few moments she was following Julian's green car down the Kirk Newton road.

Peter, who had been resting, came limping out to meet them and flung both arms round Damaris.

'Mumm*ee*! Oh, I wish I'd come with you. Why didn't you wake me? What are we going to do now? Shall we go and see Moppet? Uncle Julian's bought a new horse—did you know?' He turned and smiled at Tory. 'Hi, Tory! How was school today?'

Tory ruffled his hair, smiling down at him.

'You're a cheeky imp. Miss Webster to you.'

He grinned. 'I always call you Tory—you know I do. Tory's my best friend, Mummy, *and* Tommy Dawson. They're both my best friends.'

'You're a lucky boy to have two best friends,' Damaris said. 'Now go and ask Elena for some sugar for Moppet, and a nice sliced carrot, and we'll visit the stables. And then Tory's going to have a drink with us and you shall have one too.'

As they walked to the stables Tory thought how lovely

Damaris looked. She was wearing ice blue slacks and a cream silk blouse under a blue sleeveless slipover. The effect was casual yet sophisticated and with her smoke blue eyes and dark hair she was more attractive than ever. It would be impossible for Julian not to be in love with her, Tory decided, and she wondered again what obstacle prevented them marrying and was convinced, more than ever, that Peter was Julian's son.

'Now promise that if you come to London you'll let me know,' Damaris urged, when she and Tory said goodbye. 'You're to have a free seat for the play—*two* seats, so you can take a friend with you, and you must come backstage afterwards and meet some of the cast and we'll go out to supper somewhere.' She gazed beseechingly at Tory. 'I mean it, Tory, it's the smallest return I can make for all your kindness to Peter. Perhaps you'll be coming with that nice friend of yours—Ralph, is it?—and we can have a party.'

There was a small silence during which Tory and Julian stared at one another. It was obvious that Damaris hadn't heard yet that Ralph had left his job at Ravensholme.

When they spoke it was together.

'I don't think Ralph could c-come,' Tory began, while Julian broke in with, 'There's been some trouble. Ralph's left his job here.'

Damaris's blue eyes moved from one face to the other.

'Oh, sorry. I've said the wrong thing. How awkward of me! Forget it darlings. But what I've said still goes for you, Tory.' She smiled dazzlingly. 'With some other friend, so remember. It's a promise.'

'Thank you, I'll remember.' Tory hesitated. 'Peter's not going to London with you and Julian?'

'No, not yet. He'll be coming to stay soon, if not to live. Elena will look after him while Julian's away. She's so very attached to him.'

'I wondered—while you're away—if he'd like to come for a night to Wether Bell? Grandfather and I would love to have him.'

Damaris's eyes widened.

'But what a super suggestion! He'd adore it, of course,

and it would take his mind off my departure. Really and truly, Tory? It wouldn't be a bother?'

'No bother at all. Shall I collect him tomorrow or do you think he's well enough now to come to school? He needn't do much and he could come home with me from there.'

'That would be best,' Julian put in. 'He won't feel so left on his own and though he can't use his wrist yet to write I expect he'll enjoy being with his friends. Lewis will run him to school as Damaris and I have an early start from here.'

'Who's Lewis?' Damaris asked.

'He's the new agent. You haven't met him because he went home for the weekend and he won't be back until this evening. I'll tell you all about it later.'

The arrangement was concluded and Tory drove away thinking how close and amicable Damaris and Julian were together. Their relationship seemed entirely taken for granted by one another. She had a sudden remembrance of the day of the picnic when he had found her by the waterfall and kissed her, a kiss she had not found easy to forget. *Why* had he kissed her like that when he was in love with Damaris? It was all wrong. Worse, she had returned his kiss, and at that time she was involved with Ralph.

She sighed, thinking about Ralph. Wondering if he had gone from Scarsdale without telling her. But no, he had promised to let her know when he went away.

Peter stayed two nights at the farm and seemed to enjoy every moment of his visit. The weather stayed fine and Tory took him for a ride across the moor one afternoon after school. At least, Peter rode Jock, who plodded steadily along on a leading rein held by Tory while Troy panted slowly after them. She told him something of the history of the moors and showed him the old packhorse trails and why many a lonely inn was named the Woolpack, from the cloth traffic carried by the horses in olden days. She told him that the name Webster meant a weaver and names like Dyer, Taylor, Lister were once names for dyers, and Walker meant the fuller who trampled the sodden wool and the name Kempter once indicated a woman woolcomber. Peter was enthralled and if much of the information passed over his head, still he learned something of the Riding's tradition.

'Tell me some more, Tory,' he said, as they turned to go slowly back along the track. 'Tell me more names.'

Tory frowned.

'Well, there's Wick—names ending in ''wick'' mean a group of buildings, often a dairy farm.' She stopped abruptly thinking of Bramwick. Bramwick, grey and stone built, its garden running down to the river, Bramwick had been a farm long ago. Now it belonged to Ralph, it was his home.

'Go on,' Peter urged.

Tory bit her lip. Why did everything remind her of Ralph?

'Well, there's Whernside, that's a name that came from the Quern hillside where quernstones and millstones were quarried from millstone grit. Have you ever seen a millstone?'

He shook his head.

'No.'

'I'll take you to the old Mill near the Kirk Newton Bridge—and show you some of the millstones there.'

'Can we go tomorrow?'

'Perhaps. We might take some of the others from school, mightn't we? Make an expedition!'

'*Yes,*' Peter said, enthusiastically. 'I like expeditions. They're sort of adventures, aren't they?'

'In a way. The word means a journey or a tour or a pilgrimage, a ramble, a march, an excursion—that sort of thing.'

Peter sighed.

'What a lot of words you know, Tory. You are clever. Is that why you're a teacher, because you're so clever?'

Tory smiled.

'I'm a teacher because I like boys like you and I want to teach them many words and many other things. Look, there's the farm down there in the dip. Do you see it? We're nearly home.'

'It's nice where you live. It's like a house in a story—all those funny little windows and the rooms sort of queer and low. I wish I lived in your house instead of Uncle Julian's.'

'Do you? But Ravensholme is a handsome house and has a beautiful garden and a big park. And stables—where you keep Moppet.'

'I could keep Moppet here. He could be with Jock—they'd be friends.'

'But what about Uncle Julian—perhaps he wouldn't like living at Ravensholme without you.'

Peter frowned.

'P'raps not. And Mummy wants to stay at his house. She said so to him—I heard her say she wished she hadn't to leave him, but of course she had to because of the play. She's very famous, you know.'

'I'm sure she is. Now steady getting down—let me lift you off Jock—we don't want you to fall and break the other wrist, do we?'

Peter giggled as Tory swung him to the ground.

'Oh goodness, no. Can I go in to Mr. Webster?—I want to tell him about those words—perhaps he knows some more.'

'I'm sure he does. You go in and find him while I see after Jock.'

She returned to the house to find her grandfather and Peter deep in conversation and as she made the customary high tea she could hear Peter's chatter and Mr. Webster's deep answering voice. She thought that Peter's company did her grandfather good, for lately he had seemed quieter than usual, although in answer to her questions he had assured her he felt well enough, it was just that his leg ached at times.

Two days later when Tory took Peter back to Ravensholme she met Lewis Morton again. It was obvious by Peter's enthusiastic greeting to him that they were already good friends.

'I've got two younger brothers,' he told Tory. 'One of them, George, is the same age as Peter here . . . Julian's on his way home—he rang me this morning, sorry you've missed him.'

Tory wasn't sorry. As usual it was a relief not to encounter Julian—once was enough within a week. There was something about her meetings with him that always unsettled her. She disliked him. No, not exactly disliked. Resented was the word. It was his fault Ralph had left Ravensholme—she couldn't forgive him for that. And he had a way of probing without appearing to do so, he seemed to—what

was it? *unmask* her, as if he could see right into her and
know how she was feeling about things. Well, if that were
true, he would know how she felt about *him* and a good
thing too, she thought as she drove away from the house
and on to the Kirk Newton road.

She had shopping to do in the town and also a prescription
for her grandfather to pick up at Dr. Ryder's surgery. As
it so happened she saw Dr. Ryder himself, for he came
across the hall from his own room into the small office
where an assistant dealt with patients' National Health cards
and dispensed medicines or gave out the prescriptions waiting to be collected.

'Hello, Tory. You're not waiting to see me, are you?'

'Good evening, Dr. Ryder. No, I've called for Grandfather's tablets.'

He frowned—

'Ummm, yes. They're not for his leg, y'know. They're
for his heart.' He saw the shock on her face and added:
'Come in here a minute, Tory,' and led the way back to
the Surgery.

She said quickly as soon as the door closed behind them,

'How do you mean—Grandfather's heart? I didn't know—
he hasn't said—'

'He called in to see me the other day—ostensibly about
his leg, but I gave him a check-up at the same time. He's
got a tired heart, Tory. Oh, nothing frightening or dangerous, but I've warned him he won't be able to continue
working the farm as he has done. It's getting too much for
him—the fall he had and the injury to his leg put an extra
strain on his constitution and his heart won't stand up to
it.'

Tory swallowed.

'I knew he wasn't well—I could see he seemed weary,
listless at times. But he never said a word when I asked
him how he was—I mean, about coming to see you.'

'It was only a few days ago—I expect he'd have got
around to it in his own time. You can't rush your grandfather—he makes his mind up for himself. But I thought it
best to warn you, Tory, so you can keep an eye on him and
be prepared for what he might tell you.'

'I don't know how I'm going to persuade him to ease

off,' Tory said worriedly. 'Though he did say once something about selling the sheep to Sam Dyer, his shepherd. If only he would—and still be happy. The sheep mean everything to him.'

'Not quite everything, Tory. He's got you—you're the apple of his eye. Though I suppose one of these days you'll be getting married?'

She said abruptly, 'Not for years and years. I—I haven't any plans. Thank you for telling me, Doctor. I'll see what I can do to help Grandfather.'

'I know you will. You're a good girl, Tory. Don't fuss or worry over him—just keep an eye on things and try to persuade Mr. Webster it's time to give up the farm work.' He pulled open the door. 'Goodbye.'

Tory collected the pills and walked out onto the street, her anxious thoughts full of her grandfather. Of course now she understood why he had appeared quiet and tired, why he had seemed to be sitting around more than usual. She had put it down to his stiff leg, but it was other than that.

Would he give up the sheep? At least he had once hinted at the idea. It was up to her now to supply gentle but firm propaganda.

She was so engrossed that she never saw a girl waving to her from across the square and it was only when a voice said, 'Tory! You're lost to the world. What on earth are you day dreaming about?' that she looked up to see Carole standing in front of her.

'Carole! I'm sorry, I—I—I didn't see you.'

'That's obvious. I've been waving like mad—I even called out to you.' Carole tucked her arm through Tory's. 'I'm glad we've met like this. I've been thinking about you.'

Tory turned to look at the small, smiling heart-shaped face near hers. Carole was wearing a coral pink blouse above light navy cotton pants and she looked as gay and vivaciously pretty as ever.

'Have you?'

'Yes.' The smile dimmed, the shadow of a frown clouded her expression. 'I—I'm sorry about you and Ralph.'

Tory felt herself stiffen, but she said calmly enough,

'Did he tell you? That—that we'd called it a day?'

'He didn't need to. Mother and I guessed how things

were when he stopped seeing you—talking about you. And then—there was Madeline—so we knew.'

'M-Madeline?' Despite herself Tory's voice shook slightly as she said the other girl's name.

'Well, they're so *thick*. I knew she'd never let Ralph go once she got her hooks into him—I warned you once that she was going after him, didn't I? Oh, I've nothing against Madeline—actually, I quite like her. But we've been friends, Tory, you and I, and I know how you feel about Ralph and I always hoped you'd both get together—permanently, I mean.'

'We—we decided otherwise. Ralph's not sure what he's going to do about—about a new job.' Tory hesitated. 'He talked of going away.'

'Yes, I know. He said something to us about it. But I think he's changed his mind. Madeline wants him to go into partnership with her over developing a stud farm—you know she's keen on that?'

'So—so I understand.' Tory bit her lip. She was shaken by the news. 'Won't he have to—to put up some money?'

'Yes, but he has his legacy from Uncle Harold. And I suppose he could raise some money on Bramwick, if he wanted to. It belongs to him now.'

'Yes.' She took a deep breath. 'I hope whatever Ralph does turns out well for him. He was unlucky over Ravensholme—over his cousin inheriting the estate, I mean. And worried about the future.'

Carole gave her a quick sideways glance.

'And you don't mind about Madeline?'

Tory made an effort to keep her voice casual.

'Ralph's free to—to do as he wishes. We're friends—we always have been. If he chooses to work with Madeline that's his affair. It's got nothing to do with me.'

'But it will end in something more than *working* together, if I know Madeline. So it's just as well you feel the way you do, Tory. Otherwise you might mind very much.' Carole's voice changed. She said briskly, 'Where are you off to now—have you time for tea, or a coffee somewhere?'

Tory shook her head.

'Thanks, Carole, but I've rather a lot to do and the shops close around half past five. I'd better get on. I—it's been so nice seeing you again. How are things with you and Lester?'

'Lester? Oh, that's all off, not that it was ever really *on*— or only on Lester's side. He's quite sweet, but an awful *stick*—no fun at all really.' Carole hesitated. 'As a matter of fact I've met someone new—No, I won't tell you who he is just yet—it's a bit complicated. I expect you'll see us around together sooner or later.'

'Do I know him?'

'Yes, I think you do. That's all I have to say, for the moment.' Carole smiled, two dimples showing on either side of her cupid's bow mouth. 'Lovely seeing you, Tory, and I'm glad to know you're not pining away for Ralph. I got quite a guilt complex when I saw you just now. See you soon,' and she turned towards the car park.

'Yes. Goodbye, Carole.'

Tory felt her shoulders sag as she walked up the street towards Woolworths, and the smile that had felt like a mask over her face fell away. So Ralph wasn't going away to find another job, he was going to work with Madeline. Had he intended to do that all along? Even when he had come to tell her he must be free to move around? Was he in love with Madeline?

It was useless to repine, to wonder this and that. She had other problems to face, other worries that were much more important. *Grandfather*. What was she to do about her grandfather now that he was beginning to fail and would have to be persuaded to give up the farm? Tory, walking in and out of one shop after another, paying cheques and collecting packages, began to feel almost schizophrenic as, with part of her mind upon one concern, she tried desperately hard not to consider the other.

If only, she thought as, her errands done, she walked back to the car park, if only I could go away. Far, far away. Where I needn't see Ralph or Madeline or Carole or anyone connected with them. Where no one will stop to ask questions or sympathise with me. Where I can forget everyone and everything.

Impossible. Her grandfather was far from well and it was her job to take care of him, as he and her grandmother had cared for her a long time ago.

CHAPTER SEVEN

TORY said nothing to her grandfather of her talk with Dr. Ryder, but she watched him more closely and saw afresh the signs of weariness in his face and manner. School broke up for the long summer holiday and she had time in which to do little extra things for him, making his favourite meals, fetching and carrying for him in various ways and doing her best to see that he rested more than he had done.

It had been arranged earlier on that Jane and the two children should come to stay for a week, and Geoffrey would come at the weekend and stay until Monday when they would return to Whitby.

Tory glanced up from the letter that had come from Jane confirming their plans and said, 'Will it be all right for them to come, Gramps? It won't be too much for you, will it?'

He gave her a sharp glance from under bushy grey eyebrows.

'Of course it won't. Two kids and young Jane? What's got into you lately, lass? You've been running round me like a scalded hen fussing and moidering. D'you think I'm on my last legs or something?'

Tory was taken aback, but recovered to say calmly, 'Of course not. I've just been trying to—to save you from doing too much.'

'More likely you've been talking to Charlie Ryder and gettin' some notion I'm going to drop dead among t' sheep.'

'Gramps! I—I never thought any such thing.'

'And you haven't been chatting me over with Dr. Ryder? Nay, I can see by your face you have. Now listen, Tory I'm well aware of what he'll have said to you, but you can just forget it. I'm good for a long time yet. But I've been thinking about *you*. It's not passed my notice that things aren't right between you and Ralph. Have you packed him up or summat?'

Tory's mouth twisted.

'You could say he—packed me up.'

Mr. Webster swung round in his chair.

'That I'll never believe,' he said angrily. 'Packed *you* up—you, as is t' bonniest lass in't North Riding. If he has done, then all I can say is, he wants his head examining.'

For a brief moment Tory's head rested against her grandfather's arm.

'Oh, you're good for my morale. Shall we say—things finished between us by mutual agreement?' If that wasn't entirely true at least it would save her grandfather from unnecessary indignation.

'That's more like it. And I can say now what I wouldn't have said before—you're well rid of him, Tory. He wasn't right for you, but if I'd said so at t'beginning it'd have only made you more set on him.'

'But you—you liked Ralph—you always said so,' Tory protested.

'Aye, he's a good enough lad in his own way, but what I said was, he's not right for *you*. He's a bit of a weakling and he'll always take the lines of least resistance, will Ralph. You need a strong man Tory. Someone as'ull boss you around instead of you bossin' him. You'd try and boss me, but I'm not having any. Never would with your grandma and I'm not startin' with a chit like you.' His smile took the sting out of his words, and Tory, despite the criticism of Ralph, could not help but smile back, so warm and kindly was the look her grandfather turned on her.

He leaned forward and patted her hand.

'That's better, lass. You've been going around with such a glum look on your face I thought you were plannin' t'funeral. But I can see you were thinking on Ralph. Which brings me to another thing. I'm not having you hanging round me mornin', noon and night. You're to get in wi' living your own life, and that means getting away from here and having a bit of a holiday—maybe take yourself off abroad or some such thing.'

'I'm not going to leave you on your own, Gramps.'

'Now, Tory, mind what I said. There's only one boss in this household.' He paused and stared frowningly at the unlit pipe in his fingers for a moment or two, then he said slowly,

'Supposing I told you I'd decided to sell the sheep. What would you say to that?'

Tory waited a minute herself before answering.

'I'd say that in many ways it would be good thing. Oh, I know how much you'd miss the work and interest of them, but—they are a big commitment to you now, Grandfather, and you find the walking about tiring.'

'Aye.' He sighed. 'I reckoned it would come to it sooner or later. And best sooner.' He glanced across to her. 'I've come to terms with the idea on your account. If I carry on then maybe I'll knock myself up, and that 'ud be unfair to you. So I'm going to sell the flocks to Sam—well, bulk of 'em. Rest'll have to go to Kirk Newton market.'

'Oh, Gramps!' She couldn't speak for a moment, knowing what a big decision it was for her grandfather to have come to. Remembering that there had been sheep at Wether Bell Farm for a hundred years or more.

'I know—I know.' He moved his hand impatiently as if to brush away commiseration and sympathy. 'If your dad had lived things might have been different—there'd have been someone to carry on. There was a time when I fancied you marryin' a farmer, Tory, and living here, maybe with sons to work the place. But you'll not do that, I can see.'

'I wish I'd been your grandson,' Tory said.

He shook his head.

'That's never been my wish—you've been best granddaughter in the world to me—as good as any daughter.' He sat up a little straighter in the armchair. 'Well, that's settled, then. I'll have another word wi' Sam and after that I'll be a gentleman of leisure. Maybe it won't be as bad as I think—you slow up with age any way. And I've got a hobby or two—the chess games wi' Joe Taylor, and there's the astronomy. I've a deal to learn still.'

'You'll find lots to do, Grandfather.' Tory put her hand on his shoulder for a moment, then she moved away, to stare out on the rain-swept fields. The summer weather had broken up in storms and wind and now the landscape was half hidden under grey drizzle. She said slowly, 'Do you remember how you watched for Kahoutek?'

'Aye—and missed him. But you saw the comet, Tory. That's something you'll remember for many a day.'

'I'll never forget it.' She thought of that night back in Jan-uary and her meeting with Julian and how they had seen the comet together. She said over her shoulder, 'You know, that comet has changed a lot of things. Not just here, but every-where. It's been a year of strange happenings. There've been enough disasters to make all those old superstitions seem true. Strikes and troubles, a change of Government in February, scandals, floods and droughts and air crashes. And all the time the killings in Ulster. Air charter companies going crash and the economic crisis. What next I wonder?''

'And you blame yon Kahoutek for all that?' Her grandfath-er's voice was sceptical.

'Well, whoever or whatever is to blame, it's been a horrible year for a whole lot of people,' Tory said. She thought how Ralph had been supplanted over his inheritance and because of that, the attachment between them had been broken. *Attachment*. An old-fashioned word. Why didn't she say love affair, grand passion, devotion? Because somehow what she and Ralph had felt for one another didn't warrant so dramatic a description. Attachment meant the same as those other nouns, but it didn't *sound* so intense. We never were intense, Tory thought. Perhaps neither of us are intense-feeling people?

She turned from the window, pushing away the remembr-ance of Ralph, and said, as if in continuation of her earlier remark, 'Even the weather's been disastrous . . . only a few days of summer.'

The weather unfortunately didn't improve for Jane's visit, for though it was dry, it was cold with a good deal of grey cloud. Bobby and Betsy didn't seem to mind, they were too enthralled with the animal life of the farm and riding patient Jock along the moorland paths and playing games of Snap and Happy Families with Mr. Webster and Tory and their mother. Jane and Tory were happy enough in each other's company and as long as the rain kept off they could enjoy days out with the children at York or Ripon.

At the weekend, when Geoffrey arrived to stay, the sun came out at last and Geoffrey was glad to relax from his work in his busy practice and potter round the farm with Mr. Webster or take long walks up the Fell.

Somehow, by whose instigation Tory wasn't certain, it was

decided that Mr. Webster should return on the Monday with Geoffrey and Jane and stay with them for a week.

'But, Gramps, you never go away *anywhere*,' Tory remarked in surprise.

'Then it's about time I started. Do me good, and I'm looking forward to seeing Whitby and the coast again. I'm very grateful to Jane here for inviting me.'

Jane smiled and said, 'We shall love to have you, Uncle John,' but one eyebrow lifted as she glanced at Tory as if to say, 'This is as much a surprise to me as to you.'

If Tory wondered why she had not been included in the invitation she was soon to discover the reason, for her grandfather took her aside and said:

'Now, Tory, I want you to take advantage of my being away and get off somewhere yourself. Bessie's coming to sleep in and see after the dog and cat and Sam will be up every day sortin' out the sheep he's to take. I'm leaving it to him—he knows what he's doing and he'll arrange for the sale of the rest later on.'

'I see,' said Tory, who saw a great deal. 'All right Gramps, I'll go to London for a few days. My friends from college have said many times there's a bed for me at the flat if ever I want one. I'll telephone tonight and see if it's convenient to stay with them.'

She felt her grandfather push something into her hand.

'That's for your holiday. And buy yourself something—a new dress or whatever you want. There's money coming in from the sale of the sheep—you're welcome to some of it.'

When he had gone and she opened the envelope Tory found to her amazement that her grandfather had given her a cheque for fifty pounds. She felt she had not thanked him nearly enough and was overwhelmed by his generosity.

Emma, one of the girls with whom she had shared the flat in London, was delighted to hear of Tory's proposed visit.

'Couldn't be better—Freda's on holiday, so you can have her bed—no need for the put-u-up, though Freda will be sorry to miss you. How super, Tory, to see you again. I'll leave the key in the old place in case you arrive before I get home. Are you coming by car or train?'

'Train, I'm afraid,' Tory answered. 'My car's secondhand and really not too reliable for a long journey. I daren't risk it.'

For the first time in weeks Tory felt as if she had something to look forward to. London and seeing Emma again. It would be a lovely change and freshen her up. She felt she had been living in a rut lately and not a very happy one. And there would be no worry over Gramps, who would be well looked after by Jane and her doctor husband. What to take with her, what to wear? It was all such a sudden arrangement.

She was upstairs putting some things in her suitcase when she heard Geoffrey call from below, 'Tory? Where are you? There's someone here to see you.'

She hurried downstairs and found Julian in the sitting room with Geoffrey. The sight of him checked her in the doorway and she said uncertainly, 'Oh, hello.'

He inclined his head gravely. How was it that wherever he was, whomever he was with, he dwarfed the room and company? Geoffrey was tall, good-looking enough with his aquiline features and curly brown hair, but he seemed colourless and ordinary against Julian's brooding dark looks and impressive height.

'Hello, Tory. I called to see how your grandfather was and encountered Dr. Carey on the doorstep and we introduced ourselves.'

'Grandfather's out—did Geoffrey tell you? He's gone to see his shepherd.'

'So I understand. Is he keeping well?'

'Yes, thank you. Actually, he's going away tomorrow—to stay with Geoffrey and my cousin at Whitby.'

'Are you going too?'

'No, I'm going to London for a few days. Won't—won't you sit down? Will you have some tea?'

He shook his head, frowningly as if at some inner thought.

'No, thank you very much. I mustn't stay long.' He turned to Geoffrey. 'You live in Whitby? I've never been there, but I understand it's a very interesting old town.'

'Yes—very.' The two men began talking together until Bobby and Betsy ran into the room, followed by Jane and introducions started all over again. After a short time Julian glanced at his wrist watch and said:

'I'm afraid I'm going to miss seeing Mr. Webster as I have an appointment at six o'clock.' He turned to Tory. 'Please give him my best regards and say I hope to see him when he returns from Whitby. I'm going away myself tomorrow,' he added, his dark eyes intent on Tory's face, 'To London. I suppose I can't offer you a lift?—you have your own car.'

Tory hesitated, not wanting to say she was going by train, and Jane spoke for her.

'You're not going in the Mini, are you, Tory?'

Julian said quickly,

'Aren't you? Then let me take you in my car. I'm not leaving until around ten o'clock, if that time suits you.'

She didn't want to go with Julian—didn't want to drive all the way to London sitting beside him. And yet it would be impossible to refuse his offer with Jane smiling expectantly at her, and Geoffrey looking pleased at such a happy outcome.

'I was going by train,' she began slowly. 'It—it's very kind of you, of course—' she paused, still hesitating.

'I'm taking Peter down to stay with his mother,' Julian said briskly. 'Damaris has moved into a furnished flat close to Kensington Gardens and she hopes he'll eventually be able to go to school nearby.'

She sighed with a sort of relief. Peter was going along too. That was different, easier altogether.

'Thank you—very much—I'd like to come with you both, and ten o'clock suits me fine.'

'Good.' He put out his hand to Jane. 'I hope we shall meet again some time—you too, Dr. Carey.' He smiled down at the children and shook them both by the hand. 'Goodbye.'

Tory walked with him to the door.

'Grandfather will be sorry to miss you,' she said politely. 'I'll be ready by ten tomorrow. And thank you. Goodbye, Julian.'

He didn't shake her hand as he had done the others. For a moment he stared down at her, dark eyes narrowed. Then he said briefly, 'Goodbye, Tory,' and strode away across the cobbled yard.

Next day, Monday, the weather was still cool, but the sky was patched with blue and it looked as if it would stay fine. Jane and her family and Mr. Webster were not leaving until later in the morning and planned to have luncheon somewhere en route to the coast. Bessie Dyer had arrived to hear Tory's last-minute instructions about household matters.

'Stop frettin', ' her grandfather said. 'Go off and enjoy

yourself, same as I intend to do. Isn't that Julian's car coming down t'track? You'd best be off and not bring him in to start us all natterin' and holding things up. Tell him good morning for me and say I hope to see him next time he calls.'

'Yes, all right. Goodbye, Gramps darling. Take care of yourself.' She hugged him and with a last goodbye to the others, hurried away to greet Julian before he got out of the car. Peter waved excitedly and as she slid into the front seat beside Julian he leaned forward and said:

'Hello, Tory. I'm going to live with Mummy—isn't it super fab? Uncle Julian's car does ninety miles an hour—he said so, only we're not allowed to do that on the Motorway—only seventy.' He shook his head regretfully. 'I *wish* we could do ninety. I've never driven that fast.'

Tory smiled round at him.

'Nor have I. And I never want to. How's the wrist?'

He held up his right arm.

'I hardly feel it any more.'

If Julian didn't achieve quite the speed Peter hoped for, nevertheless it seemed to Tory that they made remarkably good time on the busy motorways. Julian drove with care and concentration, making only intermittent conversation, for which Tory was glad. Gradually she felt herself relax. Occasionally Peter leaned forward to say something then he too would lean back, staring out the window, watching everything they passed, sometimes quietly humming to himself.

They stopped for lunch near Wansford. Julian seemed glad to stretch his long legs and Peter to ease his injured one.

'I'll tell Damaris you're in London,' Julian said as he drove towards Emma's flat, which was in the Islington district. 'She will want to send you tickets for her play.'

'I don't want to impose—' Tory began, but he shook his head and said,

'She'll be most offended if you don't contact her. You promised to do so.'

'Yes. I—I'll ring her from the flat.'

'I want to see Mummy's play too,' Peter broke in eagerly.

'Well, I don't think you'd understand it or find it very interesting,' said Julian. 'You'll have to see what Mummy thinks about that.'

When they reached the tall old-fashioned house which had

been converted into several flats Julian lifted out Tory's suitcase and carried it up the front steps and into the hall.

'What's your phone number here?' he asked. 'In case I need to contact you.'

Tory told him, adding, 'I thought you were going back tomorrow, that you'd only come to bring Peter to his mother.'

'I might have to stay on a couple of days. I'm not sure,' he said vaguely. 'Are you here for the week?'

'I expect so.'

'Well, have a good time. And don't forget to ring Damaris—she'll be expecting to hear from you.' He put out his hand. 'Goodbye, Tory.'

'Goodbye.' She put her hand in his, and felt his clasp, warm and firm round her fingers. She had a sense of loss, as if she had expected more than this polite leavetaking. As if she wanted him to say something more. Absurd. He had done her a kindness—not involved her or encroached on her in any way, which was what she had feared might happen. And when he didn't she was disappointed? Of course not. She said lightly, 'Thank you for bringing me in your car.'

'A pleasure. Sure you can manage now? Sure I can't take your case up?'

'No, no, of course not. The lift is here.' He slid the gate open for her and she stepped inside and waved as she pressed the button, and the next moment she had moved out of sight of him.

Seeing Emma again made Tory realise how much she had missed her; missed the fun and companionship she and Emma and Freda had shared together. Emma's life seemed full of mobility and interest. She had a new boy-friend, Bruce, who worked at the B.B.C. and she seemed to go to endless parties, meeting this well-known person and that. Tory was tempted to do a little harmless name-dropping and spoke of Damaris.

Emma was impressed.

'How thrilling! I thought it was all moors and sheep in Yorkshire. When it isn't coalmines, I mean. Imagine meeting Damaris Lawton *and* Julian Rivers up there. He's *fantastic*—I saw him in a super spy play. He wasn't the hero—he played the part of the villain—but oh, boy, what a villain! Sinister but absolutely fascinating. Is he like that in real life?'

'He's—very attractive,' was all Tory could say.

Emma was even more inpressed when Damaris telephoned and asked to speak to Tory.

'Lovely to hear you're in London,' Damaris said in her soft, sweet voice after they had exchanged greetings. 'Now what night can you come and see the play—I'll leave two tickets for you at the box office and afterwards you and whoever you bring with you are to come out to supper with me.'

It was arranged, after a consultation with Emma who was in the kitchen, that they would go to see the play on Thursday evening. Tory thanked Damaris again for her kindness before Damaris rang off.

'How lucky can you get—can we get?' Emma said happily. 'I've been dying to see *Halcyon Summer*, but it's terribly booked up. And we're *really* going out to supper with Damaris Lawton after the show? I can't believe it. Bruce will be green with envy—he admires her very much.'

'I wish Bruce could come too,' Tory said.

'Oh, not to worry. He'll be glad for us to have such a treat.'

London was full of tourists and summer holidaymakers. Tory had forgotten how noisy it was, how dirty it had become. She loved London and always would; there was a zest, a pace of life here that was nowhere else. The shops were fabulous, the fashions head-turning after the tweeds and country cottons of the north. And yet from time to time she would think of the high fells and open skies and the sweet cool air that blew across the moors; the larks singing above the purple heather, and had a curious certainty that it was there she now belonged.

Tory and Emma arrived early at the theatre, springing a taxi in honour of the occasion. Emma was wearing a long dress in gaily patterned reds and pinks. She was a tall attractive girl with wavy brown hair and light hazel eyes. Tory wore a skirt of printed velvet in a rich shade of kingfisher blue; with this she wore a kimono-sleeved blouse in a matching shade of blue. It was very becoming, setting off her red-gold hair and deepening the colour of her eyes.

The theatre was packed; their two seats in the fourth row of the stalls next but one to a gangway seat, not yet occupied. The lights dimmed, there was an expectant rustle as the audience settled into quietness; the curtains parted and a small round of applause broke out at the first glimpse of the set, the interior of a castle in Scotland, and the sight of Damaris seated at a desk in a long mullioned window, writing. The evening had begun.

Tory was too enthralled with the play, with watching Damaris, who looked more beautiful then ever, and listening to her opening lines as she turned to speak to a tall ghillie entering from a door down stage to notice that someone had arrived quietly in the seat next to her. But when, during a pause in the play's action, the figure beside her turned and said in a low voice:

'Are you enjoying it?' She started in amazement to find Julian looking at her.

'J—Julian!'

'None other.' One of the actors started speaking again and a voice said warningly from behind them, 'Ssh!'

Tory caught the glint of Julian's smile, felt the pressure of his arm and shoulder against hers and looked quickly back to the stage. Julian *here*? But he had already seen the play. Why was he here again tonight?

She became aware that she was losing the thread of the action and resolutely put all queries behind her to concentrate on the play again, and although she was still conscious of Julian's proximity, she soon became engrossed in what was happening on the stage and forgot about him until the lights went up for the interval.

Emma was surprised and obviously thrilled to meet Julian. At his suggestion they repaired to the stalls bar where Julian bought a round of drinks with which, as he put it, they could toast the success of the play and Damaris's performance in it.

'I think she's gorgeous,' Emma said enthusiastically. 'It's a good play—very clever and amusing, but Damaris Lawton absolutely makes it.'

Tory was quiet, leaving Emma and Julian to do the talking between them. But as they returned to their seats Julian bent his tall head to say, 'I've been invited as your supper escort— Damaris is bringing Nigel Hampden and three other people from the play to make up the party. We're going to the Savoy.'

'Oh!' She was breathless on two counts; Julian's presence and the prospect of supper at the Savoy.

When the play ended, to seemingly endless applause, Julian guided them backstage and they found themselves in Damaris's dressing room, filled with flowers and the scent of grease paint and powder. Damaris, glowing, alive with the nervous tension that triggers off an actor's top performance, flung her arms round Tory and kissed her, crying:

'Darling, you look fantastic in that colour, I wish I had hair like yours. And this is the friend you spoke about?—lovely to meet you. Julian angel, find them somewhere to sit—the stool—and clear that couch I won't be long—just this goo to take off—and my dress to change.'

Other people put in an appearance, Nigel Hampden who had played one of the major roles, the girl who had taken the part of his daughter, Greg McKinlay, the man who played the Scots ghillie and a third man, tall and thin and grey-haired, who had the role of a doctor in the play. There were introductions all round, much talk and laughter and then the departure in two taxis for the Savoy Hotel.

Tory found Julian sitting beside her in the taxi, Emma and John Deering opposite to them, the other four having gone in the first taxi. For a second she felt his hand rest lightly on hers. He said in his deep drawling voice, 'Well, Tory?'

In the shine of neon lights and moving traffic she could see his face, see the dark eyes staring intently down at her. She said airily, to mask the tremor of excitement that ran through her veins like quicksilver, 'Well, Julian?'

'We meet again, you see. And not by chance, I assure you.'

She hoped his voice was too low for the others to hear his words.

'Why do you say that?'

'Because I want you to know I stayed on in London especially to be here tonight with you.'

She looked away to the kaleidoscope of dark streets and glittering lights.

'I—I find that hard to believe.'

'I hope to prove it to you.' The next moment the taxi swung into the courtyard of the Savoy Hotel and a uniformed commissionaire was opening the door for them.

Tory couldn't remember a more dazzling evening. The company, the food, the wine, the music all combined to beglamorise the occasion. Damaris, in a midnight blue chiffon dress with long floating sleeves, was the focus of the party, yet although she attracted everyone like a lodestar by the special gift that was her own she drew from the others a similar sparkle and charm, so that spirts ran high and to Tory the talk seemed all wit and laughter.

Emma, sitting on Julian's left, was gazing at him as if bemused, and Tory guessed that she had already fallen under his dark dynamic spell. On Tory's right sat Nigel Hampden, fairhaired, stockily built and far from handsome, yet with a personality so warm and humorous that she was immediately at ease with him and soon forgot that he was one of the best known actors on the West End stage and felt instead that she was in the company of a friend.

Across the table from Tory sat Peg Stockton, a dark-haired girl in jade green, and next to her was Henry Mathers, who had played Dr. Burdock in the play. Tory danced with him once as she danced with Nigel Hampden and Greg McKinlay, but she danced most frequently with Julian while the others sat talking together over the supper table.

'This is no novelty to them, you see,' Julian explained. 'They're glad to relax after the evening's performance, but you and I are fresh. Anyway, I only want to dance with you.'

Was he flirting with her, doing a line? He couldn't be serious, not with Damaris sitting at the table only a few feet away from them, looking beautiful and glamorous beyond words in the dark blue dress that breathed the word *couture*.

She ignored the implication of his remark and said, 'Don't you miss the life you had—the theatre, acting'—a gesture of her hand indicated the splendid glittering room, 'all this?'

He smiled wryly.

'I'm afraid my career didn't include many suppers at the Savoy. Usually it was sausages and chips in provincial digs. My acting was mostly confined to touring or rep.'

'You might have made the West End—if you'd kept on.'

'I lived in hopes of that, but it wasn't to be. Inheriting Ravensholme changed things.'

'Yes.' Her voice was abrupt.

'You don't still bear me a grudge, do you? I never asked for such a thing to happen. But I'm glad it did. Scarsdale means more to me than anything now. Well, with one exception.'

'What's that?'

'I'll tell you another time. Not now.' He looked down at her. 'When do you go back north?'

'On Monday.'

'Pity. I hoped you might have come back with me tomorrow.'

'Thank you, but—but my plans are made. I'm staying with relatives this weekend and then returning to Kirk Newton by coach. Grandfather comes back from Whitby on Tuesday—Jane will bring him as far as Pickering and I shall take the car to meet him there.'

'You're a devoted granddaughter.'

'I have a devoted grandfather.'

The music ended, but when they walked back to the table Julian kept hold of her hand, his fingers tightening round her own as she tried to free herself of his clasp. She gave him a quick upward glance and found him watching her. He said gently, 'What's the matter, Tory? You're always running away from me. Are you afraid?'

'Of c-course not. It's just that—we aren't—I don't—' She was stammering, unable to put into words what she was trying to say. That they could never be friends? That he belonged to Damaris? That she wanted to be left alone because she was still hung up over Ralph?

'Not to worry,' he said. 'There's plenty of time to sort things out when we get back to Scarsdale. I shall be seeing you again.'

Was that a threat or a promise? she thought, as he released her hand to pull out a chair from the table for her.

Reluctantly, the evening came to an end. Goodbyes were said and warm thanks expressed to Damaris. Julian escorted Tory and Emma back to the flat in a taxi and at the lift bestowed on each of them in turn a brief kiss as he said goodnight.

When he had gone and they were creaking slowly upwards Emma shook her head reproachfully at Tory.

'You never told me—you never even hinted at such a thing.'

'Never told you what?' Tory asked.

'Never breathed a word that you and Julian were such chums. You were all Ralph, when you came down here.'

'I'm still "all Ralph" as you put it. Julian and I barely tolerate one another.'

Emma went on shaking her head.

'It didn't look that way to me. I got the impression he fancied you.'

'Oh, Emma, don't be absurd.' Tory's voice held a note of

impatience. 'He's in love with Damaris—can't you see that?
I told you about Peter—how some people think he may be
Julian's son.'

'What does that prove?' Emma enquired mildly. 'Julian
could still fancy you. But all right, I won't say any more on
the subject. I don't want to spoil what's been the most fab
evening. Thanks a lot, Tory. I enjoyed every moment of it. I
only wish Bruce had been able to be with us.'

'I wish he had.' Tory stretched her arms and yawned as
Emma closed the flat door behind them. 'I've just realised how
tired I am.'

'Me, too. And I have to be up for work in the morning.
Not like some lucky holiday girls.'

'You must come and stay at Wether Bell with us and have
breakfast in bed every morning of your holiday.'

'Oh, super! I'd love that.'

Tory stayed with relatives who lived in Surrey over the
weekend, then went north by coach on the Monday. Next day
she drove to Pickering to meet Jane and Mr. Webster and the
children at the Forest and Vale Hotel, where they all had lunch
together before Tory and her grandfather set off home.

Mr. Webster looked well and rested and was in a cheerful
mood. 'I couldn't have been made more welcome,' he assured
her. 'And we had a bit of grand weather to get around in. You
look better yourself, Tory lass. I only wish you'd stayed longer
away. No need to hurry back for me.'

'I stayed quite long enough. And school starts next week.
Do you know, Gramps, I *missed* Scarsfell. I used to think
there was nowhere like London, but I've changed my mind.'

'I should think so. Everyone knows there's nowhere to beat
Yorkshire,' Mr. Webster pronounced firmly.

The following day, leaving her grandfather conferring with
Sam over the sale of the sheep, Tory set off for Kirk Newton
to stock up on food supplies now she was home again.

There was a nip in the air, the first touch of September frost
when only a few days ago it had still been summer. The market
town, with its grey houses and old Market Cross near the
church gate where once the packmen and pedlars had put down
their merchandise seemed another world from London. As
indeed it was. Tory listened to the men's deep voices and broad
accents, and heard the countrywomen's homely endearment of

'love' and knew that this was where she still wanted to be, despite her heartache over Ralph.

It seemed to Tory that she never visited Kirk Newton without encountering someone she knew and today was no exception. When at last, her shopping completed, she returned, laden, to the Mini, it was to find Madeline parking her car not far from where Tory had left hers.

For a moment, after locking the door, Madeline stood beside her cream coupé staring blankly at Tory as if uncertain whether to smile or wave. There was no question that Madeline hadn't seen her and, puzzled, Tory lifted her hand in greeting and called across the space between them.

'Hello, Madeline. You're quite a stranger.'

'Oh, hello, Tory.' Her voice was stiff, and there was a look almost of embarrassment on her pink face. Tory thought at once of Ralph. Did Madeline think she minded about his going to work at the stud farm? Well, she *did* mind, but she had no intention of showing her feelings and pride demanded that she should appear at least polite, if not over-friendly.

'I hope you're keeping well, and—and your father.'

'Yes, thank you.' Madeline came a few steps forward, still staring at Tory in a curious fixed way. She stood waiting, as if expecting Tory to say something more.

Tory, bewildered, said at last, 'I've been away for a week—just catching up on my shopping now.'

'Oh,' Madeline blinked, catching her lip between her teeth. 'Oh, then you—you haven't heard about it?'

Tory stared now, puzzled, frowning.

'Heard about what?'

'About my—my engagement,' and hurriedly, seeing Tory's start of surprise, 'I'm engaged to Ralph.'

The words were said. They seemed to roll and echo round the entire car park, mingling with other sounds, the noise of car doors slamming, engines revving, distant voices shouting. The rooks cawing overhead: 'I'm engaged to Ralph, to Ralph, to Ralph, caw, caw, ca-aw!'

Tory felt herself sinking under a cacophony of sound that threatened to submerge her. She fought her way upwards, into light, into air, into the awareness of Madeline standing before her, watching, waiting. Waiting for her to speak, to say something.

A stranger's voice, cold and remote, said from somewhere far off, 'I wish you both every happiness.'

'Thank you. I—I wasn't sure—I thought perhaps Ralph had told you, but if you've been away—' Madeline paused as if uncertain how to go on.

'No, I haven't seen Ralph.' Tory's fingers, shaking and clumsy, put the key in the car door, she opened it to almost fall on to the seat. 'I—I have to go now, Madeline. Goodbye,' and she closed the door with a click.

She watched Madeline walk away, past the cream, coupé, past the other cars, and as she disappeared from view Tory shivered and let out a long sigh.

Why was she so shocked, so surprised? Hadn't she known all along, somewhere deep down inside, that this was how it was going to end? Ralph and Madeline. Madeline and Ralph. Engaged to be married. Very suitable really. Madeline had plenty of money; Ralph's problems were over now. Mrs. Brierley would be delighted.

Being bitter wasn't going to help. At least Ralph was honest with you, Tory told herself. At least he was off with the old love before he was on with the new.

There you go again. Don't *be* like that.

But I wish Ralph himself had told me and not Madeline. Somehow it wouldn't have been so bad. Or would it? I mean, it wouldn't have hurt so much. Is he very much in love with her? But he was in love with *me*. Or I thought he was.

Her head seemed to spin with the jangle of thoughts and questions.

Madeline's in love with him; Carole said so. May the best girl win.

She examined herself carefully like a doctor looking for a painful spot. I'm not brokenhearted, she thought. It's not that. I shall survive. But it's the sense of loss, the knowing that it's over for good. I think I still hoped things would come right in the end for Ralph and me. I thought the only obstacle was the loss of his job and the uncertainty of the future. I never thought it would be another girl.

How quickly it had all happened. It was only a matter of weeks since the summer's afternoon Ralph had met her outside the school and told her he didn't want to be 'committed'. Now he was engaged to Madeline, and if that wasn't a commitment, what was?

Tory sighed again as she started up the car. She could sit here all day thinking and brooding and what good would it do her? She had to get back to the farm and her grandfather and, on that resolution, she reversed out of the car park and drove quickly away from Kirk Newton.

She broke the news to her grandfather the next day. She had put off telling him, hating to discuss it in any way, but she knew that in a small community like Scarsfell everyone would soon hear about Ralph's engagement and there would be the usual talk and speculation.

Mr. Webster gave her one sharp look from under his greying eyebrows and then said, in a non-committal voice, 'Aye, well, these things happen and folks change their minds. Don't be taking on about it, lass. I told you before, you'll be as well off without Ralph.'

Such remarks didn't exactly console, but she could only be relieved that her grandfather had no more to say on the subject.

School started again and there was plenty of work to do. Tory held her head high and tried not to think that everyone she met was wondering how she felt about the engagement. And then, just as she had braced herself to hope people regarded it as a nine days' wonder, she met Julian and her small reserve of pride and composure was stretched to the limit.

She was out on the fell one day with Troy when she saw, walking up the loose scree below her, the figure of a man and knew at once that it was Julian. It was useless to pretend she hadn't seen him, for he lifted a long arm in salute and turned up the scree towards her. Jason, boisterous as ever, loped ahead of him to circle round Tory, barking a greeting, while Troy, elderly and staid, flopped to the ground and lay with head on paws, unmoving except for his watchful eyes.

'Quiet, Jason!' Julian reprimanded. 'I'm sorry he's a nuisance—he hasn't learned good manners yet.'

'Troy doesn't mind. He can take care of himself.'

She knew her voice sounded stiff and unfriendly, as if their last happy meeting had never been, but she couldn't help it. She felt prickly, on the defensive, as she had been all week, ever since she had heard the news of Ralph's engagement.

Julian didn't appear to notice. He said casually, 'Are you

going back to Wether Bell?' and at her nod added, 'I'm walking that way too,' and turned with her along the track.

They walked in silence, the dogs following after them. The
day had turned chilly, they had to bend their heads against the
wind that blew off the moor. It was a day to match Tory's
mood, grey and dull and sunless.

She was aware that Julian gave her a sideways glance from
time to time, but she ignored his looks and walked steadily on
until they came to a dip in the fell which gave some shelter
from the endless sighing wind. Julian stopped and said:

'Shall we get our breath?' He held out a packet of cigarettes.
'Have one of these.'

Tory, who rarely smoked, took one, feeling that the mere
action of smoking would calm her. It was difficult to light, for
errant gusts of wind still persisted, and after one or two fruitless
attempts Julian said, 'Here—let me,' and taking the cigarette
from her fingers put it between his lips and managed to get it
alight. 'There.' He put it to her mouth and smiling down at
her said, 'Puff away.'

He seemed to bulk out the daylight, standing so close to
her, a powerful figure in tweed jacket and polo-necked brown
sweater, a narrow check cap on his dark hair, long corduroy
clad legs pushed into rubber boots.

Tory turned from him and leaned against the stone wall at
her back and stared resolutely at the cloud-wracked sky and
gaunt grey hills. After a moment she was conscious by a movement of stone dislodging itself from the wall that Julian had
propped himself up against the wall beside her. They smoked
in silence until he said slowly, 'I don't need to ask if you've
heard the news. I can see by your face that you have. Did
Ralph come and tell you?'

She said, without looking at him, 'I don't want to talk about
it. Least of all do I want to hear you say "I told you so".'

'How can I help it? I warned you.'

She swung her head round sharply.

'And I'm supposed to be grateful? Well, I'm not. So please
shut up about it.'

'That's better. I'd rather see you angry than moping around
after someone who never deserved you in the first place. The
fact is, your pride's hurt more than your heart. You were never

really in love with Ralph—you just drifted into a cosy sort of relationship with him.'

She said through gritted teeth,

'What do *you* know about how I feel or what my relationship was with Ralph? You come here, an—an absolute outsider, and you try and take over other people's lives, and you never see for one moment that it—it's *you* who—who's spoilt everything. If it wasn't for you, Ralph would have—have inherited the estate and everything would have been different.'

'You mean you'd have married him and lived happily ever after because he wouldn't have had to go touting after another girl for money?' Julian shook his head grimly. 'I don't think so, Tory. You'd have woken up one day to realise what you'd missed—a man who would love you with every fibre of his being, Ralph didn't. If he had, he could never have acted as he has toward you.'

She nearly cried out, in pain or in anger. Or hatred even, hatred of this overriding arrogant man who in a few words had torn away the shield of pride and self-sufficiency and revealed the bitter hurt underneath.

She threw away the end of cigarette and thrust her hands deep into the pockets of her jacket to hide their shaking. For a moment, unable to speak, she stared straight ahead of her, seeing everything through a rage of tears. The landscape ahead cleared, became visible again, and at the same moment Julian spoke again.

'If I've rubbed salt in the wound, Tory, it's in an attempt to heal. Face the truth and you'll feel better.'

She found her voice again.

'Why should you give advice? Your own life doesn't seem all that satisfactory. Are you in love with Damaris, or have you too, drifted into a "cosy relationship", as you put it?'

As soon as she had spoken she regretted her outspokenness and wished she could recall the words. But Julian appeared unruffled by her rudeness and answered calmly enough.

'No, I'm not in love with Damaris, and I never have been. Oh, I know the gossip and speculation that's been going around, but it doesn't worry me. I'm used to it. And just for the book, Peter is my godson, *not* my son, in case you were going to ask me that too. You obviously think the best form of defence is attack, but I'm invulnerable, so don't waste your breath. I hope we've cleared the air a bit, anyway. Now, I suppose you'd like to get on. But remember what I've said, Tory, and brace up.'

She didn't answer, but turned and started up the other side of the dip in the direction of Wether Bell Farm. When they came within sight of the farm she said stiffly, 'You're a long way from Ravensholme. Are you intending to walk all the way back there?'

He glanced at his wrist watch.

'No. Lewis dropped off at Rylstone earlier on, I said I'd be walking across the fell to the road here by four o'clock. He should be coming to meet me with the Land Rover any time now.'

She was relieved not to have to invite him to the farm for, reluctant though she might be to extend their meeting, the tradition of fell hospitality died hard.

'Oh! Then I'll say goodbye.'

'Yes. Goodbye, Tory. See you again soon.'

'I expect so.'

She watched him stride away. She remembered also what he had said about Damaris. He wasn't in love with her after all and never had been. Damaris must have been, perhaps still was, in love with Peter's father? One thing was obvious—she and Julian were good friends.

Well, it was none of her business. She had problems of her own.

CHAPTER EIGHT

IT was a week since Tory had met Madeline in the car park at Kirk Newton, a week in which she dreaded yet expected to have some word from Ralph. He couldn't let the news of his engagement go without writing or speaking of it. Surely they had been too close to one another for such a thing to be ignored as if it hadn't happened?

Should she herself write to him, to wish him happiness? Madeline no doubt would have told Ralph of her meeting with Tory. Perhaps he expectdd her to make the first gesture?

She braced herself to write a letter of congratulation, but got no further than the stiff opening phrases. And then, as she came home late from Miss Ewing's where she had stayed to go through some papers with the headmistress, a shadow dislodged itself from under the high wall surrounding the School House Cottage and Ralph's voice said, 'Hello, Tory. I've been waiting a long time for you.'

She turned abruptly and saw his face, a pale blur in the dusk of the late afternoon. She swallowed and said shakily, 'H-hello.'

'I meant to come before this, but I kept putting it off.' He paused, staring uncertainly at her.

She said quickly, 'I was going to write to you. I—I believe congratulations are in order. I do wish you and Madeline every happiness.'

'Thank you. I'm sorry Madeline was the one to tell you. It should have been me.'

'Yes, I would have preferred it that way. Not—not that it matters now.'

'Oh, Tory!' His hand came out to her in a helpless gesture.

She wanted to say, 'Don't. Please don't sound regretful—remorseful. You've chosen this, not I.' She wanted to ask him if he was deeply in love with Madeline, but what a stupid question. Of course he was. Would he be intending to marry her otherwise?

When she was silent he said slowly, 'You'll always mean a great deal to me, Tory. You know that. We've known each other a long time, and I was—I am—' He stopped and then added in a firm matter-of-fact voice, 'Madeline's a wonderful girl. And she likes you very much. I see no reason why we shouldn't still be friends, do you?'

'No—no reason at all,' Tory answered bravely.

'And you'll come to our wedding? We're asking everyone, all our friends.'

'Is—is it to be soon?'

'Some time before Christmas.' In the dusk she saw him frown, saw his mouth tighten. 'The other thing I have to tell you is that I'm selling Bramwick.'

She couldn't speak for surprise. At last she said stammeringly, 'Selling Bramwick? But—but won't you want to live there? You—your mother—where—what will she do?'

'Mother's going to live at Harrogate—I'm buying a flat for her, near Aunt Madge, her sister. Madeline and I are going to live at Lindley Grange, with Mr. Langford. He—wants us to. And Madeline would like to stay on there because of the stables and the stud farm. The house will be divided into two—not flats but into two separate houses.'

'I see.' She saw the pattern forming: Madeline paying the piper and calling the tune. 'I hope it will work out well for you.' She added, her voice heavy with the heartache that filled her, 'And—I hope you'll be happy, Ralph.'

'Thanks, Tory.' He put out his hand and caught hers. 'You've been a darling about everything, and wonderfully understanding.'

For a moment her hand lay in his clasp; she felt his fingers, close and warm round her own in the way they had been linked so often. A last caress between them. Slowly she withdrew her hand and asked:

'Are you going to work at the stud?'

'That's the general idea. I shall have money of my own from the sale of Bramwick.' He hesitated as if about to say something more. 'I'm glad we've had this talk, Tory. It's cleared the air.'

Someone else had said that to her, only two days ago. Julian.

'Yes. I'll have to go now, Ralph. I'm late as it is.'

'Of course. Have you got the car or can I run you home?'

'Thank you, but the Mini's parked round the back of the school. Goodbye.'

'Goodbye, Tory.' He stared down at her before adding, 'Madeline will send you an invitation to the wedding.'

She couldn't say anything more, only stand and watch him walk away. A few moments later she heard the sound of a car fading into the distance.

The wind blew cold about her. She felt chilled and desolate, as if it were winter already, instead of early autumn. 'You'll come to the wedding,' Ralph had said. Just like that. She was to go and smile and look happy and join in the congratulations and good wishes to the bridal pair, conscious that most of the guests would know that she had been all but engaged to Ralph herself.

I *can't*, Tory thought. It's impossible. I can't pretend I'm just another guest entering into the gaiety of the occasion. But she knew, even as she stood there hugging herself against a cold that came from something more than the bitter moorland wind, that, short of an epidemic or an earthquake, she would have to go.

The sheep were gone from Wether Bell. There would be no more baby lambs lying in front of the range, no more plump ewes baaing plaintively at the gate leading into the farmyard. Mr. Webster gazed sadly out of the window at the fields, empty save for where one cow and a young heifer grazed.

'Doesn't seem like the farm any more without t'sheep. Makes a man feel old before his time.'

'On the contrary, you look better already,' Tory told him. 'More rested. And I'm sure your leg seems easier.'

'Aye, well, maybe it does, now I'm not walkin' around all day. But it's my mind that wants occupation. A man can't sit about idle.'

'You've got your astronomy. And what about those games of chess you planned with Mr. Taylor?'

Mr. Webster smiled wryly.

'You're doing your best to console me, lass. I can see that. Stop worryin'. I'll get used to new ways in time.'

She hugged his arm.

'Darling Gramps, of course you will.'

He put out a rough hand and pinched her cheek gently.

'What about you? You came home from your London holiday looking rosy-faced and happy. Now you're looking washed out and t'school term only started a few weeks ago. You're not frettin' after yon Ralph?'

She shook her head.

'No, Gramps. It's over and done with. He and Madeline are to be married soon—I told you.'

'Aye. Well, I'll not be at the wedding even if I'm asked, and there's no need for you to go either, Tory, if you haven't a mind to. You can always take yourself off to Jane's or somewhere.'

'And run away? I'd like to do that. But everyone will say I funked things.' She sighed. 'Somehow I'll have to put a face on things and go—for Ralph's sake.'

The invitiation came two days later, thick gilt-edged paper emblazoned with silver lettering informing Tory that Mr. George Langford requested the pleasure of her company on the occasion of his daughter Madeline Rosemary's marriage to Ralph Gordon Brierley on Thursday, November 28th.

She read it through twice and put it on the sitting room mantelpiece beside the ancient black marble clock for everyone to see. A few days later she sat down and wrote her acceptance, and in the finality of the act discovered a resignation to the event she hadn't expected.

She went over to York and bought a new outfit. Pride demanded that if she had to go to the wedding she should hold her head high, and a chic little suit and a pretty hat were to be worn like armour, as protection against curious eyes.

Mr. Webster refused his invitation on health grounds, but though Tory knew her grandfather would gladly have saved her from the ordeal of attending, he was secretly pleased that she had decided, on her own account, to go. His pride in her showed in chance remarks, in a nod of the head and a brisk pat on her arm when she displayed the new suit and hat to him.

'That's the way. Put a good show on. You're a true Webster when it comes to it, and you'll still be t'bonniest lass there, make no mistake.'

November the twenty-eighth dawned a clear cold day with

pale sunlight gilding the countryside. The parish church of Kirk Newton was old, its central tower rising above gable stone roofs. Some old stocks stood near the lychgate, where already a crowd of people had gathered to wait for the guests' arrival.

It was daunting to have to walk in on her own, but Tory tilted her chin and squared her shoulders and somehow made her way up the aisle to where a smiling usher guided her into a friend-of-the-groom's pew. She knelt down and said a small prayer, then sat back to stare straight ahead, seeing nothing for a few moments but the rich painting in the mediaeval east window.

Two people came and sat beside her, smiled and murmured a greeting. Tory knew them slightly, friends of Mrs. Brierley's. An elderly man took the place on her other side; she was aware of relief at being surrounded, even by little-known people. She felt less vulnerable, less exposed. The sense of tension eased and now, unobtrusively, she glanced about her.

Mrs. Brierley was up in front wearing a sapphire blue velvet hat above a sleek fur coat. Next to her sat Carole in raspberry red with a cream sombrero hat. And beside Carole was Ralph. The knot of pain round Tory's heart tightened, she stared down at her clasped hands in an effort at composure. A tall figure sat two pews behind the Brierley family—Julian. And next to him, dark and thin, surprisingly elegant in grey morning coat, was Lewis Morton.

The organ swelled in sound, Ralph had risen, was standing in the jewel ray of colour that shone from the great Norman window, the thickset figure beside him of Harry Clegg, the best man.

An expectant rustle moved across the congregation, and heads turned, as through the arched doorway came the white-clad bride on the arm of her father. Madeline's dress was made of tiers of lace, a long lace train was held by two small pages dressed in gold velvet suits. Her thick fair hair was dressed in Edwardian style, full and waved, under a headdress of white flowers and gold velvet holding her veil in place.

A dazzling bride, all white and gold to lighten the grey church, the winter day. Tall and statuesque, she moved slowly up the aisle, to reach Ralph's side and turn her head and smile at him.

A voice was saying, 'Dearly beloved, we are gathered together—' and Tory fell on her knees with a sigh of relief, hiding her face in her hands.

It was over and they were outside the church, the photographers busy forming and reforming the wedding group while the guests, sheltering from the cold wind, exchanged greetings. Thankfully Tory found herself with friends and she stayed talking to them until the bride and groom left for Lindley Grange. She gave a lift to her friends' daughters, teenagers, and stood with them in the slow moving reception line. She had a confused impression of white lace and golden hair under a gauzy veil, cool fingers on her own and Madeline's voice replying to her good wishes.

'Thank you. Thank you so much. Lovely you could come,' before finding herself standing by Ralph. She couldn't meet his gaze, only shake hands and murmur words of congratulations and go on to where Mrs. Brierley, a regal figure in blue printed velvet, nodded and smiled with unwonted affability. A last handshake with Mr. Langford, the echo of his booming voice in her ears, and Tory stumbled rather than walked away into the throng of laughing, chattering guests.

Glasses of wine and sherry were being proffered. Tory reached out a hand to take one and swallowed a few mouthfuls. She felt it warm the back of her throat, felt a reviving glow in her chilled veins. As she lifted the glass to her lips again she sensed that someone had come to stand alongside and looking up, encountered Julian's sardonic dark glance.

'So you're here to dance at the wedding?'

Tory's chin tilted defensively, she took another mouthful of wine before answering.

'Why not?'

He shrugged.

'I commend your attitude, though I'm not sure whether it stems from genuine indifference or sheer bravado.'

'Whichever it does, it can't possibly concern you.'

'That's where you're wrong. I'm interested in your reaction to all this.'

'As a butterfly collector is interested in pinning a specimen?'

'You're harsh in your judgements, aren't you? Why do you always regard me as the villain of the piece?'

The wine was making her feel reckless.

'Not necessarily the villain. More of an—intruder, shall we say?'

His eyes narrowed.

'Because my coming here upset your personal applecart, do you mean?'

She turned away, half afraid of what she might say next. A waiter appeared with another tray of glasses and Tory put down her empty one and took a fresh glass at the same moment that Carole approached.

'Tory, how nice of you to come! I saw you earlier on, but you were all engrossed. I love your suit—that cinnamon colour with that red fox is *most* becoming, and what a super fur hat to match.' She glanced round at Julian for confirmation. 'She looks ravishing, doesn't she?'

Julian inclined his head, his ironical glance on Tory.

'I intended to say something on those lines myself, but Tory didn't give me a chance.'

'Here's Lewis,' said Carole. 'You know Lewis, don't you, Tory?'

Tory nodded, surprised at the eagerness in Carole's voice, the warmth of her smile as she looked up at Lewis.

The arrival of Carole and Lewis eased the tension between Tory and Julian, though it didn't entirely remove it. Something—a spark of antagonism—still burned beneath the surface pleasantries until at last Carole said with a grimace, 'Everybody's starting to eat. I'll have to go and sit with the family at the big table. See you later, Lewis.'

'Rather!' To Tory's amazement their fingers locked in a brief caress and then Carole was gone.

'Shall we sit here?' Julian gestured to one of the small tables set around the room. He saw Tory's questioning look and added: 'I'm not sitting with the immediate family. Take this chair. What about you, Lewis?'

Immediately they sat down they were joined by other friends of Julian's and the party was complete. Attentive waiters brought delicious food, champagne was served and soon the first of the toasts were being made amidst much laughter and applause.

Tory was glad to be sitting at the far end of the room. From here Ralph's handsome face was only a vague blur, Madeline's complacent smile scarcely distinguishable. Mr. Langford made a long speech, laying a broad hand on Madeline's shoulder when he referred to her as 'My dear little girl.' Ralph spoke well, his voice clear and humorously deprecating. Harry Clegg, the best man, toasted the bridesmaids while Tory sat, her head bowed as if she were listening to it all. The strain was unbearable; the smile felt as set and hard as a plastic mask.

It ended at last, the toast and speeches and the laughter, the cutting of the great iced wedding cake, the endless cups of tea and coffee.

The bride reappeared, radiant in a glove-soft suede coat of palest antelope, a fluffy lynx collar framing her golden hair. Ralph in a grey suit and tweed overcoat was at her side, his arm linked through hers.

'Honeymooning in the Caribbean, I understand,' someone said to Tory. 'Flying away to all that sunshine, lucky things.'

The smile on Tory's face almost cracked with the effort of it all.

'Lovely,' she agreed.

The final goodbyes were said, people ran scrambling after the happy pair, throwing confetti, calling out good wishes. Tory remained behind with some of the older, more decorous guests amidst the debris of the wedding party.

She felt someone touch her arm and looked up to find Julian at her side.

'That's over. Feeling better?'

The ache in her heart, the confused emotions of the afternoon gave her voice an edge of sharpness.

'I feel fine, thanks.'

'I wondered if you'd like to come out to dinner with me somewhere? There's always an anti-climax after a wedding.'

'So you can see me squirm?' and at his lifted eyebrow added, 'You said you were interested in my reaction.'

'Don't be absurd!' He sounded angry. 'I'm only trying to help.'

'Don't be *sorry* for me. I don't *want* your help. Nor do I want to go out to dinner with you, thank you all the same. I'm going to say goodbye to Mr. Langford and to your aunt and Carole. I'll say goodbye to you now.'

He shrugged. The well-cut morning suit set off his height and powerful build, emphasised the sophistication of sombre dark looks and saturnine features. Tory acknowledged his attractiveness and admitted to herself that she was grateful for his company through what had seemed an interminable afternoon. He had served a useful purpose, but that was all. It was as far as her regard for him went.

Perhaps he sensed her withdrawal, for he inclined his head and said calmly,

'Goodbye, then,' and allowed her to walk away.

Saying goodbye to Mr. Langford was easy. What was more difficult was shaking hands with Mrs. Brierley and repeating her thanks and good wishes. Did she imagine the older woman's smile held an edge of triumph as she said,

'How sweet of you, Tory. Thank you for your good wishes. Yes, it has been a wonderful day. Seeing one's only son married is a milestone in a mother's life, but I couldn't wish for a more delightful daughter-in-law. They looked blissfully happy, don't you think? And now they have this fabulous month's honeymoon in Grenada as a wedding present from Mr. Langford.'

'It—it's fantastic,' Tory managed to say, and went on smiling and speaking for another five minutes before, feeling almost suffocated, she escaped.

There was no sign of Carole, but on the way out Tory came face to face with her in the doorway.

'Oh! Oh, sorry, Tory. Are you leaving already?' Carole asked breathlessly.

Tory managed a smile.

'It's more than time to go, I think. I'm so glad I've caught you. I wanted to say how much I—I've enjoyed it all.'

'Have you, Tory? I hope so. I felt—oh, never mind.' Carole glanced at her wrist watch. 'Heavens, it is late after all. Some of us are going over to Harrogate this evening, to a dinner dance. I didn't think to invite you?'

Tory shook her head.

'Thank you, but—but I couldn't have come.'

'Lewis is coming, Julian too, I expect. I've just been arranging times and transport, only don't breathe a word. Mother and Ralph are so down on Lewis because he works for Julian.'

'Lewis?' Then—then are you—?'

Carole's smile was conspiratorial. 'I told you about him, the day we met in Kirk Newton. I'm in love with him.'

Tory could only stare.

'Oh, Carole—!'

'Exactly. Oh, Carole, indeed.' Her voice sobered. 'He's so sweet—the nicest person. And—and I think he likes me too.'

'I'm glad for you—I hope things will work out. With your mother, I mean.'

'I hope so too. I must fly, Tory. Bless you for coming today. Let's meet very soon and catch up with all our news. I've so much to tell you.' She hugged Tory warmly. 'Goodbye for now.'

Carole and Lewis, Tory thought as she drove home to Wether Bell Farm. It spelt complications. But Bramwick was sold and Mrs. Brierley was going away: Ralph would be living at Lindley Grange. That might simplify matters.

She would probably never go to Bramwick again, Tory told herself. Once she had imagined herself living there. So much for dreams and hopes, she thought as she turned in at the farm gateway.

CHAPTER NINE

Two days later the weather broke. Throughout the morning and afternoon the wind rattled and banged at the school house shutters and the air seemed alive with banshee voices howling and wailing under doors and down the chimney stacks. It was a north wind, the landscape cold and sullen under a yellow sky. Snow clouds, Tory thought, watching their ominous darkness moving unhindered over the moors. It will come early this year.

She shivered in a chill that bit to the bone and huddled over the hood of her navy duffle coat as she said goodbye to Miss Ewing. *Grandfather*. She must get up to him before the snow came, otherwise remembering past winters, Tory knew he could be marooned there at the farm alone.

The first flakes were falling as she came up the hill from Scarsfell. To begin with they were no more than a nuisance, a feathery dampness that shrouded the windscreen and kept the wipers working overtime. But gradually, as the moors opened out and the shelter of walls and stunted trees fell behind her, the snow came faster and faster until, within a matter of minutes, she was driving through a blizzard.

The thing to do, Tory told herself, as she peered out the space of glass which the creaking windscreen wipers somehow cleared and then cleared again, was to keep going. She knew the road well enough to remember every bend and dip, to sense where the hard surface ended and the edge of the moor began, but early darkness had fallen and to the hazard of night driving was now added that of the snow-storm.

It was slow progress. In the ordinary way she would be halfway home by now, but Tory doubted if she had come more than a couple of miles. She saw pinpoints of light some way off the road. That would be Sam's cottage; four miles to go. The car droned on up the hill, slipping and sliding on the treacherous surface of snow. She had gone a little way farther when, with a protesting screech, the windscreen wipers stopped, and in a matter of seconds the entire window was covered in snow. Hurriedly, Tory got out. The wind caught the door and hurled it out of her hands so that it banged back against the side of the car. She struggled to close it, and with clumsy gloved fingers wiped away the load of snow from the wipers so that they would function again. She had left the motor running; to her relief the wipers resumed their slow half-circle to and fro, and once more she could see through the windscreen.

Back in the car, to release the handbrake and move the gear, and now the back wheels churned and ground helplessly, sliding across the freezing snow. For a moment Tory was aware of a sense of panic. If she couldn't get moving again she would be stuck permanently.

She was on the edge of despair when, slowly, miraculously, the car started to creep forward and she breathed again. Her relief was shortlived, for as she went on the whirlwind of falling snow grew denser, blown hither and thither by a wind of gale-force proportion.

Grimly she kept on, sitting rigidly upright at the wheel, peering with strained eyes through the snow-flakes whirling endlessly in the beam of the headlights. Every moment she expected the windscreen wipers to pack up again or the car to be turned over by the buffetting wind. Then, with a lift of the heart, she felt the road begin to slope down and guessed that she had come to the hollow in which stood Wether Bell.

It was almost impossible to make out the gateway and she turned by instinct rather than sight into the opening that led to the farm. The snow had already drifted across the track, there was a moment when she thought the car would not get through, but somehow she pushed on and came almost inch by inch into the farmyard and so into the shelter of the barn. She dragged the doors across and fastened them, then plunged through feet-deep snow to the house.

The back door was unlocked. Stamping the snow from her boots and shaking her duffle coat, she went into the kitchen. All was in darkness. She pushed open the sitting room door and found it empty and unlit save for the dull glow of the wood fire. She switched on the light and Topaz sprang from the armchair in which she had been sleeping and came towards her with a mew of greeting, while Troy rose from the hearthrug, wagging his tail and stretching.

Tory called sharply, 'Gramps!—Gramps, where are you?'

With Troy padding after her, she raced upstairs to Mr. Webster's bedroom. Darkness and emptiness again. The small room where he kept his telescope and instruments. No one. The bathroom, her own bedroom, the two spare bedrooms. Nothing and no one.

Tory had a panic vision of her grandfather lying somewhere in the yard or in one of the outbuildings. She dragged on her coat again and taking the big flashlight kept handy for such emergencies, plunged once more into the snowstorm.

Bridget mooed plaintively when Tory opened the door of her shed and the calf beside her turned a placid brown head. Jock's stable next, to find it empty. Her grandfather had taken the pony out with the trap.

But where to? And why? Was it possible they could be somewhere on the wild snowy moor? Turned over in a drift? A dozen disasters presented themselves to Tory's anxious mind.

She battled her way into the house and removed her snow-soaked coat. Everything was neat and tidy, no signs of a meal having been prepared at midday, no dishes in the sink. Had her grandfather gone out early, then? But he had made no mention of visiting anyone.

What shall I do? Tory asked herself. If only her grandfather had not been so obdurate against installing a telephone.

Topaz crouched beside an empty saucer of milk. Troy sat in the middle of the kitchen gazing expectantly at her as if asking where his supper was.

Food, thought Tory food, and Bridget to be milked. Then I'll have to think what to do. Her heart sank in dread as she contemplated getting the Mini out and setting off across the moor, and even as she thought about it she wondered if it would be humanly possible.

She fed the animals and put fresh logs on the fire and stoked up the range. As she had thought, Bridget needed milking. The snow was falling thick and fast now, blowing in deep drifts against the wall and doors of the outbuildings.

She struggled out of the yard to the track beyond and stared through a whirling greyness up the hill. Without chains the

Mini would never get to the top road, and even if she managed to get them on the back wheels it would be impossible to drive to Scarsfell in such a storm.

If only I knew where Grandfather was, Tory thought despairingly, as she fought her way back to the house through blinding snow. If he's safe somewhere, I don't mind anything else.

She busied herself making tea and scrambled some eggs, for she was hungry as well as cold. She had just sat down to supper on a tray when she head a loud knocking on the back door, and in a second she was out of the room and pushing back the heavy bolt. The wind hurled itself through the opening as she did so, blowing snow across the scullery floor, all but blowing a tall figure into the house with it. She tried to shut the door and the man turned and pushed his weight against it. Tory slid the bolt into its socket and said breathlessly, '*Julian!* What—why are you here? Is it—where's my grandfather? Is he all right?'

For a moment Julian leaned back on the door as if to catch his breath.

'Yes, I came to tell you. He's at Miss Ewing's.'

'Miss Ewing's?' She stared. 'But I left there only a few hours ago.'

'I know Miss Ewing told me. What happened is this. Your grandfather went down to Sam Dyer's this morning in the pony trap—he was worried about the change in the weather and he wanted to give Sam a hand with the sheep. Sam had gone to Kirk Newton Market and Mrs. Dyer had arranged to fetch him home by car. Your grandfather left Jock and the trap in Sam's stable and went with Mrs. Dyer to Kirk Newton. They missed Sam because he'd decided to leave early and get a lift in the postman's van back to Scarsfell. He was worried about the worsening weather too, you see.'

Tory could only stare in bewilderment.

'But—but how do you know all this?'

'It's a long story. Sam left a message with the landlord of the Market Inn to tell Mrs. Dyer he'd gone to Scarsfell. As you know, it was bitterly cold and I gather Mr. Webster didn't feel too good, so he and Mrs. Dyer stayed to have a drink and some food to warm them before returning home. When they got back to Scarsfell it was snowing. Miss Ewing told your grandfather you had already left. He was anxious about you being on your own and he telephoned me and asked me if I could take him back to the farm—he said he didn't know who else to ask at a moment's notice. Of course I was only too glad to help. When I got to School House Cottage in the Land Rover the weather was grim and I felt it unwise for your grandfather to face the drive over the moor if there was any chance we might get stuck in the snow. I managed to persuade him to stay with Miss Ewing while I came to fetch you.'

'Thank you,' Tory said. She frowned. 'Grandfather—he—he's not ill, is he?'

Julian shook his head.

'Just overexhausted. Miss Ewing's making up a bed for him.'

'How good of her. She's very kind.'

'I dropped Mrs. Dyer off at her cottage—she said her nephew would see after some cow or other—is that right?—and I was to bring Troy and the cat back with us.' He looked down at her. 'Better get a move on, Tory. Conditions are pretty bad out there.'

'I know.' She glanced up at him. 'I don't know how *you* got up here.'

He grinned lopsidedly.

'I don't quite know myself. Or how we're going to get back. But we'll have to try. We might have to finish up walking. Wrap up well while I go and see if I can turn the Land Rover—I left it by the gates, not daring to attempt the drive down to the farm. I'll be back for you in a few minutes.'

When he had gone, disappearing into a whirling maelstrom Tory hunted round for the cat basket and put the protesting Topaz carefully inside it. She snapped Troy's lead and placed the high guard round the fire, eating mouthfuls of cold scrambled egg as she moved from room to room. A nightdress and toothbrush in a hand case, thick tights and an extra woolly, a few cosmetics and she was ready, waiting for Julian to return.

The grandfather clock ticked away the minutes while alternately she sat or walked restlessly about. She could hear nothing but the wind, howling and whining around the house as if seeking entry. Why was Julian taking so long? she demanded desperately of the clock as it ticked relentlessly on. What was happening out there in the snow?

At last the thump of the back door, a gust of bitter cold that blew upon the sitting room door and lifted the edges of the carpet off the floor. She rushed out calling, 'I'm ready!' then stopped dead. Julian was sliding the bolt into place and as she turned he said frowningly:

'It's no use, Tory. I tried to move the Landrover, but the drifts are so deep now that when I reversed it slid off the road and got bogged down. I've been trying to dig the back wheels free, but I can't shift it. I'll have to leave it there until morning and then try again when it's stopped snowing.' He shook his head. 'Even if we could have got away I doubt if we could make it across the moor to Scarsfell, and it would be no joke to be stuck out there all night.'

Tory bit her lip, looking up into Julian's tired, strained face.

'I was afraid this might happen. I know what it can be like up here when there's a blizzard.' She sighed. 'At least, Grandfather's safe.'

'And he'll guess I got to you—that you're not on your own here. I think that's why he sent me, to bring you back or stay with you.'

The words echoed through Tory's brain. *Stay with you.* Julian was here and he was staying with her. Tonight and— Her thoughts jerked away from the idea of Julian being with her here at Wether Bell Farm for longer than that, refusing to face the fact that they could be snowbound for more than one night.

To hide the sudden self-consciousness that engulfed her, she knelt down and unfastened the cat basket, and Topaz leapt out with a meow of relief while Tory said briskly, without looking up, 'I'll make coffee and get you something to eat.'

'Thanks.' He shook his coat out over the sink and put it across the back of a chair before sitting down to drag off the heavy boots he was wearing.

'There's a fire in the other room,' Tory said over her shoulder. 'Go and get warm.'

He came over to where she was putting cups and saucers on to a tray.

'Let me help you.'

He made her feel nervous, towering above her, black hair

shining wetly about a face glowing from his efforts and exercise in the cold. She said jerkily, 'There's nothing to do. Are you hungry—would you like sandwiches and something hot—soup?'

'Sandwiches and soup would be great. I haven't eaten since lunch-time.' He met her quick upward glance and something in his look, a gleam of amusement in the dark eyes, added to her sense of confusion. For a moment they stared at one another, then Julian lifted the tray from the table and carried it through to the sitting room, saying over his shoulder, 'May I go and clean up—wash my hands? I think I remember where the bathroom is.'

'Yes, of course.' She made two rounds of sandwiches while the soup heated up. She buttered cheese scones and found some cold apple pie. When Julian came downstairs again she had laid the table and the log fire was crackling with flames.

He smiled from the doorway.

'What a cosy scene. I like it.'

Tory gestured with the formal politeness of a grand dame hostess.

'Please sit down. Will you have bread with the soup?'

He inclined his head gravely.

'Thank you. Aren't you having soup?'

'No. I—I had scrambled egg just before you arrived. I'll have coffee and a sandwich.'

They ate in silence. Troy came and laid his black head on Julian's knee and gazed hungrily up at him.

'Is it allowed?' Julian held up a corner of sandwich in his fingers.'

'I'm afraid not. Only in the kitchen.'

The wind whirled suddenly down the chimney stack, blowing clouds of smoke into the room, scattering red sparks on to the hearthrug.

'It's a hell of a night out there,' Julian said as he stamped his foot on the embers. 'I wonder how long it will go on like this?'

'The storm will blow itself out by morning. You'll be able to get the Landrover mobile again, or the snow-ploughs may even get up here.'

'So soon?' Julian's voice was gently mocking.

'Certainly,' Tory said with an assurance she was far from feeling. She stood up. 'If you'll excuse me I'll go and make up the spare room bed. It is aired.'

'Thank you. You're most hospitable.'

He was laughing at her, in some way pinpointing the tension that threatened to overcome her.

When she came back to the kitchen the table had been cleared and he had started to wash up.

'Please don't.' She took the mop out of his hand. 'I'll finish this.'

He picked a tea towel from the rack.

'I'm very domesticated. Didn't I tell you?'

She made her voice light.

'I don't think you did.'

'I have other unsuspected talents. Perhaps while we're here together you may discover some of them.'

'It's hardly likely. There won't be time.' She glanced at the kitchen clock. 'I'd better put Troy out before we—before I go to bed.'

'Already? It's only half past nine.'

She said hurriedly, 'We—Grandfather and I go to bed early at Wether Bell Farm. We have to get up so early, you see. But you're welcome to—to stay down in the sitting room and read or watch television, if it's working. It may not be, with this weather.' She turned away. 'Come on, Troy. You must struggle out into the yard somehow.'

The snow was piled high in the porch and against the back door, so high indeed that it reached Troy's back when he tried to flounder through it. Tory battled to close the door behind him, then went to fill the kettle for hot water bottles.

'I hope you won't be cold in your room,' she said with matter-of-fact briskness. 'I'm afraid we haven't got central heating or electric fires, they would overload the generator. But there's a small oil stove in the bedroom ready to be lit.'

'Thank you. You think of everything.'

Above the rattle of the wind she heard Troy's bark and went to open the door for him.

Julian was there first.

'I'll do it.'

He put a hand on to the latch at the same moment that Tory did and their fingers touched. She jerked back as if the contact scorched her skin, and sensed him give her a swift glance as he pulled the door open to allow Troy to stumble into the scullery looking like a dog snowman. His coat and black head were covered in snow, his paws encrusted with lumps of ice. He shook himself vigorously, scattering snow in all directions, and Tory shivered as she rubbed him dry with an old towel.

'It must be absolutely freezing out there. Heaven help anyone on the moor on such a night.'

'Thank God we didn't try to get back to Scarsfell. We shall be safe here for a few days.'

'A few days?' Tory straightened up, staring in dismay. 'We—we won't be here for all that time!'

Julian shrugged.

'No? If it freezes hard tonight I doubt very much if we'll be able to get the Landrover on to the road again until it thaws out.'

Tory was filled with consternation, and some other emotion she couldn't pin down. The thought of staying at Wether Bell alone with Julian was disquieting, to say the least. Only a moment ago the touch of his hand on hers had triggered off a reaction as sharp as the ringing of an alarm bell. If they were to be cooped up here for any length of time she would have to be wary of him. She would make it clear that she expected him to stay on the other side of the demarcation line she would lay down. Screwing on the top of the hot water bottle, she said firmly, 'I'm going to bed now. When you come up would you mind putting one of the big logs on the back of the fire then it will keep in overnight. And please leave the guard round. Troy sleeps in there, on the rug.'

He was looking down at her, but she refused to meet his gaze. From the doorway she said politely, 'Goodnight.'

'Goodnight, Tory. Thank you.'

She hurried up the steep stairs. Her grandfather's room was next to her own; across the landing was the bathroom and next to it the small room that was Mr. Webster's den. At the end of the passage two steps led down to a minute square of landing with two rooms facing one another, which were the guest rooms. In one of these Julian was to sleep. A safe distance away, Tory thought, coming out of the bathroom a few minutes later and closing her bedroom door carefully behind her.

Undressed and in bed, she curled like a hedgehog against the cold, the hot water bottle hugged close to her. The sound of the wind was the voice of a demon, howling and screeching across miles of open country to fall in fury upon the old house where it crouched, low-roofed, thick-walled, stout as the oaks from which its ancient timbers had been felled, ready to withstand storm and wild weather as it had done for hundreds of years.

Grandfather is safe at Miss Ewing's, Tory thought sleepily. And we are safe here, Julian and I. And tomorrow—tomorrow the snow will be gone.

The light woke her—a luminous brightness reflected into the room as from a mirror. Tory shivered as she jumped out of bed and, pulling on her warm wool kaftan, crossed to the window to draw back the curtain which had been left closed against the chilly draughts.

The wind had dropped and it had stopped snowing, but the landscape before her was one vast world of whiteness. Not a tree nor a hedge, not a wall was to be distinguished in the sweeping snow-covered land before her. It rolled towards a grey horizon where smoke-coloured clouds crouched low, threatening yet more snow.

The road above the farm had disappeared, lost under endless drifts. The roofs of the barns, the cowshed were white lumps rising above other white lumps, door and window hidden under the snow piled up against them.

She shivered again and hurried out of the room to the bathroom. The water ran warm, but she would have to keep an eye on the generator that pumped water from the well. Brushing her teeth, splashing her face and hands, she thought that she must remember to tell Julian to be sparing of its use.

When she emerged from the bathroom, pink-faced, her damp hair fastened on top of her head, it was to meet Julian coming along the passageway.

'Good morning. I heard you around—I decided it was time to get up.' His dark eyes flicked over the turquoise kaftan. 'You're not dressed yet?'

She shook her head, aware of being caught very *en déshabille*.

'I shall only be a few moments. Did you—did you sleep well?'

'So-so. Oh, the bed was most comfortable, not to mention the hot water bottle you'd so kindly put in it. But the wind kept me awake for a while—I thought the roof was going to blow off.'

Tory smiled slightly.

'Not at Wether Bell. We're used to wild winters.'

'So am I—or should be. There was plenty of snow in Canada. But things seemed better organised.' He frowned, rubbing a hand over a face and chin dark with stubble. 'Does Mr. Webster have a spare razor, or must I grow a beard?'

Tory looked up at him. She had a fleeting thought that a beard would suit him. With his strong features and black hair and brows he would look—what was the word?—*piratical*. But all she said was, 'I think I can find an old one of Grandfather's. I'll get dressed first,' and she turned to go in the bedroom.

She put on warm check tweed slacks and a polo-necked sweater of rust-coloured Shetland wool and after supplying Julian with an old razor, hurried downstairs. When she pulled back the heavy velvet curtains it was to find the room dark from the snow which had drifted to the height of the window sills, shutting out daylight and turning the living room into a gloomy cave. The kitchen was little better, but although the porch was feet deep in snow she managed to open the back door for Troy. He floundered out, sniffed at the wall and after a moment struggled back into the house.

The kettle was filled and on the range when Julian came into the scullery.

'Not a hopeful prospect, it is? It looks as if we're snowbound for today, at any rate, though I'll see later if I can dig a path up to the road.'

'The thing is, to clear the way to the shed where Bridget and her calf are so I can get food and water to them,' Tory said. 'And the hens. They'll need seeing to.'

'What about fuel—logs, coal for the stove here? Can I get those in for you?'

Tory opened a door at the far end of the scullery.

'We keep a ton of fuel in here. A door at the back opens into the yard. Logs too—they're stacked on this side.'

Julian smiled wryly.

'I see you're ready for the siege. Does this often happen?'

'Most winters we have a spell of bad weather that isolates us, if only for a few days. But sometimes it can be for weeks. Several years ago some of the fell farms were actually cut off for months. Up here we're not like towns-people, we have to be self-supporting and self-sufficient.'

He gave her a direct look.

'You're certainly the latter, Tory. In every way.' The tone of his voice made her doubt if he intended the remark as a compliment. She turned, saying, 'Would you like bacon and egg for breakfast?'

'Very much, thank you.'

They ate it in the kitchen, Troy waiting expectantly beside them for crispy bacon rinds, while Topaz, having drunk a saucer of warm milk, performed a careful toilette in front of the range. After the meal was cleared away and washed up Tory went upstairs to make the beds and tidy round while Julian, supplied with the big spade kept handy in the coal cupboard, went out warmly clad, to dig a clearing across the snow-filled yard, to the barns.

She came downstairs and he was still digging—she could hear the endless scrape, scrape of the spade. He had cleared the snow from the kitchen window, so she was able to glimpse his powerful frame bent double between tall walls of piled up snow. She busied herself peeling vegetables and cutting rashers of ham from the smoked gammon hanging in the larder and then, glancing at her watch, saw that it was eleven o'clock. Julian had been digging for nearly two hours. She opened the door and called to him, 'Come in and have a rest. I've made coffee and afterwards I can give you a hand, if you like.'

He stood in the porch, stamping crusted snow from his gumboots.

'That's some snow you've got out there. D'you know it's drifted up to eight feet in places? I'm nearly through but I'd no idea it would be such a job.' He came in, pulling off his wet gloves. 'At least Troy has a run out now.'

She poured the coffee and set a plate of buttered scones

before him and as he ate one he said, 'Umm. You're quite a cook, Tory.' He cocked a black eyebrow. 'You'll make a good wife for someone.'

She didn't answer and after a moment he said, 'I'm afraid it's snowing again.'

'Oh *no*!' She swung round to see the first light flakes drifting silently past the window.

'I'd better finish the digging before it gets bad again.'

'I'll come and help you.'

'It's too heavy a job for you. I can manage.'

She insisted, struggling into boots and duffle coat and arming herself with a stout shovel worked beside him while the snow, at first gentle and intermittent, began to fall faster and faster about them.

The shed was reached at last and Tory was able to look after patient Bridget and her small calf, Honey, putting down food and fresh water while Julian raked muck and soiled straw to one side. By the time she had fed the hens and collected the eggs it was to find the yard hidden under whirling flurries of snow and the sky darkened over as if night had returned.

Julian frowned.

'Not much chance of digging out the Landrover today. I'll try first thing in the morning.'

'Yes.' Tory's voice was abrupt. She moved away from him, feeling his presence in the small scullery somehow overwhelming, 'I'd better make the lunch.'

'O.K. I'll see if I can get a weather flash on the radio.'

He came back into the kitchen after a time, shaking his head.

'The outlook sounds grim. Snow and more snow to come.'

Tory bit her lip.

'What are we going to do?'

'Do?' He shrugged. 'What can we do but stay put? You told me yourself you're used to this sort of thing and that it can go on for days—weeks even.'

'I know—but—' She stopped, unable to go on and say what she was thinking: '*I was with Grandfather, not you.*'

He was looking at her with his dark sardonic smile as if he could read her thoughts.

'What's worrying you? You know your grandfather is

being taken care of. We're warm and sheltered, with suffi-
cient food, so you assured me. The animals will be seen to
and you've got company—me. Relax, Tory.'

You, she thought. It's you that's worrying me.

She said in as casual a voice as she could muster, 'There's
soup and cheese for lunch. I'll cook something hot for us
tonight.'

'Splendid.' He lowered his great height on to one of the
kitchen chairs. 'Lucky for me you're so domesticated. I
certainly won't starve.'

Throughout the long afternoon it snowed, slowly and purposefully. Every time Tory looked out of the one window
that was clear and saw the endless white flakes she felt more
and more claustrophobic. It was absurd, because there had
been times like this before at Wether Bell. She remembered,
even as a child she and her grandparents being isolated at
the farm for weeks on end.

She turned from the window, aware without looking that
Julian was watching her. She said brightly, 'Thank goodness
Grandfather's given up the sheep. He'd be worried sick about
them now, and so would I. But Sam will be able to look
after them and he has his nephew to help him. They'll know
where the sheep go to shelter out of the wind. And the dogs
help to smell them out. Grandfather always said the thing
to do was to keep the sheep moving, looking for their food.
That way they get exercise.'

'In this?'

'Yes. Buried under the drifts they can survive for a week
or more. Of course, if it's very hard or the frosts go on for
too long a lot of them die. It's dreadfully sad—and even if
they live through it, not many of them will lamb in spring.'

'Poor devils.' Julian stood up, stretching a little as if he
too, like Tory, felt hemmed in by the four walls of the farm
and the dark day closing in on them. He went over to the
window and gazed moodily out. 'Damned nuisance I can't
have a go at the Landrover. But I wouldn't be able to see a
foot in front of me.' For a moment he was silent, then he
turned his head to look at her and said, 'Do you realise that
while we're in the middle of a non-stop snow-storm Ralph
and Madeline are basking in the sunshine of the West In-

dies?' He added slowly, almost deliberately, 'On their honeymoon.'

Tory's chin jerked up defensively.

'Why do you say it like that? As if it meant something. It doesn't, not any more.'

The dark eyes narrowed.

'I'm glad to hear it.'

Across the space of the room they stared at one another while the silence between them stretched in unbearable tension. It was Tory who broke it, moving to the door and saying, 'I'm sorry. I've got something to do in the kitchen.'

She dreaded that Julian would come after her, but he remained in the sitting room and after a few moments she heard him go up the stairs.

She let out a long sigh of relief, banging crockery and clanging lids as if to prove her own activity. Why did she have this mounting feeling of tension? Did she think that like some villain in a melodrama he was going to spring on her, make love to her against her wishes?

You're crazy, she told herself. Snap out of it. It's all in your mind, not Julian's. You're getting an obsession or something.

It was because he had kissed her that time. She kept wondering what she would do if he repeated the experience. Scream, shout—have some fearful scene?

Or submit? Even—co-operate.

Never. She must be mad to even allow such fantasies to invade her. I must keep busy, she thought. Busy and composed and very, very cool.

It was night outside. Time to draw the curtains against the ceaseless blizzard. The wind had risen again, battering into each nook and corner of the house. They were closed in together for another night.

When Tory came from the kitchen into the sitting room Julian was standing by the side table. He turned his head to say, 'Do you play chess?'

'Yes, with Grandfather. He's an expert.'

'Are you?'

She shook her head.

'No. But Grandfather sometimes allows me to win. Do you play?'

He smiled.

'A little. Like you, I have to be *allowed* to win. Shall we have a game after supper?'

'Yes, I'd like that.' She had a sense of relief as if playing chess was some sort of escape. From what?

After the meal was finished the chess board was set out on a low table by the fireside and the game begun. The fire crackled in the big grate, a log fell gently from time to time, emitting a shower of sparks and the scent of burning apple wood into the room. Troy lay stretched out on the hearthrug, his black nose twitching from time to time, his legs jerking, as if in his dreams, he chased some rabbit or fox. Topaz crouched on a stool, paws tucked neatly out of sight, her green eyes narrowed to slits in her yellow face.

They were soon absorbed, sitting with deep concentration, speaking only intermittently as in turn they moved the pieces about the board. Yet Tory's interest in the game didn't prevent her awareness of Julian; of noticing his long well-shaped fingers as they placed a knight or queen on the chosen square, or seeing the lock of black hair that fell across his frowning forehead, the thick black lashes that cast a shadow on the high cheek bones.

Once he glanced up and stared at her for a moment in silence. Then he said, 'I hope you're not daydreaming. It's black's turn to move.'

She came to with a start and gazed down at the board, conscious of her warming cheeks. They had reached the stage of the 'middle game', after the exchange of some pawns and two or three pieces, on each side. Now the queen who had been kept back so as not to risk being snapped up by some minor piece or pawn would come into strength. What was it Grandfather declared? That the great aim should be not to capture one's opponent's men but to mate his king. The queen being a powerful piece, she had to be employed to the fullest possible extent.

In the end Tory won, for she was undoubtedly the more experienced player, though her moments of aberration had put her in danger more than once.

'We'll play again tomorrow,' said Julian. 'I need practice. Now it's time for bed.'

She glanced up, momentarily startled and he added gently,

'*Your* bedtime. It's after eleven o'clock. I'm afraid you've missed your chance of retiring early tonight.'

She stared in astonishment at the clock.

'Have we been playing all evening? It's hard to believe the time's gone so quickly.'

'Time does, when one is enjoying oneself.'

'Yes.' She stood up and carried the chess board over to the side table. 'Would you like something to eat—or drink?'

'No, thank you. You cooked too good a supper. Shall I put this big log on the fire?'

'Yes, please do. I'll put Troy out.'

The whole scene was so heavily domestic she hurried away from it. We're like an old married couple, she thought as she took the kettle from the range and filled the hot water bottles. Like a Darby and Joan or something. She said from the safe vantage of the sitting room doorway, 'I—I'm going up now. Will you let Troy in, in a few minutes?'

'Certainly. Goodnight, Tory.'

'Goodnight.'

She hurried to put the hot water bottle in Julian's bed, pushing it down with the far-too-small pair of her grandfather's pyjamas that she had lent him. Was he able to get into them? She didn't want to know.

She was out of the bathroom and safely tucked up in bed by the time she heard the creak of Julian's footstep coming up the stairs. She snuggled down as if she were hiding herself, which was absurd because he wasn't likely to come into her room.

The moaning wind swept around the house, it was still snowing. How much longer were they going to be marooned here together?

Next morning the sun was shining. It glittered on the roof-tops, on the blue shadows cast by the outbuildings, on the landscape that stretched, as far as the eye could see, in rolling white waves.

'I'm going to try and dig a way out to the Landrover today,' Julian declared at breakfast.

'I'll help you.'

'No. You've enough work of your own to do. Let me see how I get on.'

Despite the sunlight the air was so cold it caught at Tory's throat like iced wine. She gasped and swallowed when she picked her way between the walls of snow to the barn. Julian was already digging, she could see his arms and shoulders moving in an endless rhythm, as he bent and lifted and bent again.

He came in at mid-morning for warming coffee and a short rest and then went out again, firmly refusing Tory's offer of assistance. The stock of bread was getting low. She got out flour and dried yeast and the wide earthenware bowl in which her grandmother had taught her to make bread, and when, just before midday dinner Julian came stamping into the scullery the dough was rising near the warmth of the stove.

He sniffed.

'Something smells good. Like new bread.'

'It is new bread. I'm baking.'

He stared at her.

'I don't believe it! You can't make bread, as well as everything else, including beating me at chess?'

'It's an occupational hazard of living up here on the fells in winter. Most of the farmers' wives make their own bread from time to time.'

He shook his head.

'No deep-freezes?'

'Not for us, I'm afraid. Just a cold larder, and a cellar if we want to use it.'

'Tory, you're a girl in a thousand. Quite apart from the fact that if we stay here together long enough I shall have to make an honest woman of you, for the sake of your reputation, I can't afford to let you go. You're too valuable an asset.'

As usual he was teasing her. She turned away, saying as lightly as she could, 'Wait until you taste the bread before you commit yourself.'

When lunch was finished Julian went out to do more digging while Tory attended to her bread-making. The dough had expanded like a balloon and now she turned it on to a floured board and kneaded it vigorously for several minutes before shaping it into loaves and putting it in greased tins for a second rising. When the dough had risen again she popped the loaves in the oven and putting on her duffle coat and boots, took the shovel and went out to the track to see if she could help Julian.

He was working like a machine and had already cleared a pathway two-thirds to the top. He scarcely stopped in his labours to speak to Tory, merely nodding to say, in answer to her query, 'All right. It will help if you push back the lumps of snow I've left as I've gone along, then they won't freeze hard into the ground.'

She worked with him for almost an hour. The wind was biting and as the sun went down in a smoky red sky everything began to freeze up again. Tory was already breathless and tired after an hour's stooping and digging. She couldn't imagine how Julian was able to continue at such a steady remorseless pace. Reluctantly she said, 'I'll have to go in, I'm afraid, to see after the bread. How long will you be? It will soon be dark.'

'I shall be here until I can't see the spade in front of me. Thanks for your help,' he added curtly without even looking up.

The bread was baking and well browned—the kitchen full of its delicious aroma. Tory turned the loaves out on to a wire tray and left them to cool. The fire had sunk, so she put on fresh logs and filled the kettle, ready to make tea for Julian when he came in from the cold. She left the curtains undrawn so he would see the lights from the house, for it was so dark now, she couldn't even see him.

She went into the scullery when she heard the sound of the back door closing. He looked exhausted standing there dragging the sheepskin coat from his shoulders, but he gave her a lopsided grin as he said tiredly, 'I finished the track and reached the gateway. Tomorrow I'll be able to dig out the Landrover.'

'Oh, well done, It must have half killed you.'

'I wouldn't say that.' He moved to the sink and began to wash his hands under the tap. Tory, going to the larder to fetch some scones for tea, caught a glimpse of water running red and stopped in her tracks.

'Your hand is bleeding. Have you cut it?'

'It's nothing. Just a gash.'

'Would you like a plaster or something?' She went over to him. 'Let me see.'

He turned away.

'Don't bother.'

'Here's a towel.' Tory held it out to him and then she saw

the fresh blood trickling from the side of his hand and said sharply, 'What have you done? That's more than a gash.' Before he could stop her she had taken one of his hands gently in her own and turning it upwards she saw the bleeding cuts on the blistered palm.

'Oh, Julian!' For a moment she couldn't speak. 'Let me see the other one. It's just as bad. How could you have gone on working with them like this? They must be hurting terribly.' She stopped, unable to go on, aware of a most curious pain, as if it were *her* hands that were so cruelly lacerated. She could have cried over them, she had the strangest impulse to hold his fingers against her face.

'Don't fuss,' Julian's curt voice cut through the air. 'They look much worse than they are.' He pulled his hands free of her clasp. 'Have you any iodine?—if I put some on it will cleanse and harden the skin.'

'There—there's iodine in the bathroom cupboard.'

'Good. I'll get it,' and he turned and walked out of the doorway.

She stared after him, hurt by his sharp and unexpected rebuff, as if he didn't want or need her sympathy. She had only tried to help, to ease what, despite his assertion, must be a burningly painful state of affairs.

Oh well. She went to lift the kettle off the range. At least he would be glad of a cup of tea and wouldn't snap at her for offering *that*.

When he came downstairs she found he had covered some of the deepest cuts with strips of plaster. He said half apologetically, 'I found some of these in the cupboard too. Hope I haven't robbed you.'

'Of course not.'

He gave her a rueful grin.

'It's so I can play chess again. I have to beat you tonight.'

She smiled back, strangely happy again.

'You can try.'

The new bread was a great success.

'I've never tasted anything so good,' Julian declared. 'What was I eating before—baked blotting paper or foam rubber? Take that loaf away, Tory, before I devour it at one sitting.' He paused frowningly. 'These super meals keep turning up and I never ask you where it all comes from. How are the supplies going? You say you haven't a deep-freeze, so what about meat?'

'We keep sides of bacon in the cellar—there's a brace or two of pheasants, some partridges. And I've shelves of tinned stuff stocked for just such emergencies.' She smiled at him. 'We won't starve.'

'I'm sure of that. Anyway, if I can reach the Landrover tomorrow we shall have a good chance of getting back to civilisation.'

'Is that what you call it?' Tory said lightly. She was aware of an odd sensation, a feeling of what? Disappointment, deflation? 'I expect they've been worrying about you at Ravensholme.'

'Lewis will cope. He knew I was coming up here, so he'll guess what's happened—that we've been marooned. I'm glad, though, Peter's not still there. He'd have been lonely—with no school, no one to visit him.'

'Yes. It's better he's with Damaris.'

He gave her a quick glance.

'Damaris is thinking of getting married. Did I tell you? A very decent bloke. He works in the theatre—directing and producing. He's a little older than Damaris and he's been married before. No children of his own and he's truly fond of Peter.'

'I'm glad—for Peter and for Damaris.'

'She was going to be married before—to Peter's father. He died very suddenly, in South Africa, where he was working. Damaris had been on tour out there and had gone back to England, pregnant, as it so happens. John was coming over to marry her, but he fell ill and was gone in a matter of days.'

'I'm sorry.' Tory was silent for a moment. 'I hope she—she will be happy now.'

'Yes. It's been rough going. Damaris and I have been friends for a long time.' His smile held something of its former sardonic quality. 'I know what you thought—what everybody thought, but it wasn't so. I was never in love with Damaris, nor she with me.' He added, suddenly brisk, 'Now, what about that chess game?'

It was the mixture as before. The table in front of the glowing fire, the chessboard set out with the men placed in order along the back row; the pawns occupying the two ranks in front of them, the rooks in the outermost position, and then, coming inwards in turn, knights, bishops and finally the king and queen.

The same as the previous evening. And yet—somehow different. A different atmosphere. As if the climate between them had changed and the barometer, despite the winter night outside, was 'set fair'.

It was after eleven before the game was ended and still Julian hadn't managed to win.

'You're too good,' he said 'But your luck will change tomorrow night.'

'We may not be here tomorrow—if you get the Landrover moving.'

'That's a thought.' He looked down at her from his great height. 'Perhaps I shouldn't bother—it's so very pleasant being together here like this.'

She met his dark glance and felt a strange stirring somewhere deep inside her. Earlier on she had admonished herself to keep 'very, very, cool', but it wasn't going to be easy. She was like a piece of steel being drawn towards a magnet and it was with the greatest effort that she managed to break the spell and say, hurriedly, 'Troy's waiting to go out. He—he's by the door,' and swinging round, rushed to open it.

When she came back to hover nervously in the doorway it was to find Julian had put the chessboard away and was standing by the fire smoking a cigarette. He said, casually, 'I take it you're going up? I'll see to the fire.' Night, Tory.'

'G-goodnight, Julian,' she stammered with relief, and thought how ridiculous she was. Always imagining situations that didn't exist.

Or did they? she wondered, remembering that deep dark look, and the strange feeling of tension that it seemed to engender. All she knew was that being near Julian was like being near a bomb; any moment the fuse could blow and she would go up with it.

There was no snow in the night but a savagely hard frost.

'The track's like glass,' Julian said after he had been out with the shovel. 'I shall have to put some ash down—it's hard to keep upright.'

Tory found the yard equally slippery and slid along the path to the sheds as if she were on a skating rink. The wall of snow on either side was frozen hard as a rock and when she had attended to Bridget and Honey and to the hens she put down food and water for the few birds who perched, hunched and hungry on wall and roof top.

When she had finished she struggled up the ash-strewn path to the road at the top where Julian was hammering away at the ice-hard snow covering the Landrover.

'You need a pick-ax to this,' he gasped when Tory, clambering over the deep snow, reached his side.

She stared doubtfully at the bulky outline of what looked like some prehistoric monster left from the ice age.

'Do you think you'll ever get it to go again? Won't it be frozen up?'

He shrugged, pausing a moment in his labours.

'There's anti-freeze in the radiator—it should be all right.'

Tory looked over her shoulder at the snowy wastes surrounding them, where not a landmark, not a tree or a wall or a house broke the undulating whiteness.

'Even if it starts how can you drive in this?'

He grinned.

'I'll have to dig a way clear every hundred yards or so.'

'It's not worth it.'

'I'm inclined to think that, too. But I must try. Anyway, you never know, they might get those snow-ploughs you spoke about working up here.'

'How are your hands? You won't be able to do too much with them today.'

'I've got plasters on and gloves. And there's not much more digging to be done—just messing about with the innards.'

She stayed to help him chip the frozen snow from the roof and sides of the Landrover and watched it gradually emerge out of the drift. When he started to tinker with the engine he turned to say, 'This is going to take time. Don't stand about in the wind, Tory. Go back indoors. There's nothing you can do to help at this stage.'

'Are you sure? I could sit in the driving seat and do anything you told me.'

'Not at this stage. I'll probably have to bring some of the plugs back to the house to warm and dry them before I can get anything started.'

She went back to the farm, slipping and sliding down the

track, glad of the ash which helped and gave some sort of grip on the frozen snow.

It was a long time before Julian returned and then he brought part of the motor with him which, after cleaning, he put to dry on top of the range while he ate his lunch. Afterwards he went back to work again on the Landrover, but without success.

'I can't get it started,' he said frowningly when at last he abandoned his efforts. 'I don't know what's wrong—I'm afraid I'm not a good enough car mechanic to be able to solve the problem.'

'Tomorrow's another day,' Tory said consolingly. 'You'll be able to try again.'

'Yes, I must.' He looked at her. 'What about your job at the school?—they'll be missing you a lot.'

'At least Miss Ewing knows where I am. I expect some of the children are away too. It usually happens.'

'I'll see if I can get a weather flash later. Maybe the thaw's on its way.'

Tory was listening to the wind which seemed to have risen again.

'Maybe. But somehow I doubt it.'

She was making pastry to put over a can of stewed steak she had opened for supper when suddenly, without warning, the light in the kitchen flickered and went out.

Startled, she turned, and fumbled her way to the door leading into the hallway. It was in darkness too.

She went towards the sitting room one hand stretched out in front of her and as she did so she heard the door open and in the glow from the fire saw Julian's tall figure outlined in the framework. His hand caught hold of hers and he said, 'Tory! What's happened? Have all the lights fused?'

'I think the generator's gone. We—we'll have to see to it.'

'I'll get the flashlight. It is in the kitchen?'

She was very conscious of his hand holding hers tightly in her own, aware of his powerful body close to hers.

'Y-yes. I-I'll light one of the oil lamps.'

One arm came about her shoulders.

'Lead on—you know the layout better than I do.'

They made their way slowly back to the kitchen, where Julian found the flashlight and flicked it on while Tory lit one of the old oil lamps.

'The generator's in the cellar.' She opened a wooden door at the far end of the kitchen. 'Down here.'

'Let me go first—I'll carry the lamp and you bring the flashlight, for good measure.'

The cellar was cool but dry—it smelled 'cellarish', a mixture of ancient stone and earth but not unpleasant. On an immense slate-topped table were slabs of butter and a huge cheese wrapped in muslin and a half used side of bacon: eggs in racks and an earthenware bowl of milk on which the cream had risen. Unplucked game hung from the rafters, gammons of ham, herbs and onions and bunches of dried milk. A low archway led to another smaller cellar to which Tory gestured.

'In here.'

Julian put down the lamp and stared frowningly at the silent generator.

'Now what? I haven't any experience of these things.'

'I've seen Grandfather take these out,' said Tory, indicating the wrenches. 'I think it's to drain the fuel tank. He takes the air out of the feed pipe or something and then connects it up again.'

'Simple. If you only know how.' He bent down, shining the flashlight onto the side.

'Grandfather keeps tools in that box over there.'

'Good. I'll see what I can do.'

For some minutes he struggled with the wrenches and then removed the fuel line. Tory tried to remember what her grandfather had done and so instruct Julian. When he had completed the procedure he started to crank the generator, but nothing happened. It remained obstinately silent. He went on cranking until he was breathless, but still no response.

'I can't have done the thing properly. What next, I wonder?'

'Perhaps it's something mechanical. Some part broken?'

'I don't think so. Everything here seems intact. I'll try again.' He began to crank the generator again, but still there came no answering 'chug-chug'. He straightened up, saying worriedly, 'I don't want to bust the thing.'

Tory hesitated.

'Shall we leave it for the time being? I can light oil lamps and we have the range to cook by. There's an old hand pump by the sink in the scullery, that can be worked to keep the tanks filled, and we shall just have to be as careful as we can in the use of water.'

Julian shrugged his broad shoulders.

'It sounds like a return to the Stone Age. But it's my fault. I should have learned to repair electric generators instead of memorising lines from Shakespeare and Ibsen. All right. I'll come back later and have another try.'

Tory led the way, flashing the flashlight across the darkened cellar, Julian following her with the oil lamp held high in his hand. He paused to gaze round at the hanging birds, the rich brown hams.

'Some store you've got here.'

Tory glanced over her shoulder at him.

'It will be Christmas soon—we're beginning to stock up.'

She turned back, shining the flashlight on to the shallow stone steps that led up to the kitchen. What happened next she could not quite remember. Perhaps she wasn't concentrating. Perhaps she didn't see the next step clearly or perhaps she slipped in its worn groove, but suddenly she stumbled and fell, missing her footing and sliding backwards while the flashlight dropped from her fingers and rolled clattering on to the stone below. She heard Julian's voice call sharply, 'What's the matter? Tory, are you hurt?' and the next moment he had put the oil lamp down on the table and was kneeling beside her where she had fallen across the dusty slabs.

She said, shakily, 'It's all right. I—I missed my footing or something. How—how silly.' She tried to get up and Julian's arm came about her to lift her gently to her feet.

'Sure you're all right? You've not knocked yourself about?'

She shook her head, very aware of the warmth and closeness of his hold. The oil lamp, wavering in the cold air, cast shadows on wall and rafters, on Julian's face, and intent dark eyes. She said with a tremor that came from something other than the sudden mishap.

'N-no. But the flashlight—is it broken?'

'Never mind about the flashlight. It's you that matter. You gave me the devil of a fright.' His arms tightened about her and he said, with a deep husky note in his voice she had never heard before, 'I'm in love with you, Tory,' and the next moment his mouth came down on hers in a close and passionate kiss.

CHAPTER TEN

SHE went with the kiss. There was no protest, no resistance left. It was as if Tory had been waiting all her life for this moment, for the thrill, the pounding delight that swept through blood and senses. Instinctively her arms tightened about Julian's neck, her whole being seemed to be flowing in a tide towards him. Conscious thought had gone, there was only feeling, an awareness of soaring rapture.

At last Julian released her, but still holding her two hands in his he said slowly:

'I've been longing to do that for three days—ever since I came here. But I held back. Now you might as well know—I love you, Tory. I love you very much!' He looked down at her his eyes black in their smouldering intensity. 'I fell in love with you right at the beginning, certainly from the day you crashed your car and I took you back to Ravensholme with me.' He half smiled. 'Do you remember? You didn't believe in "instant" anythings. But you see, it happened that way. As suddenly as the comet flashing across the sky.'

She didn't know what to say, how to answer him. She felt too overwhelmed. And, somehow, a little scared. As if she were being hurried too quickly towards something she couldn't cope with.

He said gently, 'What's the matter? You must have known, must have guessed how I felt about you. And you like me a little too, don't you?' The smile deepened. 'It seemed like that, a few moments ago.'

She felt the colour come in her cheeks.

'I—Yes, I—I'm attracted to you.'

The grasp on her hands tightened, he drew her closer to him.

'That's the most important thing. We'll take it from there.

She tried to pull back. 'I—I don't think I'm in love with you. It's just a—aphysical thing.'

'Good heavens, and when wasn't falling in love a "physical" thing, as you put it? As I told you once before no love affair that's worth the name is based on anything but a strong sexual attraction. Hasn't anyone ever told you? That's what makes the world go round.'

'You're laughing at me.'

'I'm sorry, I didn't mean to. I think you're the sweetest, most gorgeous girl in the world and I'm fathoms deep in love with you. But you're an innocent at large. I'm more convinced than ever that you were not truly in love with Ralph. But we won't go into all that now. I want to get you safely up these steps. Wait while I fetch the lamp and then I can help you.

'The flashlight is broken,' he announced when he came back to Tory and, putting an arm about her waist, held the oil lamp in the other to light their way up the steps.

'We've another somewhere—I'll look for it.'

Troy was waiting for them by the door, wagging his tail and whining as if to say 'What a long time you've been'. Everywhere was in darkness, but Tory searched in one of the kitchen cupboards and found two more oil lamps which had been stored away against just such an emergency as this.

'And we've plenty of candles,' she said as, with Julian's help, she filled the base with paraffin and wound up the wicks. She met his glance and looked away, aware of his nearness, of the tall figure that cast shadows of magnitude proportions in the flickering light. She had had this sense of claustrophobia before, but now it was intensified, as if she and Julian were closed up together in an even smaller confine, limited to the circle of light cast by the lamp, for everywhere else was shadowy and obscure.

She forced herself to turn away and saw, on the table, the half made pastry. She said hurriedly, 'I'm afraid supper will be a bit late. I'd better get on and finish the pie.'

She was glad to wash her dusty hands and busy herself rolling out dough and filling a dish with chopped meat. Julian carried logs into the sitting room and made up the fire, then pumped water into the tanks so that the boiler, served by the range, would not be in danger. He pumped up water for the cow and her calf and filled buckets to carry out to the shed.

When he returned he said to Tory, 'It's a beautiful night. No moon, but the stars are fantastic. Come and see.' He added warningly, 'Wrap up first—there's a bitter frost.'

The pie was in the oven, carrots and potatoes simmering on the hot plate. Tory bundled herself into her duffle coat and followed Julian into the yard. The air was so sharp it caught at her throat, her breath was an icy cloud when she shivered and spoke.

They walked a little way up the track to view the frozen glittering world around them. A twig snapped and Tory jumped, from somewhere a dog barked. It must have been miles away, for there was no other human habitation near them, but it sounded as if it were in the next field.

'Sound travels in the frost,' Julian said. 'Just as snow muffles everything.' He waved a gloved hand. 'Just look at those stars!'

A thousand, a million of them shone, sparkling hot and white in the indigo darkness of the night sky.

He slid his arm through hers. 'I wonder what happened to Kahoutek. Do you think he's still there but we can't see him?'

'I suppose so. Grandfather says people think that a comet is a chunk of the same primordial matter that created the solar system. Other people say there exists an enormous ''comet cloud'' somewhere in outer space that occasionally sloughs off comets. No one is really sure.'

Julian tilted back his tall head.

'Do you know all the stars by name?'

'I know some. There's the Great Bear—or perhaps you call it the Plough? Do you see the shape of it—with those seven stars? I can't remember all the names—Alkaid is one, and Mizar and Merak. Oh, and Alioth. I've forgotten the others.' She turned her head, feeling slightly dizzy with the effort of looking up. 'And that's Orion—you can't miss *him*. There are three stars of his belt—do you see? And the triangle which encloses the belt. Grandfather taught me their names. That's Betelgeuse—the reddish orange one on Orion's left shoulder, and that's Rigel, the one that looks very clear and bright.'

'Yes, I see them. They're tremendous. What about the belt? Do you mean those three in a line?'

'Yes. They're called Alnilam, Alnitak and Mintaka, and they're particularly notable ones. Grandfather told me that those three stars were supposed to represent the Three Kings, Caspar, Melchior and Balthazar, riding from the East to Bethlehem. Isn't that a lovely thought? It's strange, because it's always near Christmas time that one sees them most clearly.'

'What a lot you know. Any more?'

She raised her hand.

'There's Sirius, the brightest star in the whole sky.'

'The Dog Star—I know that one.' He smiled down at her. 'Thank you, teacher.'

She felt her cheeks warm despite the chill air.

'You asked me to tell you.'

'I know. And I'm very impressed. I think you're wonderful, Tory. The most wonderful girl in the world,' and his arms came about her and he bent his head to kiss her.

His lips were ice cold on her own, yet a warming thrill ran through her, starting somewhere in the soles of her boots and racing like a fever through the blood. Fire and ice, a dizzying combination that set every nerve a-tingle, every heartbeat throbbing like a drum.

Out here in the quiet frozen world she returned Julian's kiss in a way she would not have dared if they had been closed up indoors. Here she felt wild and free, as unrestricted as the stars that swung high above her head in the infinite space of the sky. She was a part of them, as she was a part of the night and the snow and the silent empty fells.

'I love you,' Julian murmured against her lips. 'I shall love you for ever.'

His words excited a response in her, as if, lost under his deep close kiss, she loved him too. But that was impossible. Only a few weeks ago she had been in love with Ralph. Her feeling for Julian, the maelstrom of sensation that swept through her at his touch could only be some physical reflex, a sort of rebound from her unhappiness over Ralph.

He released her at last to say, 'We mustn't stay out here all night or we shall turn into snowmen. Better get back to the house, darling.' Keeping an arm about her, he propelled her gently round and slowly, slipping dangerously on the frozen surface of the track, they made their way back to the house.

Indoors was an anti-climax. In a dream-like sequence of movement Tory let Julian help her off with her coat and tug off her boots, then she came suddenly to life, and smelt burning pastry and boiling vegetables. The magic of those moments under the stars faded quickly as she dashed to the oven door and dragged pans from the hot plate.

Just as well, perhaps. As it was she felt strangely self-conscious with Julian and was aware that as he stood leaning against the kitchen dresser his dark eyes followed her every movement. Once when he took a dish from her hand to carry it to the table he said, 'What a pity we have to eat. It's a constant interruption.'

She tried to sound casual.

'You wouldn't say that if there wasn't any food.'

'Oh, I don't know. Man doesn't live by bread alone.'

She lifted out the steak pie, its crust crisp and golden brown with only a tinge of over-cooking.

'You won't want any of this, then?'

He smiled, shaking his head.

'I've changed my mind. Who was it said

"He may live without love, what is passion but pining?
But where is the man who can live without dining?"

It was Lord Lytton, wasn't it?'

Tory concentrated on cutting into the pie.

'I don't remember. Please help yourself to vegetables.'

He reached his hand across the table and held hers for a moment.

'You're so practical, Tory. Yet a little while ago, when I held you in my arms out there in the snow, you were warm and tender and tremblingly alive, the very essence of romantic feeling.'

She looked away from him, pulling her hand free of his clasp.

'You—you caught me unawares. I think we—we should both be practical—well, sensible, anyway. And—and not talk in an emotional way.'

'That's a bit hard. Especially as I feel definitely emotional towards you.'

'You beguile with words. It—it's a part of your actor's training.'

He gave her an intent look.

'I'm not acting, Tory. I'm dead serious about being deeply in love with you.'

Why did his words trigger off a sense of happiness, as if this was what she wanted to hear? It was dangerous to talk in such a way, it undermined her defences. She said stammeringly, 'You-you're not being sen-sensible, making declarations of love at the supper table. I—I wish you wouldn't.'

'You mean there's a time and a place? Later, perhaps?'

It was like the games of chess they played—matching wits, each trying to out-manoeuvre the other, to mate the king.

Tory didn't answer him but bent her head to her plate as if to set an example of detachment.

After they had cleared away the meal Julian handpumped up water into the tanks and filled buckets to carry out to the byre and hen house in the morning. When he came into the sitting room with a pile of fire logs Tory was setting out the chess board.

'I thought we'd play again tonight. Would you like to?'

He smiled crookedly.

'I can think of better things to do, but O.K., chess it is.'

For the first time since they had started to play the game together Julian won. Perhaps Tory wasn't concentrating as she should, perhaps she was too aware of Julian sitting across from her in the pool of light cast by the oil lamp. Its gentle glow, the soft crackling of the wood fire seemed to produce a mood of inertia and fog her brain, slowing down action and reaction.

'What's the matter?' Julian demanded. 'You're not with me at all.'

'I'm sorry. The warmth of the fire has made me sleepy or something.'

He stood up and stretched his long arms.

'Shall I get us a drink? It will wake you up.'

Tory said quickly, 'No—no, nothing for me, thanks. But have one yourself, if you'd like one.'

He flung himself down into one of the big armchairs.

'I don't think so. Some coffee perhaps, later?'

'I can make some now.' Tory rose up to move to the door. To do so she had to pass the chair in which Julian sprawled, and as she tried to squeeze behind him rather than go so close he reached out a long arm and pulled her round towards him.

'No rush. Let's talk.'

She looked down at him, her hand clasped so tightly in his there was no chance of a quick retreat.

'Wh-what about?'

'Us. We've a lot to say to one another and I think this is the time and place,' and slowly, his dark eyes holding her gaze, he drew her even closer so that she was pressed against his long legs and then, with a twist of his wrist, he pulled her down on to his knees. 'That's better. Now you can't run away from me. And I can tell you all the things I want to—this way,' and catching her up into his arms he put his mouth to hers.

For a moment Tory struggled and then as his hold tightened about her she found herself, as once before, responding to his long deep passionate kiss. And kisses. She seemed to be dissolving under them, to be melting in a warm flowing tide of emotion. The touch of his lips on hers, on her face and hair and throat, was honey-sweet. Somehow they had slid round in the chair and she was almost lying in Julian's arms, the weight of his body heavy across her own. He was murmuring her name, murmuring endearments, telling her he loved her.

Something brought her back to her senses; the clatter of a falling log, the warning voice of the grandfather clock ticktocking into the room, a movement from Troy as he moved away from the heat of the fire. Shaken and breathless, Tory tried to push Julian from her and turning her head away said, 'Don't, Julian. Please, please stop.'

He moved his arm, shifting his weight as he did so.

'What's the matter—am I crushing you to death?'

She said, unsteadily, 'Please don't make love to me.'

His lips brushed her cheek, touched the lobes of her ear.

'Why not?'

She managed to straighten up.

'Because we—we're alone like this.'

He said in a deeper-than-ever voice that somehow held a hint of laughter, 'I should have thought these were the ideal conditions.'

She put the back of her hand against her hot forehead.

'Too—too ideal. I'm afraid of what might happen.'

'*Afraid*?' He tilted her chin to stare down at her his eyes black in their intensity. He said slowly, 'I thought you wanted what I want. To love utterly and completely.'

She met his look, wondering how to put her fears and hesitations into words.

'In a way I do want that. Because—because I—I am attracted to you. When you kiss me I can't think straight. I can't think at all. That's why being like this together is—is dangerous.'

He held her fingers to his lips.

'Darling—my sweet darling—I love you. I love you and want you and I want you to marry me. What's dangerous about that?'

'I—I'm not sure how I feel about you, that's why. I like you. I like you very much. You attract me physically—I admit that.' She looked away, feeling oddly shy. 'More—more than anyone I've ever known. But—am I in love with you?' She shook her head. 'I don't know. It's only a month—two months since I thought I was in love with Ralph. Everything is over between us now—he's married someone else and all that's left is a memory of the hurt.' She looked at him and said steadily. 'I don't want to become emotionally involved with you if—if it's going to be another mistake. I have to be certain. Do you understand?'

He frowned, leaning against the arm of the chair so that she was free of him.

'In a way. Though I can't believe that the milk-and-water affair you and Ralph had going between you bears any resemblance to the way *we* feel about one another. You love me. Tory. I'm sure enough for both of us. And there'll never be anyone else in the world for me but you, my darling. Please believe me.'

She sighed.

'I believe you. It's not you I doubt so much as myself. That's what I'm trying to make you see. The—the circumstances we're in are so unusual—we're thrown together twenty-four hours of the day and how long it's going to go on for we've no idea. I—I feel I'm on a roller-coaster being run away with by emotions I won't be able to control. I'm frightened of the pressures that can build up in this hot-house atmosphere. I want to be able to make any decision in cold blood.'

'Oh, Tory!' He gave something that was half a sigh, half a groan. 'My dear little innocent schoolmistressy Tory. As though anyone *ever* experienced a love affair in cold blood. But I suppose I know what you're trying to say. You want me to act like a gentleman, is that it? Instead of the low-down dog I seem to be. Don't you know the age of chivalry died the death years ago?' He shrugged. 'Well, I'll try, but it won't be easy feeling the way I do about you.'

'Thank you!'

He stood up and put a hand out to help her up.

'Only while we're here, mark you.' He gave her a half smile. 'When we get back into circulation again there'll be no holds barred. I shall "woo and win you" as the saying is, with or without honour. Wedding bells or seduction—take your choice.'

She smiled back at him a little uncertainly and held up two fingers.

'Until then—it's pax?'

He put his own hand up in an aswering gesture.

'Pax it is. *Pax vobiscum*—peace be with you—*us*, I mean. And tomorrow I'm going to shift that Landrover on to the road if it kills me—the sooner we're both out of here the easier life will be for both of us.'

She hesitated.

'Shall I make some coffee now?'

'To sober us up, you mean? It might not be a bad idea.'

She went into the kitchen, calmer but aware still of a whirlpool of emotion churning away under her matter of fact façade. She thought she had never been nearer to loving Julian than in the moment he had battened down his own feelings and responded, with the light touch, to her appeal to his generosity. He's a super man, she thought. I think I *am* in love with him. Then, hurriedly, time enough for that when the snow's gone and we can leave here.

After the coffee had been drunk in the silence that had fallen between them, as if each were thinking their own thoughts, Julian stood up and said briskly, 'I'm going to bed first tonight while you finish off the clearing up.' He gave her a wry smile. 'I'll be safely tucked away before you come up. Don't bother to bar your door.'

'Oh, Julian, you know—'

'I'm joking. Or didn't you notice?' He gestured a salute. 'Night, Tory. Sleep well—if you can.'

'Goodnight.'

She watched the door close after him and wondered how many more nights they would be alone here.

Next morning Julian was out early to attend to the Landrover. There had been no more snow and the sun was shining. If it goes on like this, Tory thought, the thaw will come soon, and had a sudden strange pang as if of regret.

But by lunch time he had still not been successful in starting up the Landrover, and the sun had disappeared into an overcast sky. The day seemed to drag—she and Julian were aloof, wary with one another as if avoiding contact.

After tea he went down to the cellar to struggle with the generator and miraculously, after a comparatively short time down there, came up to say, 'Switch on. The generator's working again.'

'Oh, fantastic! How did you manage it?'

He shrugged.

'I got so fed up with the damn thing I gave it a couple of good hard kicks and it started up. Let's hope it stays that way.'

With lights and water life seemed easier again.

'I'll wash tomorrow,' Tory announced. 'Can I do anything of yours?'

He grinned.

'What, and let me go around starkers? I'll have to stay in bed while you wash my smalls.'

She coloured slightly.

'You're so huge nothing of Grandfather's fits. But I'll see if I can find something you might be able to squeeze into.'

They played chess again that evening, concentrating hard on the game and making only desultory conversation. Julian won for a second time and for a second time went off to bed early, saying he had a book to read now that the bedside lamp was working again.

Five days. We've been cooped up here together for five days, Tory thought despairingly when she got up next morning. Julian was already downstairs, the curtains were drawn back, the fire made up and the kettle simmering on the range.

'Thanks,' said Tory. 'This is a great help.'

'I couldn't sleep,' he answered shortly.

She opened her mouth to say something and then shut it again, and busied herself slicing bacon into the frying pan. They had almost finished breakfast when Julian put down his empty cup and sitting back in his tipped chair said, abruptly, 'I was thinking about Ralph last night.' His gaze narrowed as he added slowly, 'Do you know the reason he sold Bramwick?'

She was so startled by the unexpectedness of the question that she could only stare at him for a moment before answering.

'To—to make some money, I suppose. Madeline wanted to go on living at Lindlay Grange, so there wasn't much point in him keeping the house.'

'He sold Bramwick and all the land with it to the Council—they're going to start building the new bridge over the river from that spot.'

Tory bit her lip.

'Are—are you sure?'

'Absolutely certain. Because a compulsory order of purchase has been slammed on my land—the fields which belong to the Ravensholme estate and which lie across the Scar from Bramwick. Originally I refused to sell, but now, because Ralph has let his place go, I have no alternative. I thought he might have told you.'

She was silent in her dismay. So Ralph had done what he had intended to do in the first place—sell out and allow the Dale to be changed.

'I—I didn't know. Ralph said something about it to me a long time ago. We—we quarrelled about it, actually.'

Julian's set face softened.

'I'm glad. Glad you were on the opposite side of the fence to him.' His lips curled slightly as he added, 'He's made a packet out of it. But that's of no consequence to me. What I regret is that it will open up the Dale.'

'I regret it too.'

'Some people may benefit. Let's hope so.' He stood up. 'Well, what are the chores for the day?'

While Tory washed up and made beds Julian went out to see after Bridget and the calf and clean out the barn before feeding the hens. Tory washed some clothes, and as she did so she thought about Ralph. So he had sold Bramwick and 'made a packet', as Julian put it. The old house would be razed to the ground and where it had once stood the new bridge would be built. Things would change in the Dale, there would be cars and people, more traffic. It was odd to think that Ralph who had been part of Scarsdale for most of his life didn't care about that, but Julian, the stranger and newcomer, had fought to preserve its beauty untouched.

She shook her head as if putting the thought of Ralph from

her. Already he seemed a dim and far-away figure, someone she had known in another life.

The window above the sink was steamed up from her laundry efforts. Tory climbed up on to a chair to wipe it clear, and she had just finished and was stepping down when she heard the back door open and over her shoulder saw Julian come in. His sudden appearance unnerved her. She moved back too quickly and as she did so the chair tilted dangerously. She would have fallen if Julian hadn't dashed forward and with a warning '*Careful!*' caught her in his arms.

He lowered her to the ground, but didn't release her. Instead his hold tightened about her and he said, 'Darling, you do do some silly things. Like falling down cellar stairs and crashing off chairs,' and without warning he bent his head and kissed her.

It was heaven, it was rapture to be kissed all over again. Tory almost kissed him back, but somehow she resisted and putting both hands against his broad chest she pushed hard saying, in a muffled voice:

'Please, Julian—pax. You promised. Pax, *please!*'

Reluctantly he let her go, pushing a hand through his thick black hair in a gesture of frustration.

'I couldn't help that—you were such a temptation.'

'We've both got to try.'

'Both?' His voice was rueful. 'I'm glad you feel tempted too. I thought it was a case of mind over matter with you.'

She said with more assurance than she felt, 'We'll be out of here soon. I'm sure it's warmer today.'

'Maybe. Anyway, I intend to set to on the Landrover again after lunch.'

'I'll help you,' Tory offered as she had done once before.

Soon after midday they went up the track to where the Landrover, now dug free of snow, lurched unsteadily over the edge of the road. The sun was shining and the snow sparkled like frosted icing on a wedding cake, and the sky had cleared to a brilliant blue. For a time Julian struggled to get the motor started, but there was no response, while Tory cleared some more snow out of the way for where the Landrover would reverse.

'It's hopeless,' Julian said frowningly. 'The battery seems dead. I'll give it a rest and then have a final shot, but I haven't much hope. Here, give me that shovel and I'll do some of the clearing while you sit down.'

Troy, who had come out with them, rolled in the snow as Julian cleared it away and sniffed and gambolled more like a puppy than the elderly dog he had become.

'One more try,' Julian declared, laying down the shovel and climbing back into the Landrover.

Tory was in the passenger seat and she stayed beside him while once more he jabbed at the accelerator with the choke pulled full out. Then suddenly, miraculously, the engine spluttered feebly into life and he gave a whistle of delight.

'Keep your fingers crossed—this may be it.' He nursed the motor along until it was running steadily and then he said, 'Will you jump out, please.' Tory, and see I keep on level ground as I come back.'

The ash on the road that Julian had put down some days ago helped the tyres to grip so that the Landrover was able to reverse slowly but surely up on to the road and then swing round so that the front was pointing towards Scarsfell. Leaving the engine ticking over, Julian jumped down to throw his arms around Tory and hug her to him.

'We're mobile again, sweetheart. You'll be back at Scarsfell with your grandfather tonight, if not tomorrow.' He looked down at her. 'Are you glad or sorry?'

She shook her head, half smiling.

'I'm not sure. Relieved is the word, I suppose.' She broke off, turning her head as if listening. 'What's that?'

'It's the motor running—the engine's warming up.'

'No—no, it's not the Landrover. I can hear that as well. Listen!' and she held up a warning hand. Julian looked and for a moment they stood in silence. Then Tory said slowly, 'It's the snow-plough. It must be. It's a noisy grinding sort of sound. Yes, there it is—can you see? Something coming over the top of of the hill.'

They stared together and saw a black speck silhouetted for a moment on the snowy ridge before it began moving at snail's pace down the slope of the hill that led to Wether Bell. Slowly, grindingly, it approached, casting flurries of snow ahead of itself as it cleared a path along the road.

'It's not the snow-plough—it's *Sam*. It's Sam driving the tractor,' said Tory. 'He's come to rescue us.'

'We'd almost rescued ourselves,' Julian said ruefully. 'But it will certainly be a help to have a track cleared through over the fell.' He caught her hand in his as he looked down at her. 'I wonder what would have happened if we'd had to stay on here at the farm?'

Tory could afford to be lighthearted in the moment of rescue.

'We shall never know.'

Julian sighed, but he was smiling too.

'I'm not sorry to see Sam and his tractor. Once we're away from here I'm free to pursue you without redress. You know that, don't you?'

She smiled back at him, her hand warm in his clasp.

'I don't suppose I shall run very fast or very far.'

She saw the flash in his dark eyes.

'Oh, Tory!' Then, 'Damn, I can't kiss you right under Sam's nose. He'll fear the worst. But I shall make up for it later on.'

She freed her hand, said softly over her shoulder, 'I hope so,' and ran across the snow waving and calling to Sam as he climbed down from the tractor and started to walk towards them.